IF YESTERDAY COULD TALK

SONJA GUNTER

I'd like to dedicate this book to my son, Danton Gunter, who passed away in 2011, at the age of 18. He would listen to me talk about my characters and watch me type my stories into the computer. He also encouraged me to keep writing and to get published. He never saw my achievements, but my other son Travis Pfeiffer has. I did give up on my dreams of being an author for a while to only remember the joy Danton would have experienced knowing his mother was a published author.

I'd like to dedicate this book to my son, Danton Gunter, who passed away in 2011, at the age of 18. He would listen to me talk about my characters and watch me type my stories into the computer. He also encouraged me to keep writing and to get published. He never saw my achievements, but my other son Travis Pfeiffer has. I did give up on my dreams of being an author for a while to only remember the joy Danton would have experienced knowing his mother was a published author.

Chapter One

Not a good sign.

Mark Christmenn, the owner, and president of MAC Industries, sat in the comfort of his black limo. He clenched his jaw and tightened his grip on the door armrest. He watched FBI Agent Tom Nelson approach Hal, his personal pilot. The federal agent had requested, no, demanded, Mark meet him in one hour at the Flying Cloud Airport and have his company jet, *Dream Catcher*, ready. The agent had been abrupt and hadn't even given him a chance to ask any questions before hanging up.

Mark's temper soared, and his thoughts raced dangerously. The moment the limo stopped, he opened the door. Philip, his bodyguard, sometimes chauffer, and best friend, joined him. Throwing back his broad shoulders and stiffening his arms so they wouldn't swing, Mark took long and purposeful steps toward the waiting pair.

"Agent Nelson, what in God's name is so urgent that you felt it necessary to drag me out here at two o'clock in the damn morning? You're lucky I recently moved my corporate jet from the Minneapolis/St. Paul International, Lindbergh Terminal."

"Steven Massaro."

1

Instantly, Mark took a step back and his hands clenched into fists automatically. He clenched his jaw and narrowed his eyes. His emotions went into overdrive with revulsion. He flexed his hands, hating the way his body reacted to the mere mention of the man's name. Mark cleared his throat. "Massaro?"

"Yup, he just arrived in San Diego. We weren't expecting him for another month or so, but we got word he's meeting with several known Mexican drug cartels. We think he's trying to get them to join forces with the Italian mob. Right under our noses. The rendezvous is taking place tonight at the Grill Restaurant. We need—"

The roar of jet engines cut off Agent Nelson, and Mark moved closer to hear.

"We need you in San Diego today. All the previous plans have been pushed forward. Undercover agents will meet you at the airport with updates. We're very optimistic your presence and the sting will hang it on him."

"Hang what and on whom?"

"Oh, sorry. We hope to set Massaro up with you," Agent Nelson said.

"Who do you want me to meet?" Mark was so furious the negativity clouding his thoughts and didn't care if the roar of the engines hid the anger in his voice or not. "Are you insane? The man wants me dead!"

"That's why it's so important for you to go. We're betting Massaro will confront you." Agent Nelson paused. "Don't worry, the FBI, along with the DEA special teams, will take extra precautions for your safety. Any questions?"

"Have you been inhaling some of the drugs you've confiscated? Because it sure seems like it. You want me to be in the same room with a known killer and mobster. The same man who has issued a hit on me because I reported him to the FBI. This is a no brainer. No. No fucking way. I'm out of here. Come on, Philip, drive me home." Mark turned and made his way back to his limo.

"Mr. Christmenn, calm down." Agent Tom Nelson grabbed Mark's arm. "You have to understand, I wouldn't have asked if I thought for a moment you'd be in harm's way, and you did agree to help us fight this scum."

Mark shook his head and ran a hand through his hair. *Is my company's reputation worth dying for? Or am I willing to die? This isn't what I agreed to do.* He brushed Agent Nelson's hand off his arm and motioned to Philip to come over to him. "This isn't what the original plan was! We were to interview some new coffee brokers. Place a large order so the FBI could watch the incoming shipments for drugs."

"I know, I know," Agent Tom Nelson said.

"I didn't agree to see the man who wants me dead in person!" Mark shook his head. The FBI wanted hard proof, so what? He'd agreed to a very plain and simple plan. Now they wanted him to actually be in the same fucking room with Steven Massaro.

Sweet deal for whom? Not for me! The question is, do I want to be looking over my shoulder for the rest of my life?

"You have to trust the FBI and the DEA. If these guys are taking payoffs and are responsible for placing the cocaine in your shipments, we need to stop them," Philip said.

"What if—?"

Philip cut Mark off. "There aren't any 'what if's'. Either we do this, or we don't. It's up to you."

He shoved his hands into his pockets in defeat. Philip was right and could always talk him down from his temper. He walked back to Agent Nelson. "All right, I'll agree under one condition."

"I'm not here to make deals."

"If you want me, Agent Nelson, then I want my bodyguard Philip West, as part of the undercover unit." Mark motioned once again for Philip to come over to them.

"I can arrange that. I think that's a great idea. Your actions here this morning and tonight are really appreciated." Agent Nelson extended his hand.

Mark hesitated, still suspicious of the agent's motives, and then shook his hand. "Before I change my mind, is there anything else you need to tell me?"

"There is one thing. We've arranged for you to meet with one of our agents, Harvey Johnson. The coffee world knows him as a buyer of exotic coffee beans." Agent Nelson started toward the *Dream Catcher*. "We've used his cover before, which is what led us to the coffee brokers."

"You're positive Massaro won't suspect anything?" Mark raised his voice over the drone of the engines.

"Yes. You're both big in the coffee business. Of course, it wouldn't be unusual for the two of you to be seen together. I have to finish a couple of things here before I head out. I'll meet with you later this afternoon." Agent Nelson held out a file. "Take this file. You'll want to read it."

Mark nodded and accepted the file, even though he was tempted to throw it back in Agent Nelson's face and walk away.

"The other part of my team will be at the San Diego Airport when you arrive. They'll take you to a secure location until I arrive. Mark, Philip, have a nice flight." Agent Nelson left.

Mark tucked the file under his arm and stepped up the stairs into *Dream Catcher*. Philip followed with the luggage.

"Are you okay with all this?" Philip asked once they were inside the plane.

"No! I mean, yes, I want to get on with my life, run my business, and put this damn nightmare behind us. We'll be fine," Mark added, more to assure himself than Philip.

He didn't want Philip to worry any more than he already was. He sure as hell hoped they'd be okay. With Philip as extra protection, nothing could happen, could it?

Once in the air, Mark used the time to open the agent's file, and quickly read the reports. He wasn't a cop or an FBI agent and here he was about to embark on some sort of mission. Guns, being wired, a bulletproof vest, and an earpiece. It all seemed unreal.

When he saw Philip approach, Mark closed his eyes and pretended to be asleep. He didn't want to talk, and he sure as hell didn't want to argue. He sensed Philip passed by him and then heard the cabin door shut again. So many thoughts about his life, his lack of relationships, and the business empire he was running came and went as he waited for the three-hour flight to end.

Too soon for comfort, Mark saw the flashing yellow lights signaling their approach into the San Diego Air Force Airport and wished he had more time. But he'd never hidden from anything in his life, and he wasn't going to start today.

When he and Philip disembarked, a group of men were waiting. A man with black hair and sunglasses stepped forward.

"Welcome, Mr. Christmenn and Mr. West. I'm Agent Johnson from the Narcotics Division Special Services. Thanks for agreeing to help us."

"I can't say I'm pleased, but I'll do whatever it takes to get this guy out of my life," Mark said.

"I understand. We'll take you to the hotel right away and meet with you later in the afternoon. It shouldn't take long to get you wired and into the bulletproof vest. If you think of any questions, I'll be able to answer them at that time," Agent Johnson assured him.

The new information, along with the knowledge that the Narcotics Division was now involved, calmed some of Mark's concerns. The division was known for monitoring drugs. They had their own vice enforcement team that worked closely on organized crime problems specializing in narcotics. They'd been the ones that had found the cocaine in one of his shipments last year and had set this nightmare into motion.

"Do you think he'll try to kill me?"

"We've gathered some rather interesting information that confirmed him as a very, ah, should I say, just a little bananas about the foiled hit on you last fall," Agent Johnson paused for a moment and then added, "We're betting Mr. Massaro will attempt to take you out. We're very confident his Italian temper will get the better of him and we can bust him."

His earlier anger returned, and he swallowed hard. "Just who is betting on my life?"

"No, no Mr. Christmenn, it's not like that. Sorry, bad choice of words on my part. The waiters and the food staff are the Cavalry. Sorry, undercover agents. Actually, everyone but Mr. Massaro and his guests will be agents with the exception of the chef and owner."

Mark felt Philip's presence behind him.

"Isn't Massaro going to suspect something if he doesn't recognize the staff?"

"It's all part of the sting, Mr. West. When our informants told us they were using this restaurant as a meeting place, we moved in several months ago. The owner has several violations pending, which we used as leverage, and he was more than happy to allow us to step in," Agent Johnson said.

"That's reassuring to know unless he tries to double-cross you. I hope I'll be able to act this out for you. I don't want to let anyone down," Mark said, using as much sarcasm in his tone as he could.

"Don't worry, you'll do fine. Agent Nelson has told us a lot about you. We're done here. If you don't have any more questions, we'll take you to the hotel now." Agent Johnson signaled to a waiting black SUV Cadillac.

Mark blew out a breath. His churning gut told him something about the plan was way off. He had to stay focused for any signs of anything out of place.

"One last thing," the agent continued. "A special taxicab will pick you up and take you to the restaurant. I'll keep in touch if we have any last-minute changes. Try to relax this afternoon."

Adventures were something he had never really enjoyed, even as a kid, and this one was now at the top of his list of what things not to do.

"Mark, you nervous? Because I sure am," Philip said once they were alone inside the car.

"Hell, yes. It's not as if we put our life on the line every day. Well, I should say, I don't, but you do. I can't handle this much stress," Mark replied, and wiped his sweaty hands on his pants. Normally he wouldn't confess weakness to anyone, but he'd known Philip for years and literally trusted the man with his life.

"You don't have to do this. We could back out."

"No, I have to. I can't say I don't have a bad feeling, but on the other hand, I can't sit by and allow scumbags like Massaro, and other drug cartel leaders attempt to import drugs into the United States by shipping them concealed in imported goods. I'm not going to live my life in fear of them or their organizations. I have to do what is necessary to protect my companies and their reputations and help other importers."

"I want you to know that if I thought there was even a slight chance, I couldn't protect you and you might be killed, we wouldn't be here right now."

"Want to play a couple of hands of blackjack, once we get to the room?"

How his friend knew the right thing to say and do, he didn't know. He rubbed his fingers over his tired eyes, somewhat comforted by Philip's words. "I *am* fine. You're worse than Mrs. Weber. I just want to lie down. I need to be by myself."

They remained silent the rest of the ride to the hotel. When they arrived, an agent escorted them to their room.

Mark picked up his own bag without saying a word, strode into the bedroom, closed the door, and threw the bag onto the only chair. Fully clothed, he plopped down onto the bed, placed his hands behind his head, and stared at nothing.

What in God's name am I doing? I could be dead in a few hours. Then what? The end? No! I'm not going to die this way. I have to stop thinking that way.

He focused on the shadows on the ceiling, letting them take on shapes. They formed into what resembled a Chinese dragon dancing and moving around.

Dragons were his good luck charm and all through his life whenever one would turn up in his dreams something good always happened. He'd even gotten a dragon, with wings outstretched and green eyes, tattooed on his back right shoulder. Most of the women he'd dated loved it and had given him the nickname Dragon. Could this be a sign that everything was going to be okay?

He closed his eyes and willed sleep to come to quiet his roaming thoughts, but it never did. He lay there for a couple hours unable to relax. A knock on the door kick started his heart.

"Mark, the agents are here," Philip called out.

"Okay, I'll be out in a minute."

Show time. Ready or not.

———

As the Grill Restaurant came into view, waves of acid welled up in his throat from his belly. To calm himself, Mark thought of the upcoming mission as one of the video games he'd played years ago where he'd held the main controller and was in charge of everyone. The winning move was to find the bad guy and walk away alive.

Simple.

Painless.

He peered over his shoulder to eye the car following them, encouraged by the fact Philip was in such close proximity. As promised, Agent Johnson had assigned Philip a position outside the front of the restaurant in case of trouble.

That would place Philip near the action and close enough to come to his aid, if needed, but far enough out of harm's way. The mere thought of Philip getting hurt if this all went down bad caused his chest to tighten. He couldn't lose his bodyguard and close friend over a loser like Massaro. Not to mention the media hype of a civilian involved in a shoot-out.

Quicker than Mark had expected, the parking valet opened the car door. The games were about to begin for real. With one foot placed confidently in front of the other, he moved up the stairs and through the double-wood doors. Right now, *he* felt like the avatar and someone else was holding the remote control.

"Welcome to the Grill Restaurant."

A pretty redhead in her mid-to-late thirties with a wide smile and friendly eyes greeted them.

Mark stared at the hostess for a moment, cleared his throat, and willed his heartbeat to slow. "Hi, I'm meeting someone. I'm not sure if he has arrived."

In one swift glance around the room, he spotted the clean-shaven, dark-haired Massaro and froze. Mark's adrenaline kicked into high gear.

Shit. Now what?

He swallowed dryly, ready to turn and run when their eyes locked. To his relief, Massaro was the one who shifted his glance away first, but not before giving him a murderous glare.

"Your party is already seated. Please follow me," the hostess said.

Mark wrestled to reel in his racing thoughts while his mind screamed for focus. He needed to stay alert, but he was so damned uncomfortable. And he was sweating like a damn pig. The bullet-proof vest they'd made him wear was heavy, and he could feel the sweat trickling down from his armpits to his hips.

"You're doing great, Mr. Christmenn. We've got his attention," a voice in his ear said.

Mark flinched at the volume. Trying not to look conspicuous, he said under his breath, "You're too loud."

"Sorry. How's this?"

"Better," Mark said. Taking a deep breath, he settled his nerves as he followed the hostess, who led him past Steven

Massaro's table. It was all part of the plan. The agents had wanted to make sure Massaro knew he was in the restaurant.

Who were they trying to kid?

As they cleared Massaro's table, the sounds of curses and glass breaking caused Mark to slow. He felt the hairs on the back of his neck stir and was tempted to glance back.

Am I a dead man walking?

Inhaling deeply, he stiffened his back, focused on Agent Johnson's face, and continued toward the table, feeling certain things were going to happen sooner than everyone thought. The vacant chair across from Agent Johnson seemed to be yards and yards away. When he reached the table, Mark sank into the welcoming seat, grabbed for the glass of water, and drained it.

Keeping his eyes lowered, he wiped the perspiration from his forehead. The vest was beginning to suffocate him, and the tape they'd used to secure the wires was beginning to itch.

The voice in his ear addressed him again. "Great job. You can now start to talk business. Talk loudly so Massaro will be able to hear."

His pulse roared in his ears, and he couldn't talk. His mouth had gone dry. Not wanting to show his panic, Mark turned his head and stared at Agent Johnson.

"Mr. Christmenn, I hope you had a pleasant flight. I'm glad we were able to meet tonight. I'd like to discuss combining our coffee bean purchases. This, I'm sure, will benefit both our companies. When will I be able to take a tour of your company's processing plant?"

His uneasiness subsided as he concentrated on Agent Johnson. However, when he answered, what came out was barely audible.

"I..."

"Mr. Christmenn, you need to calm down and start talking," the voice in his ear demanded.

Mark glanced around for something else to drink. He took the only thing left on the table, a glass of wine, and drained that. He could do this, dammit. He was a multi-millionaire with a successful business. Massaro and his deadbeat gang weren't going to have the last bang. He lifted his head higher. "How about tomorrow, Mr. Johnson? I'll give you a personal tour and I'm confident you'll be very pleased with my processing plant."

"Good. Good. Keep talking," the voice in his ear said.

With this encouragement, Mark was now able to do what he needed to do. What he did every day to keep his business thriving. He kept up a lively conversation and even laughed to bring the attention to their table, surprising himself. He felt as if he was watching and doing things from outside of his body. Just when he was beginning to feel confident, an uneasy feeling came over him. Wanting to turn his head to look at Massaro, he fought the urge and remained facing Agent Johnson whose face was a mask, revealing nothing about what was going on behind him.

The meal came and went with no interruptions from the other tables or the damn voice in his ear. He'd worried this had all been for nothing. Massaro wasn't taking the bait.

Did he suspect it was a set-up?

Would Massaro come after him another time because of this?

The voice spoke again in his ear, startling him. "Change of plans. Now in place, Plan C."

Mark groaned inwardly. Plan C was for him to walk by Massaro's table as they exited. He was to stare at Mr. Massaro the entire time and promptly exit the building.

The Grilled Chicken Caesar Salad he'd just eaten turned sour in his stomach.

Where was his antacid when he needed one?

Agent Johnson shifted the conversation to the roasting process of coffee beans just before tapping the table three times, which was the signal to leave.

"Okay, everyone's in place. Take your time. Walk slowly," the voice instructed.

Right, walk.

Run was more like it, and he wouldn't look back.

The man behind the voice was going to die when he did make it outside.

"That would be great. I, um," Mark stumbled over his words as he watched Massaro push back his suit coat to reveal a shoulder holster gun. "I could arrange for the plant to stay open longer. We run several public tours on the weekends."

They reached the front of the restaurant without incident and proceeded out to the waiting cars. Mark located Philip a few feet from him. He wanted to leave ASAP. Nothing had happened. The whole damn trip had been a waste of time. Turning to face Agent Johnson to tell him what he thought, but the voice sounded one last time in his ear. "Take cover! Duck."

Instead of doing as he'd been told, Mark instinctively turned to see what was going on. As if in slow motion, he saw Steven Massaro standing at the top of the stairs with his gun drawn and pointed right at him. Then came a bright flash. He heard the gunshot and felt the bullet whiz by him. To his utter shock, the next bullet hit him in his chest. It sent waves of pain unlike anything he'd ever felt through his torso.

I've been shot. I knew it. Just like that.

For a moment, his dismal life flashed before him, all his dreams, and all his unfinished plans.

"Shit, I've been shot."

The power behind the bullet knocked him backward. He landed hard on the pavement. It knocked the wind out of him. His head hit the ground. A black haze slowly took over, while gunshots, shouting, and Philip yelling for him to stay down, was the last thing he heard.

Chapter Two

Monday, day two hundred thirty-seven, looking for a new job. Interviews eighteen and nineteen, bombs. Overqualified and not enough experience. Not even sure how that works. Where have all the good jobs gone?

Rane Schoen ended her post on Facebook with a sad face emoticon. She set her laptop off to the side and Thor, her rather sizeable white ragdoll cat, soon took the empty spot.

"Thor, what am I going to do? I only have one more interview tomorrow." She rubbed her face against the cat's. "But I have a good feeling about it."

Meow, meoweee.

"I know, I had good feelings about all the others, too."

Rane pushed the power button on the remote, scrolled down, and then up to find a movie or some TV show to watch. Before she'd picked something, *ping* sounded from her laptop, followed by several more, *ping, ping, ping.*

"That didn't take long. I'll bet you a catnip treat there's a message from Val."

Thor yawned. He could be finicky at times, but he was always there for her.

Rane started reading the replies.

I guess they've gone to the Black Hole in space.

You're not alone.

Hang in there, girl.

And the best post of all read:

Why work at all? Less stress. Just find a man to entertain you nightly. You'll be too tired to work.

She laughed so hard, Thor got up and lay on the couch. The last post *had* come from Val, though, which meant she owed Thor a treat. Without thinking, she clicked on Skype.

The screen said '*Calling*'. Then Val appeared on the laptop screen with her hair in a scrunchie on top of her head while she applied makeup.

"Hey, I knew you'd be calling," Val said. "I don't have much time. So, it didn't go so well, huh?"

"How'd you guess? The last man who interviewed me kept looking out the window. Didn't give me the time of day, said I was over-qualified," Rane moved the laptop screen to get a better picture of Val, who kept moving in and out of the camera.

"It's okay. Don't you have another one set up?"

"Yeah, in the morning, with the MAC Company. Will you stop moving around and sit."

Val laughed and did. "Just for a moment! I have a big meeting with Mr. R."

"Which one is he? I've lost track."

Val, her best friend since grade school, was an attorney and worked for a huge law firm, with a client list that would have any star-struck fan in awe. They ranged from professional athletes, from the Minnesota Twins, the Vikings, and the Timberwolves, to actors and actresses living in the area. The players were forever being sued for the stupidest things, which was lucky for Val and the firm.

"You know I can't say, but remember what my-ex used to watch?"

"Oh WWE-Really? Who is it? I bet it's Seth "Freakin" Rollins."

"Right and wrong. Have to go. Sorry about the interview. We need a movie night soon."

"Betcha, I think it's your turn to pick. Text me later."

"Okay, really gotta go."

"Bye."

Rane clicked '*end call*' and the screen went blue-green. Her smile disappeared, replaced by a frown. Being single had its advantages, but finding the right man wasn't easy. She didn't want another one like her ex-husband, David Moore.

Right after her divorce, things had been great, but now with her new mission and outlook on life she wanted a man. Not just any man like Val had suggested. One who would treat her special and maybe want to have a baby.

Having to start over at thirty-two was not her idea of being successful. It was because of David, her deceitful, unfaithful ex-husband, she was out to better herself. This time she was going to do it right.

Step one: interviewing. Step two: dating.

Her newly received master's degree in marketing resource management wasn't helping. The degree was getting her foot in the door, but then she'd been told they had several applicants. She just wanted someone to give her a chance. Once she got a job, she'd be able to work on her next goal, which was finding a meaningful and lasting relationship.

She wanted a man who'd love her, who'd spend time with her, and who wanted children, lots of them. Her biological clock was ticking, and she couldn't turn it back. She was childless because David hadn't wanted any. He'd insisted she take the pill, saying they didn't need to establish a family while in college.

Ping!

She touched the shift key, which brought her screen to life.

Another post. Maybe her mother was responding. Refreshing the posts, her excitement died.

Baby, you don't need to work. Come back to me!

Rane stared at the words in horror. A sudden chill hung in the air.

David.

Why was he bothering her? Now, of all times.

She felt the color drain from her face as alarm and anger rippled up her spine.

Chapter Three

In the darkness of Mark's mind, a huge dragon sat next to him and there was blood everywhere. He reached out to stop the flow, but his arm wouldn't move, and he couldn't find where the blood was coming from.

He felt trapped and a heaviness lodged in his chest. Suddenly, the dragon roared, making its blue eyes sparkle. Mark wanted to call out to the creature, but it faded away.

Out of nowhere, a light broke through the blackness surrounding him, but the shrieking in his ears remained. The sound intensified as he focused on the light.

The harsh reality that he'd been shot came back to him as his mind cleared. He heard Philip's non-too-gentle voice burst through his befuddled senses.

"Am I dying?" he muttered and carefully opened his eyes, afraid he'd see his imminent death reflected in Philip's face.

"No, but you're going to be the death of me. Are you okay? Did you break anything when you fell?"

When he didn't answer, Philip shouted, "Mark, can you talk? Can you hear me?" After a pause, Philip yelled again, "Mark!"

"Why are you shouting? I hear you and I can see you. Will

you just shut up and help me?" Mark demanded impatiently, wincing in pain. The fog clouding his thoughts lifted a little more.

He'd had on a bulletproof vest. He couldn't be wounded.

There was no pain when he touched his chest.

Thank God for modern technology. Relief flooded through him. He struggled to get up before standing with Philip's help, but the world spun out of control.

He held on tightly to Philip, reached up to find the source of the ache, and located a large lump on the back of his head. He touched it gingerly and winced in excruciating pain when his finger made contact.

The pain went right to his forehead. He closed his eyes, willing the pain to go away. When it didn't fade, he opened his eyes to see the scene going on around him, all the sirens, the police, and the yellow tape.

Totally chaotic.

Agent Johnson forced a handcuffed Steven Massaro up against a squad car, and Massaro's bodyguards were face down on the ground in a line. Paramedics treated the wounded, an FBI agent and a couple of Massaro's bodyguards.

Surreal.

He could have wandered onto a movie set filming an episode of *CSI*. He leaned up against a car, still unsteady on his feet. "Philip, what happened?"

"Everything went bugs. You and Agent Johnson had just come outside when it all went down. Massaro and his bodyguards rushed out of the restaurant with their guns drawn. We had to get back and couldn't fire until Massaro or his bodyguards shot first."

"What?" He knew he'd hit his head and Massaro had fired at him, but he didn't understand what Philip was talking about.

"Man, it was bananas! Massaro's first zap whizzed by your head. If he'd hit you, you'd have been a chump. I thought for sure you'd taken a ride."

"You're not making any sense. Bananas, chump, zap, and what ride? What are you talking about, Philip?"

"Oh, sorry, that's all the police slang. It all started coming back to me. When you came outside, Massaro and his bodyguards followed. Massaro shot at you. I yelled for you to take cover, but one of the bullets hit you. Thank God for the vest."

"Thanks for the reassurance," Mark said.

Philip continued as if he hadn't heard his remark. "It was perfect. You turned, and that's why the first zap missed. His second zap hit you. And, *timmmbbberrr*, you fell. Man alive, it was right out of a textbook."

"You're sick. You wouldn't be so excited if it had been you who fell."

"Hey, now, I knew you'd be safe on the ground," Philip said defensively.

Mark gave him a look that would've had anyone, other than Philip, squirming in his or her shoes.

"Anyways, Massaro's bodyguards started zapping, sorry, *shooting* at everyone when they realized it was a sting set-up. Agent Johnson took Massaro down without having to fire a single shot. They've confiscated enough firearms and ammo here to start a war. It was all over in a matter of minutes. None of the agents can believe Massaro actually fired at you. Someone like him would use hitmen, but he must have thought no one would see him kill you. And you missed it all."

Mark crossed his arms over his chest and nodded. Checking his watch, he saw that only seven minutes had passed since he'd left the inside of the restaurant.

"Are you okay?" Philip asked again.

"Yes. Would you quit asking?"

Philip let out a gasp and pointed. "Look at the size of the hole in your suit coat!"

Mark followed Philip's gaze to the burn hole in his coat and then his shirt. He stripped down to the bulletproof vest where he saw the bullet stuck in the vest, flat as a pancake.

The cold reality stuck him hard. If he hadn't been wearing the bulletproof vest, he'd be a dead man right now. The bullet would have hit him in the heart.

The thought made his stomach roil. He and Philip gaped at each other and shook their heads in unison.

"I see everything is fine over here. We're still piecing together Massaro's actions by firing at you. Nothing adds up," Agent Johnson stated. "You might get a good-sized bruise from the impact of the bullet, but other than that, you seem to be okay. Should I have the paramedics look you over a second time?"

"No, no, I'm fine and I'll take a few painkillers when I get home," Mark said.

Philip cut in, "Don't you even try to say no. Send one over. Mr. Christmenn has a lump on his head, and he did black out."

"Sure, I'll get one here right away." Agent Johnson smiled and waved over a paramedic as he walked away.

"Philip, you're not my damn mother! Leave it alone. I'm fine. It's just a little bump," Mark added. "Did you see if Agent Nelson is all right?"

"He's inside. He said as soon as you're ready to leave, we could head home, but we're not leaving until the paramedics look you over.

Once given a clean bill of health, minus a few lumps and bruises, they took Agent Nelson's suggestion and headed to the airport. Mark wasn't feeling completely safe, but after the tires of his plane left the ground, he did. The fact he'd almost died wouldn't leave him. The idea nagged at him as he waited for the green light to come on, signaling it was safe to move about the plane. Guns, shooting, FBI agents, and then Massaro drifted into his thoughts.

Had it only been twenty-four hours ago he'd been in the comfort of his bed?

Who'd believe, Mister Executive, Bachelor of the Year, multi-millionaire, owner of MAC Enterprises, Mark Christmenn, would put his own life on the line to save his company's reputation?

No one.

It was out of character for him.

He solved daily worries with numbers and the everyday simple pressures of meetings and phone calls. Not guns.

Placing a hand on his chest, he winced. Having a gun pointed at him and then seeing it explode had been the most terrifying moment of his life.

His life flashed before his eyes in the seconds he fell to the ground. The horrifying thought he'd been dying was something he didn't want to ever experience again. He felt empty. Lonely.

What if I had died?

The endless list of 'what ifs' went on and on and on. It made him see just how alone he was, and he'd never realized it until now. He'd been a confirmed bachelor for so long because he'd chosen to wait all these years for some woman, whose name he couldn't remember, who he'd met once, to show up on the twentieth anniversary of the year they'd met at the agreed-upon location.

Stupid!

Who would wait two decades for a woman?

Pathetic!

Love was for dreamers. On the other hand, had the mental picture of her been his excuse for his long line of insignificant relationships? The grim reality boiled down to the fact he didn't have any children to carry on the family name. He didn't have a wife. He didn't have anyone.

What do I have?

The answer came too easily and quickly.

Money.

A successful conglomerate of companies.

A huge house.

His own line of coveted coffee beans.

A short list, and all material things. What about the emotional ones?

He had a mother who didn't care about him, a father who'd died when he was twenty-two, a secretary who treated him like a son, a bodyguard who was his only true friend, and a long line of unfulfilled relationships.

Nothing to be proud of, he realized.

The disturbing truth came rushing out unexpectedly. He wanted kids and he wanted someone to share his days and nights with until they grew old.

Glancing at the annoying red light, he moved impatiently in his seat. The plane jerked again, and his head ached more than ever. The throbbing prompted him to take out a bottle of ibuprofen.

The paramedics had said he was okay but advised him if his headache didn't go away, he was to see his own doctor. The pain wasn't as bad as it had been before, but it still nagged him.

The light flashed green bringing him out of his self-pity. Immediately, Mark got out of his seat and headed to the back of the jet. As he passed through the galley, he grabbed bottled water and strolled into the bedroom, determined to come up with some sort of plan to find a wife.

The first step was to let go of the memory of a girl gutsy enough to ask him to marry her and her damn promise to meet him in twenty years.

Talk about lasting impressions. This one sure had left its mark on him. He'd only been deceiving himself and all his past relationships. He'd never given any of the women a fair chance to win his love. It was time to move forward and time to forget the past and begin his search for Miss Right.

Mark fell into a light sleep, disturbed by visions of a knight protecting a dragon with green eyes.

Chapter Four

Rane turned into the MAC Company's private parking ramp. Her interview was at eleven o'clock, which meant she'd arrived a half hour early. With some reservation, she pushed the button on the speaker.

"May I help you?"

"Yes, I'm here for an interview."

"Thank you. Please continue ahead into space fifteen. Have a nice day."

Before the guard finished speaking, the parking ramp door opened. The sight made her nervous, but excited, all at the same time. *This is my time! Damn it!*

David's Facebook friend request and his comment still made her sick. Why would he come out of the woodwork now? Almost five years had passed since their divorce.

Val had said to ignore his post and block him from her page.

Rane did and hoped it would work. Anger swept over her, causing her stomach to twist into knots. She reached for her brief-case to make sure her resumé and letters of recommendation were all in place. Slowly the waves of resentment subsided, and she lifted her chin in defiance, vowing David, the cheating pig, wasn't going to get into her head today.

She slid out of her car and slammed the door shut. Moving her shoulders in a shrug, she pivoted and sauntered toward the elevators with her head held high and newfound confidence.

The doors opened to a huge lobby with shiny marble floors and columns. She strolled forward to the reception desk. "Hello. I'm Rane Schoen and I'm here to see Mrs. Wallen for an interview at eleven o'clock."

"Mrs. Wallen is on the sixth floor. Please use the set of elevators to your left, not the ones you just exited from."

"Thank you."

Rane gave her a friendly smile, which had come easily. But with every step she took, inadequacy, failures, and other shortfalls emerged from the corners of her mind as she waited for the doors of the elevator to open. She imposed an iron control on herself and pushed the poisonous thoughts back to where they'd come from.

Confidence restored, she rocked backward gracefully on her heels, which was a bad habit and had cost her a pretty penny. She'd thrown away many expensive shoes because of broken heels. Her lips turned up in a half smile. She bowed her head to rummage through her briefcase and yanked out the printout of job qualifications. Focusing on the ad and determined not to let David's old verbal abuse haunt her, she knew deep down she had many good qualities.

The elevator beeped, signaling she'd reached her destination and heard the doors open. Still looking downward at the paper in her hand, she took a step out of the elevator.

"Oh, no!" She'd suddenly come to a halting stop and stumbled backward, having run into something. Thinking she'd hit a brick wall as her file slipped unceremoniously to the floor, she saw the *It* wore polished black shoes, which meant the *It* was a man.

In a matter of seconds, her gaze traveled slowly upward. When it reached the man's athletic broad shoulders, abruptly, a hand was firmly clutching her elbow. She swallowed dryly, expelling the breath she'd been holding.

"I'm so-so sorry! I wasn't—I wasn't looking where I was going."

To recover from looking like a blubbering fool, Rane stepped backward, forcing the man to release his hold on her. She bent to retrieve her file and papers. One paper had slid a few feet away, so she straightened and started toward it. Then she actually took a second to look up at him. She stopped in mid-stride.

Oh my.

Wow, was he a Viking God?

She blinked as her sex-deprived body screamed, *Take me now, you hunk*, reminding her she hadn't had sex with a man in over a year. She couldn't help herself as she looked at him provocatively and lazily appraised his assets.

Her thoughts continued in that direction, and she wondered what he'd be like in bed. The hunk had to be at least six feet tall, in his late thirties to mid-forties, and wore a light gray suit, which fit his physique like only a tailor-made one could.

Yummy, yummy, she thought and unintentionally licked her lips. He could have strutted out of a GQ Magazine.

She couldn't escape from her unexpected sexual daydream as she stared blatantly at the most delicious-looking male she'd seen in a long while. Her tongue moistened her dry lips as she continued to stare at him. His long and thick eyelashes almost hid the blueness of his eyes.

No mascara could make lashes look that long and thick. He was a lucky son of a bitch.

Why was it that men always seemed blessed with them?

The man's hair was so black it reminded her of a moonless night. It appeared casually brushed to the left side, as if he'd been out in the wind. His nose made everything come together with his high cheekbones, giving him the look of a masculine male model. She was sure any actor or actress would pay millions to have this man's nose.

"No, I'm sorry," he said.

His deep voice brought her out of her daytime soap opera dream. Rane watched in stunned silence as his arm stretched toward her. She braced herself for the contact, but it never came. His arm went past her to stop the elevator door from closing. The man stepped around her half-crouching form into the waiting elevator.

She continued to stare at him and followed his retreating figure, her fallen papers forgotten. He turned as the doors closed and their gazes met. She watched his incredible pair of lips move and could only imagine what they were capable of doing.

"I do hope you're all right."

This time when he spoke, she was prepared, even though his voice sent her heart racing. The doors closed and the Adonis disappeared, leaving her staring into space.

"Oh my God, breathe," she mumbled.

What had gotten into her?

Who was she trying to kid?

It wasn't every day you literally ran into a man who could make all your sexual fantasies come true. Her pulse was still lurching out of control. Using the Pilates techniques she'd learned recently, she took several deep breaths and let the air rush out slowly. Instead of calming her as she'd hoped, it only caused her body to become more heated than it already was.

The man had been wearing Drakkar cologne.

It was her favorite masculine fragrance. She fought the urge to start sniffing the air like a dog before the cologne lost its intensity.

Once she'd given a bottle to David as a gift, but he'd refused to even try it and told her Drakkar smelled like dead fish.

What did he know, anyway?

Men. Who needed them?

She sure didn't.

As an after-thought, she added maybe not a man like David, but she'd sure like to get to know the man she'd literally run into.

"Are you all right?"

Startled, Rane glanced around for the person behind the concerned voice, as all thoughts of David and the mysterious man momentarily faded away. Then she spotted a smiling face near the reception sign.

"Yes, yes, I'm fine." Rane placed a hand to her heated cheeks and crossed over to the reception desk where the young woman sat. "I think my pride is hurt more than I am, but thanks for asking. I'm here to see Mrs. Wallen for an interview."

"Are you Ms. Schoen?"

"Yes," Rane said.

For a second time she raised her hand to her cheeks, hoping her face had returned to its normal color. Being caught staring, no ogling, a good-looking man wasn't exactly what she had envisioned her first impression to be.

What if the man had been the woman's boyfriend? Or worse, her husband.

The young woman handed an application to her. In a matter of minutes, she'd completed the form and watched an older woman with curly white hair walking toward her.

"Ms. Schoen?"

She stood and shook the woman's outstretched, slender hand. "Hello, yes, I'm Rane Schoen."

"Nice to meet you. I'm Mrs. Wallen. Please follow me."

Rane gathered up her belongings and pushed the lingering thoughts of the sexy man away before following Mrs. Wallen to an open office.

The interviewing process took on a normal tone with questions about her schooling, previous positions, and her career change. Mrs. Wallen explained the position the MAC Company was offering. Everything seemed to be going well. The position sounded challenging, but she knew she'd be able to make a difference for the company. Presuming the interview was over, she was about to take hold of her briefcase, when Mrs. Wallen excused herself and left the room.

While she waited, Rane tallied the pros and cons of the position. It was her specialty, helping companies gain control over departments. Some businesses didn't realize their lack of organization until it was too late, much too late. From what Mrs. Wallen had said, the MAC Company appeared to have many departments that needed reorganizing.

But coffee?

She didn't even like the stuff, although many people paid mega bucks to drink it annually. It was the MAC Company's only product. They had their own coffee plantations in Hawaii, Costa Rica, Columbia, and Kenya. They harvested the beans, exported them to the U.S., and then processed the coffee beans for their private and own branded special blend labels.

She hadn't realized how complex it was to get a simple cup of coffee. It all sounded very interesting, and she was tempted to give coffee a chance since she'd never acquired a taste for it. Then the vastness of the job hit her, and doubt kicked in.

The door opened and Mrs. Wallen returned with a man.

"Ms. Schoen, I'm Mr. Hansen, Director of Human Resources. Would you mind if I asked you a few questions?"

"No, I'd be glad to answer them."

As Mr. Hansen sat down, she watched Mrs. Wallen quietly exit the room. After another round of endless technical job and personality questions, he stood up, excused himself, and left.

This could be it.

The Mac Company was interested in her. She'd made it to a second-round interview on the same day as her first. Her search was almost over. The door opened and to her surprise, it was Mr. Hansen again, not Mrs. Wallen.

"Ms. Schoen, thank you for being so understanding. I still need a few more minutes of your time. Would you be able to stay a little longer?"

"Yes, of course."

Thinking he was going to ask more questions, she stared at Mr. Hansen in disbelief when he offered her a position with a salary in the low six-figure range, plus bonuses. The company also offered medical and dental insurance coverage, three weeks paid vacation, and, amazingly, added two more weeks after only four years. And it came with the title of Director of Corporate Resources. She had to be dreaming.

What a sweet deal. Wow.

"A position as Director of Corporate Resources?"

"Yes," Mr. Hansen stated and added. "Would you be interested in the position, Ms. Schoen?"

Then reality came crashing down on her, hard. A larger-than-life image of her spineless fish of an ex-husband popped up. His words still haunted her. *You'll never amount to much. You needed reassurance for everything, baby.*

David could go screw his little nurses, which was probably exactly what he was doing now. She was going to take this job and shove it in his face.

Sitting up straighter in her chair, Rane said, "Yes, I will accept your offer. When would you like me to start?"

"Tomorrow at eight-thirty."

Through her haze, she couldn't believe he had said tomorrow. She nodded in acknowledgement, unable to find her voice.

"Mrs. Wallen will be able to tell you more. You will be an asset to the company."

She pushed away the creeping doubts and found her voice. "Thank you so much for this opportunity."

They shook hands to seal the deal and he escorted her into the hallway. "I'll leave you in the very capable hands of Mrs. Wallen and welcome to the MAC Company family."

Rane stared after him, still in a slight state of shock. The enormity of what she'd done, of what had just happened burst through her excitement.

"Welcome aboard. I'm sorry the interview took so long, but when I see someone that the MAC Company would benefit from having as an employee, I don't hesitate to jump," Mrs. Wallen stated.

"Thank you so much for the opportunity. I know I'll enjoy working here."

"Stop by the reception desk tomorrow morning."

"I will. Thank you." Rane said and held out her hand.

They shook hands and Mrs. Wallen walked away, leaving her at a total loss and completely dumbfounded. Feeling like she was in some sort of time warp, Rane took a moment to enjoy the feeling of self-worth.

Holy shit, she'd landed a job.

David had been wrong. She didn't need anyone's approval to make her own decisions.

As she came to the receptionist's desk, she saw the elevator, which brought back the image of the hunk she'd collided with. Her curiosity got the better of her. "Excuse me, the man I ran into earlier. Does he work here?"

"Why, yes, he does," the receptionist said and added. "Did you get hurt, or was there a problem?"

She didn't miss the woman's slight twitch of her lips. "No, I'd like to leave him a note to say I'm sorry again."

The receptionist handed her a piece of yellow notepaper and Rane wrote, '*Hi, I'm sorry about this morning. I hope you didn't get hurt. I guess I owe you. Ms. Schoen*'.

Short and sweet.

If he wanted to read between the lines, he could. Handing the folded note back to the receptionist, Rane turned and drifted over to the set of elevators. She wished she'd had been gutsy enough to write, '*Mr. Hunk, I'm glad we bumped into each other. You have a wonderful body. I'd love to see what's beneath the clothes*'.

The thought of that man in her bed made Rane smile all the way to the main level. She returned her visitor's badge and was informed her temporary employee badge would be ready in the morning.

They sure did work fast here.

Still unable to believe what had happened, Rane headed to her car.

She'd done it. It was indeed a very good day.

An image of David tried to surface in her mind, but she pushed it away. He wouldn't ruin her triumph. The dirtbag wasn't wrecking her day.

As she exited out of the parking ramp, a black stretch limo delayed her turn. She was busting at the seams to share her great news with someone. But who could she call?

Val.

No, she was still in New York.

Her mother would still be at work, and this was Grandma's bingo afternoon.

Part of her enthusiasm dissipated while she drove home. She was alone, which meant she was going to have to settle for a night of Facebook posts or text messages to Val. Then it would be off to bed with the only male in her life, Thor, since she didn't have a hot-blooded man to celebrate with. Maybe luck was still on her side, and she'd have one soon. The Viking god she'd met today.

Chapter Five

The MAC company black limo stopped in front of the company headquarters as a red sports car drove out of the parking ramp. Not waiting for his driver or Philip, Mark opened the door himself. With Philip behind him, Mark entered the modern structure his father had designed.

"Good afternoon, Mr. Christmenn."

"Thank you, Karen. I hope you had a nice lunch." Mark smiled as he passed her desk. "I'll be fine. Take care of things here and come see me when you get some info. I'm not pleased with the whole Massaro bullshit," he said to Philip, who had been about to follow him into the elevator.

Immediately, the most alluring perfume Mark had ever smelled engulfed him. He took several deep breaths and allowed his senses to take in the wonderful aroma. He couldn't put a face to the perfume, which surprised him. He was able to recognize the perfume of all the female employees and who they belonged to. It was his business to know smells. Yet this particular one was new, but not new at the same time. Instantly, as the doors opened, a face flashed before him.

The blonde. No, he corrected, the stunning blonde-haired

woman with a light shade of emerald eyes that he'd bumped into earlier. He'd been so deep in thought about his pending lunch meeting with some of the MAC Board members, he'd literally run into the woman as she'd stepped out of the elevator.

The incident made him smile as he recalled how her breasts had smashed against his chest. It had shocked him how his body had rippled with sexual tension then and was beginning to do so again now. His body ached with longing to hold her again. On the other hand, was it just to hold a woman? Any woman? His reaction reminded him precisely how long he'd been alone.

Too fuckin' long, that is for sure.

Who had the woman been?

He couldn't recall meeting her or seeing her before today, but he felt as if he should know her. Had she been a salesperson? It was a possibility, because they were actively looking for some new packaging designs for their private label coffee beans. Could she have met with the Marketing Department?

Curiosity got the better of him and he made a mental note to have Mrs. Weber, his personal secretary, find out who the perfume woman had come to see.

Before going to his office, he stopped at the executive floor receptionist's desk and waited for his messages.

"Here you are, Mr. Christmenn," Linda said, "Mrs. Weber is still at lunch."

She handed him a stack of small pink messages, which were usually solicitations. Linda, who'd been with the company for almost three years, always did a good job of screening his calls for Mrs. Weber.

"Thank you. Can you tell me who the woman I made drop her files was here to see?"

Beep, ring. Beep, ring.

His question about the mysterious lady went unanswered as he watched Linda take the incoming call. She held up her finger to him, indicating he was to wait. Instead, he waved and headed to his office.

He opened the door and stepped over to the rectangle conference table. After setting his briefcase on it, he scanned through the pink slips. He'd been correct, most were from salespeople. About to toss the stack into the wastebasket, a yellow folded piece of paper caught his attention. Pulling it from the pile, he unfolded it and read the stylish handwriting.

Very old school.

Who took the time to hand write an 'I'm sorry' note, nowadays? Someone with a passion for right and wrong. It was a welcoming delight to receive one.

He smiled.

What an interesting turn of luck.

The face, along with the unforgettable perfume, now had a name.

Ms. Schoen.

It wasn't a name he knew. Who was she, and why had she come to his company?

The questions nagged at him. Her ring finger had been bare. He always checked when he encountered someone interesting. It was a bad habit of his, but he refused to get involved with married women. He knew all the wives, ex-wives, mistresses, fiancées, and daughters of his executives' staff.

Ms. Schoen wasn't any of them. It meant she was fair game in his book.

Even as he said her name in his head over and over, there was something about her he couldn't quite figure out. Knowing her name would allow him to find her phone number. He grinned at the possibility. He'd be able to ask her out for dinner. Which could lead to her naked body pressed against his naked body, while their lips devoured each other's—

Ring, ring.

"Mr. Christmenn, I have Agent Nelson on the line for you.

Would you like to take the call?" Mrs. Weber asked over the intercom.

"Yes, I've been expecting a call from him."

His erotic fantasy vanished as fast as it had developed in his mind. The phone rang again, signaling the incoming call. Stepping around his desk, he hit the speaker button. "Agent Nelson, you're back from San Diego?"

"No, I actually wanted to give you a highly important update. Some of Massaro's bodyguards broke under the pressure. We've learned Massaro placed another hit on you when he was released from jail. It's supposed to take place in a few weeks. We don't have all the specifics, but we'll keep you informed."

"Another hit? Why was he released? I put my life on the line."

"I can't go into details, but he was released on bond. When you have Italian mob money backing you, it was hard to keep him in jail. I'm sorry. I wanted to let you know firsthand. I'll be back on Saturday, but don't worry. My team is on top of it."

"They better be. In the meantime, I'll have Philip contact the head of your team for more security."

"Have him call. He should have my number, but in case he doesn't, feel free to share it with him."

"Thanks for nothing," Mark said and hung up. Taking out his cell phone, he texted Philip to come see him.

"Yes, Mr. Christmenn?"

"You know I don't like it when you address me like that when we are alone."

"And-never mind, I was eating lunch. What's up?"

Mark paced around the office. "You're not going to believe this. There is another hit out on me. Agent Nelson called to let me know. I was expecting everything to be fine, but no. Massaro was released on bond. Can you fuckin' believe it?"

"Christ, this isn't good, Mark. I'll beef up our security."

"Whatever you need, do it. Call Agent Nelson if you want or need more help. When is this going to end? I want to get on with my life." Mark sat in his chair behind his desk. Disgusted and emotionally spent, he raked his hand through his hair and winced. The lump on the back of his head had subsided, but the spot was still tender to the touch.

"What life," Philip stated. "Should I call Ms. Alicia?"

"Really? That is your solution to my dilemma, a quick screw." He sat up straighter. "No thank you. I'm very capable of getting that done on my own."

"Just checking," Philip chuckled and added, "You're acting like you need one."

"Piss on you."

His raised voice should have warned Philip to tread lightly, but in case it didn't, he stood and pushed his shoulders back to show who was taller. He paced the room again and realized he was grinding his teeth. Sighing, he stopped and turned to Philip. "Don't you have something you should be doing?"

"Mark, I will always have your back. I'll call Agent Nelson right away. What time do you want to leave this evening?"

"When I'm good and ready."

Mark ignored Philip's laughter as he left. His best friend was right. He did need to get laid. No, not just laid. He needed to find a woman who'd be his life-mate. No one had come close except for his very first girlfriend, Lucy.

She'd been the typical girl next door, with one special exception. They'd shared the same birthday. The two of them hadn't been able to fight their unique bond. The two of them had done everything together. Climbed trees, played baseball, and they would have campouts in her backyard until they had gotten older, and her parents put a stop to it.

He could still remember how pretty Lucy had been even with mud stains on her cheeks. However, all good things always ended. During the summer of their fourteenth birthday, his father had once again ruined everything by sending him away to school in Europe. The night before his departure, he and Lucy had discussed the future and the possibility of getting married when he returned. To prove his love, he'd given her a promise ring.

Four years later, after graduating, he'd returned home to the girl he loved, ready to plan a wedding. The sweetheart he'd remembered, with dimples and ponytails, had turned into a beautiful young woman with a devious and manipulative heart.

Clearing his head, he realized the past would always haunt him. It still made him sick to think about her, but time had taught him to forgive. Lucy, however, had provided a lesson he was grateful for — to be very pessimistic of all women.

Could he ever fall in love again?

Love.

Who was he trying to fool?

Love was for the young and foolish but being shot made him contemplate finding a partner.

He'd lost faith in love a long time ago, except for the damn picture on his desk. This was the twentieth year. What if he showed up and she didn't? On the other hand, what if she showed up and he didn't?

Shoving his hands into his pants pockets, not sure what he wanted to do, he felt the folded personal message he'd placed there earlier. With purposeful steps, he headed to Mrs. Weber's office. She would need to figure out who Ms. Schoen was and who she'd come to see.

The main objective was to obtain her phone number.

Screw Philip.

Chapter Six

The major interstate into downtown Minneapolis was a mess. Traffic barely loosened up before her exit. If the streetlights were good for her, she'd still be able to arrive early like she'd planned.

She hadn't been able to sleep, so she'd given up and had gotten ready for her first day on the job. Thor had ignored her except when she picked up her purse. He knew she was leaving and beamed at her with wide, green eyes and meowed. Feeling guilty, she left him some extra treats and kissed the top of his head.

The modern MAC building came into view and Rane pulled into the parking ramp with ten minutes to spare.

"May I help you?" a voice from the speaker asked.

"Hi, I'm Ms. Schoen. This is my first day. Can you tell me where I should park?"

She felt exhilarated to say the words aloud. She was now on her way to being independent. Every month, when David's alimony check arrived, she cringed with disgust. The courts had made him pay dearly for his years of verbal abuse and unfaithful conduct. Thanks to his successful career as a doctor, she now had plenty of money. She'd tried over the last couple of years not to need or use it. However, something always came up, and she had to dig into the funds.

"Your parking space is number twelve," the voice said, and the huge ramp door opened.

Nerves caused her stomach to act up once again. She drove inside and turned into her parking space, feeling important, but a little voice inside her head had her doubting herself.

With her briefcase and purse in hand, she slid out of the car and slammed the door shut, secretly wishing David's face had been wedged between the metal. Her temper cooled with the image of his perfect face, bleeding and swollen.

Ex-husbands. Who needed them.

Proving David wrong had become her mission since their divorce, but why, in God's name, had he'd been so damn handsome? Determined not to let the past or David dishearten her, she lifted her head higher. It was one of her downfalls, good-looking men, but she was learning to overcome that handicap with Val's help.

A cheery welcome broke through Rane's surly demeanor as she stepped out of the elevator. Karen, whom she'd met yesterday, was waiting for her to approach. It called attention to the fact she was starting a new job and a new beginning.

She smiled as she walked closer to the desk. "Good morning."

"You're here early, Ms. Schoen. I have all the paperwork ready for you to sign. And I have your employee badge."

"Thank you. I was worried about the traffic."

"Some days it can be stressful. I also have the parking ramp key for you. Please keep it with you at all times."

Rane signed the papers and couldn't help but beam at the name badge. It looked so official. "Thank you again for your help."

Shoving the key into her pocket, she clipped the employee badge to her jacket before heading to the other set of elevators. There were several people waiting for them too. When the doors opened, the mass of people sauntered in, and it was as if everyone was a contestant on the *Price Is Right* game show. They began calling floor numbers as music played in the background. She joined in and called out the sixth floor, since no one else had.

By the time the elevator reached her destination, she was the only person left to exit. Not wanting a repeat of yesterday, she kept her head up to see where she was going when the doors opened. Her stomach took several dips as she recalled how her body had pressed up against the man's and how muscular he had felt. That sensation was imprinted in her mind.

As she exited, she quickly looked around to see if the man from yesterday was anywhere near, having gotten a whiff of Drakkar, as if he'd recently walked by. Not seeing anyone who resembled the hunk, she headed over to the receptionist.

"Hi, I'm here to see Mrs. Wallen again," Rane said.

"Yes, I see that. I'll ring her. Please take a seat."

As she waited for Mrs. Wallen, she kept an eye out for the mysterious man.

"Good morning, Ms. Schoen."

"Good morning, Mrs. Wallen." Rane stood, nearly dropping her briefcase.

"Please come with me to my office."

She allowed a tiny smile to form on her lips as she followed. It became apparent Mrs. Wallen didn't like small talk. Their entire journey was done in silence. Not sure if it was a good or a bad thing, but it gave her time to glance around and take in her surroundings.

The areas they were walking through had modest décor with several offices, conference rooms, and a lot of windows, all which had escaped her attention yesterday. When they neared the end of the hall, an aroma of freshly brewed coffee filled the air.

"Mmm, that smells good. Reminds me of home," Rane mumbled.

"Wait until you go on one of the field trips to the processing plants. The smell can be overwhelming at times."

"Field trip?"

"Yes, field trip. It's in the employee handbook I'll be giving you," Mrs. Wallen said, then went quiet again.

They took yet another turn, this time to the left. They'd only taken a few steps halfway down the hall before stopping. Mrs. Wallen signaled for her to enter the office. "Have a seat. I hope everything went agreeably this morning when you arrived?"

"Yes, it did, thank you. I received my parking space and my employee badge." Rane held the badge like a trophy.

"Good. I'm glad your first day is beginning without any problems. That's what I like to hear. Watch for an email scheduling your time to get your picture taken. We'll add it to your employee badge. We can now get down to business. I'll need to see your driver's license and social security card."

Pulling out the requested items and handing them to Mrs. Wallen, who then began enumerating company policies and benefits. She was like a machine. How did the woman remember everything?

She lost count of how many forms she signed. The next items Mrs. Wallen handed her was the job description and the employee handbook. As she listened, Rane wondered if the woman ever varied from her speech. Smiling and nodding here and there, her mind drifted.

Would she catch a glimpse of the man from yesterday?

Did he have an office on this floor? He'd been very well dressed, so he could have been one of the VPs or a director.

Had he found her interesting enough to ask out?

"Ms. Schoen, are you all right?"

"Yes, yes," Rane replied, realizing Mrs. Wallen had asked her a question. Why was she thinking of dating? This was her first day on the job and she was daydreaming about of all things a man. She scolded herself to stay focused. If she wanted to make a good impression, this wasn't the way to do it. The hunk was going to have to wait. "I'm sorry. The smell just got to me a little."

"It can do that. You'll get used to it. I carry around mints. They help me when the smell gets overwhelming. I'll give you a short tour of the floor before I take you to your desk. Ready?"

Together they left Mrs. Wallen's office and proceeded down the hall which opened into a large room filled with numerous cubicles. Despite the high noise level, Rane saw a lot of work was being done. Smiling at some of the other employees, she didn't spot an empty cubicle destined to be hers. To her bewilderment, Mrs. Wallen kept walking through the open area to a doorway at the other end of the room. They walked into yet another corridor and down the new hallway. To her surprise, they ended up back at the reception area.

They'd made a complete circle.

It was then she noticed all the office doors. Finally, Mrs. Wallen stopped.

"This is your office."

"My office?"

"Yes, all directors have their own. Someone from Systems and Mr. Adams should be calling you soon. If you need anything, here is my extension," Mrs. Wallen said and handed her a phone list with her number highlighted.

"Thank you, I-I should be fine."

Attempting to hide her surprise, didn't go well. All she could do was smile after Mrs. Wallen left. Never once had she expected her own private office. Rane took a couple of steps into the office that was larger than her kitchen and almost cried. It wasn't a corner office, but she did have a great view of downtown Minneapolis.

Grinning from ear to ear, Rane went to the window. She could look down onto Nicollet Mall, the main street which used to have heated sidewalks during the cold wintery months. Some of the skyways that connected one building to another were still in use, but everything was changing with the times. The IDS Building, which was the tallest structure in Minnesota, reached into the sky several blocks away. She even saw the new home of the Minnesota Vikings, the US Bank Stadium, after the Hubert H. Humphrey Metrodome was demolished. The Minnesota Twins had already bailed out and had a new outdoor stadium, Target Field, which she couldn't see. The panoramic landscape was awesome.

Turning away from the window, Rane admired her new office. She had an urge to dance a Scottish jig even though she didn't know how. The previous company she had worked for had given her a cubicle connected to eight others. It barely had enough room for a chair, let alone for a person.

"My very own office. David, you piece of crap, look at me now!"

If only he could see her. How dare he tell her she'd never be successful? Her grandma's advice rang in her head. *Good things come to those who wait.*

She had.

The days, weeks, and months of tears and sleepless nights were well worth the cost of all the tissues. She'd waited and made herself strong in the process.

The phone rang, jolting her out of her memories. Clearing her throat, she picked up the receiver. "Hello, this is Ms. Schoen."

"Hello, Ms. Schoen. This is Richard Adams, your supervisor. Mrs. Wallen informed me you were in your office and we're to meet after the Systems people have a chance to get your computer set up."

"Yeah, that's what she told me."

"They're behind, which is the norm for them, and won't be by until after ten. In the meantime, would you care to go to the break-room? I'm sure Mrs. Wallen didn't include it on her tour," Richard said.

"Ahhh, no, she didn't."

Hearing his rich baritone laughter made her smile.

"Mrs. Wallen always fails at that end of her, ah, what should I call it, her routine? Would you like to get something to drink? I hear today's flavor, Vanilla Chocolate, is very tasty. I'm on my way for a cup right now."

"Please call me Rane. And yes, I could use something to drink."

"I'll be there in a minute to show you where the breakroom is. You can pick out your own flavor."

He disconnected, and she placed the receiver into its cradle. While she waited, she used the time to make the desk her own. Shifting her briefcase to the desk, she removed a coffee cup penholder, some brightly colored sticky notepads, colored paper clips, and a picture of Thor. She was studying the placement of everything when the door opened. She lifted her head and smiled, ready to greet whoever it was.

A very tall man in his early forties with light brown hair entered. He was good looking, but she immediately caught sight of a wedding ring. Married. She could check him off as unavailable. No married men for her, but then scolded herself. She wasn't here to find a man, she was here to do a job.

He walked toward her and held out his hand. "Hi, I'm Richard. I'm sorry I wasn't able to meet with you yesterday. But from what I've read in your resumé, you're more than qualified for what I was looking for."

Rane reached across the desk and took his hand in hers. "Richard. I'm Rane. It's nice to meet you. I'm excited about being added to your team."

"Welcome aboard. I don't like to discuss business before my morning dose of caffeine. Follow me. I prefer an espresso latte to the plain straight coffee. What about you? Do you favor the Caffe Lattes, Cappuccino's, or Frappuccino's?"

"I hate to admit it, but I'm a *Coke* drinker. I haven't developed a taste for coffee yet. Does loving the smell count?"

"Oh, I see, a newbie," Richard said and chuckled. "No, enjoying the smell of coffee brewing doesn't count. I'll give you two weeks before you turn into a redcoat."

Not drink *Coke?*

Never in her lifetime.

"I'm open to trying new things," she said, not wanting to sound impertinent.

He didn't seem affected by her reply as he kept up a lively rendition of what the MAC Company did. He described some of the problems she was expected to fix. So much for not wanting to discuss business before his coffee. She nodded and replied with an okay when she needed to.

Without warning, he stopped and held open a door. "This is the breakroom. All you could want. As you can see, it has several espresso machines, and on Mondays, Wednesdays, and Fridays we have our very own Barista server. The soda fountain is over here, along with the most important machine of all, the candy/snack one."

"Gotta love those," she said as she entered the room. At first glance, she noted several long tables with chairs. There were four microwaves and three large refrigerators. It was an employee's heaven.

"Every morning you'll receive an e-mail informing every one of the day's coffee blends. Sometimes when the company, or I should say Mr. Christmenn, is testing a new blend, you'll be asked to fill out a survey."

"New blends? Are we required to try them?" Her stomach churned a little at the thought of having to try different coffees all the time.

"No, but how can you resist? Doesn't the aroma call to you? Doesn't it make you want to sample the drink so you can taste the smell you smell?"

Rane shook her head.

He laughed. "If you want hot food for breakfast or lunch, you'll have to use the lower-level cafeteria."

"A cafeteria? Isn't this the lunchroom? Mrs. Wallen didn't mention anything. What do they serve?"

"Almost anything your heart desires. If it's not on the menu, they can make it for you."

About to inquire more about the cafeteria, she stopped and reminded herself not to. When she became nervous, she had a bad habit of asking a lot of questions and not allowing the person to answer them. They made their beverage selections. He chose a latte, and she ordered a hot chocolate.

"Would you like a lunch date on your first day?" he asked as they walked to the door.

"That would be lovely."

"How does twelve-thirty sound? The main rush should be finished by then."

"Sounds great, and thanks for the offer. It's very nice of you to ask. I'm surprised at how big this building is. I know I would've gotten lost if I had tried to find this room on my own. Thank you again," she said.

"No problem. I'll also be able to take you on a tour of the building after lunch."

As they made their way back to her office, Richard stopped several times to introduce her to other employees. When they reached the elevators, he excused himself and went to talk to a man standing at the reception desk.

Rane waited off to the side, sipping her hot chocolate, giving the two men privacy. She had a feeling she and Richard were going to work well with each other. And he'd be a great boss.

Not sure if she should continue waiting for Richard, she was about to go back to her office when he motioned for her to come over. As she did, he moved aside, giving her a closer look at the other man he was talking to.

Shit.

It was him.

Mr. Hunk. Mr. Brick Wall. Damn.

She had no choice but to go and be properly introduced to him. Taking a deep breath, she stepped over to the two men.

"Mr. Christmenn, this is Ms. Schoen, our new Director of Corporate Resources. Ms. Schoen, this is Mr. Christmenn, the owner of MAC Enterprise."

The bowl of cold cereal she'd eaten for breakfast threatened to come up. This man couldn't be the owner. The owner of a company this large would have to be old and hunched back.

Why was this happening to her? She felt so stupid for having acted like some babe looking for a good time. Yesterday, she'd given him the once-over look, like he'd been some male stripper showing off his wares. How could she have done that to the president of the company?

Triple damn.

Shit.

He did recognize me.

She'd seen his eyes light up when she'd come up to them.

Play it cool and take charge. Rule Number Fifteen, according to Val's rule book.

"I'm pleased to meet you, Mr. Christmenn," she said before he could and held out her hand.

"Ms. Schoen, it seems we've met before."

The Adonis god spoke and shook her hand. The contact sent sparks of heat throughout her body, causing her hand to perspire immediately. But she'd heard the sarcasm in his voice.

"I guess you could say we have."

Holy shit. He'd definitely recognized her.

This was it. He was going to fire her.

She withdrew her hand and fought the urge to wipe it on her pants. All she wanted to do was crawl away and hide. No, run and never look back.

"I'm pleased to be formally introduced to you. Call me Mark. Welcome aboard. Mrs. Weber, my secretary, will set up a meeting to go over your findings. I'm very interested in how you think you can improve my company."

Someone was on her side. Thank God. Her new career wasn't

47

over before it started. Before she could respond, he dismissed her by turning his body and directing his next statement to Richard. "I believe we have a meeting at three-thirty today."

"Yes, we do."

"I'll see you then, Richard." Mark looked back at her. "Ms. Schoen, I'm pleased to have met you."

Her reply went unsaid. He hadn't given her a chance to, as he simply walked away. She had to blink and forced herself to refocus, unable to block the sight of him strutting.

"Do you know Mr. Christmenn?"

"No, but I did run into him yesterday, not knowing who he was. He was, uh, helpful," she said, unsure how to say she'd literally run into him.

They walked to her office in silence. Even though she was tempted to look over her shoulder at Mr. Christmenn's retreating figure, she didn't. She had to acknowledge to herself it hadn't been a misfortune to run into him. Any woman would have found it sweet to have done so. However, she knew she had to definitely check him off her list of eligible men.

Rule Number One from Val. Never date the boss.

Taking another sip of her hot chocolate, his words hit her. "I didn't think I'd meet the president of the company so soon. You don't think he really wants to have a meeting this week or like next week? I'm good, but he made it sound like he wanted to meet today."

"No, he comes across like that, but he knows his business. Don't worry, he'll be fair. I see Systems has left you your sign-on and your password. Let's get started."

Rane too noticed the yellow sticky note on the computer screen. Pushing aside her thoughts of how Mr. Christmenn's hips had moved when he'd swaggered away, she turned her attention to Richard, as he began instructing her on her new job.

Chapter Seven

"Do you want to share what's funny?"

Mark stopped grinning and looked at Mrs. Weber. Sometimes her tone held such a deceptive calmness it set him on edge. But he knew she meant well. She had gracefully aged over the years. Her hair now sported what she called earned gray strands. She'd had to get glasses a few years ago and they hid the crow's feet around the corner of her eyes.

He forced all the emotions from seeing the perfume woman, whose name was Ms. Schoen, away and put on the stony mask face people feared. "What?"

"You were smiling. And I'm wondering why. It's a rare sight."

"No one, I mean-nothing. I just saw Richard and confirmed our three-thirty meeting but I xeant to cancel it."

He slid his hands into his pockets and shook his head to clear his mind. The woman had really upset his normal control of emotions and thoughts.

"Are you feeling all right? You're just standing there."

"Yes, I'm fine. I was preoccupied. I have a lot on my mind. Please call Richard and apologize and reschedule our meeting for next week. Do you have everything ready? I want to leave at about two o'clock."

"As if you'd have to ask. Your overnight bag is packed. Hal has the flight plan and Philip has been informed. Did I forget anything?"

Now her tone had taken on a casual quirkiness. He couldn't ignore it and placed his hand over his heart. "No, but I'm wounded, remember? Maybe when I bumped my head, some humor was knocked into me."

Without waiting for a reply, he rushed into his office before she could question him further. He couldn't believe his luck. The beautiful woman with the incredible perfume who'd bumped into him was an employee.

When she had come over to stand next to Richard, his heart had stopped. He was sure of it. He'd been able to tell she'd recognized him. The surprise on her face had made her eyes widen.

What an interesting turn of events. At first, he'd been a little taken aback when she hadn't acknowledged him. She'd simply acted like this was their first encounter and their bodies hadn't touched. Most women he knew would've taken advantage of the incident and played up to him when they found out who he was.

She hadn't. She'd been cool and collected.

Very unusual.

She intrigued him even more.

He needed to find out more about Ms. Schoen, his newest employee.

As was his habit, he began pacing his office. When his mind tried to solve problems, he did it. The more he tried to figure out a way to stay here, he couldn't. Too many people were counting on him this weekend. The coffee plant in San Francisco needed him. They'd come up with a new flavor and needed his approval before the roasting process could start.

Time was an issue.

It always was.

Why they couldn't have called him a couple of days ago was beyond him. He could've flown to San Francisco from San Diego and met with them yesterday morning. But if he had, then he wouldn't have had his run in with Ms. Schoen.

Fate? Was it on his side this time?

He stopped pacing and sat in his chair, then hit the intercom button on the phone. "Mrs. Weber, I need you."

"Yes, Mr. Christmenn."

Mark waited and drummed his fingers on his desk. She came in and sat in her usual chair with her notepad.

"Will you have the Development Team run some stats on the cost of introducing a new flavor this close to the holiday season?"

"Right away. I heard you met the new employee, Ms. Schoen."

Her comment caught him off guard. Was there gossip about his encounter with her yesterday already? He lowered his head to hide his surprise. Clenching his jaw, determined not to show her how concerning her comment had been, he raised his head.

"I did. I believe my request of finding out who she is has been resolved."

"I'm glad. I was able to obtain her employment records from Mrs. Wallen. I put the file in your inbox. It's the one on top. If that's all for now, I'll contact the Development Team."

"Thank you."

She stood and then walked out, and he glanced over at his in-basket. There on top was a file with a yellow sticky. Ms. Schoen was written on it.

The file called to him.

Again, he thought about canceling his unexpected trip. He could do a Zoom meeting and tell the plant to go ahead. It would open up his afternoon. He could request to meet with her.

No, he had to do the tasting in person.

His responsibility of running a successful company took precedence. He had to fly to California. Taking the file, he slipped it into his briefcase. The new employee was going to have to wait.

When two o'clock arrived, so did his requested reports and Philip.

"Mrs. Weber, feel free to leave early. I'll see you Monday morning," Mark said as he walked out of his office.

"Thank you, I just might."

Even though she said she would, he knew she wouldn't. She was his life blood to the company when he was away on business. Nothing got past her. He didn't know what he'd do without her.

As he and Philip neared the elevators, Mark glanced over toward Ms. Schoen's office. There was no sign of her in it. He paused for moment, feeling a little disappointed he hadn't been able to see her before leaving. Entering the elevator, he took one last look in Ms. Schoen's office direction and sighed. Monday would arrive soon enough for him to act, which would allow him plenty of time to do some soul searching this weekend.

————

Sitting in her office, Rane heard several dings from the elevator in a matter of ten minutes. She checked the time on the computer.

Four-thirty-seven.

She couldn't believe it. Her first official day had ended.

The weekend had arrived, and she only had an hour before Val was to meet her at her townhome. She clumsily searched for her notes on how to log off the computer. Finding them, she successfully shut it down and watched the screen go black.

She grabbed a handful of manila file folders, paper clips, and reports and placed them in her briefcase, knowing she'd be able to find time to work on them at home. As she exited *her office*, Rane took one last good look around, smiled, and then closed the door.

When she left the parking garage, she called her mother, a weekly duty. Their conversation usually began with her mother's usual questions. 'How are you doing? Are you eating enough? Are you dating? When are you coming to visit?'

Rane always changed the topic, asking about her Grandma Gretta even if it caused her mother to go into her usual guilt trip about having to leave her in Minnesota by herself.

However, to her surprise, she got her mother's voicemail. "Hello, Mom. My first day at the new job went great. I'm sorry I missed you. I'll try calling you tomorrow. Bye."

Thankfully, the drive home only took about a half hour. The sight of her two-story brick twin-home made her smile. She'd bought it with the money from her divorce, the payback for putting David through medical school. Noting the bare flowerpots by the front door, she reminded herself to make a trip to the garden store.

As if on cue, her cell phone rang the minute she stepped inside the house. Slipping it out of her pocket, she saw it was Val. "Hey, Girlie, I just got in. Are you on your way?"

She bent down to pet Thor who'd come to greet her.

"Yeah, I'm about five minutes away. I have the movies, ice cream, and, of course, our usual mini Korbel champagne. I'm ready to celebrate!"

"Me, too. Me, too. I'll have everything ready. Oh, you're never going to guess what happened today. Remember the man I told you about yesterday?" Knowing she had Val's full attention, she paused before adding, "Oh, it's going to have to wait, see ya in a few."

Rane heard Val laugh before the connection ended. Thor wouldn't leave her alone, so she picked him up and got his purring approval. She took out his canned food and grabbed a bag of special treats. "You're going to get to celebrate too."

He sniffed at the odd shaped treats before eating all of them.

She stood and walked upstairs to the bedroom with Thor in tow. Taking off her suit, she hung it up and took a pair of comfy pajama pants from her dresser drawer. Debating if she should take off her bra, she opted not to and slipped on an oversized tee shirt.

Just as she was coming down the stairs, Val arrived in less time than she'd indicated and entered the house talking. "Okay, I drove like a madwoman to get here. Now out with it, before I die. Did you see the man again?"

Rane smiled, not able to get a word in edge wise. She and Val were like two peas in a pod. Val took off her coat and carried the bag of goodies into the kitchen.

"You're never going to guess who he is." She turned when the popping of the champagne bottle scared Thor, making him run off. Opening the cabinet, she took out two tall glasses.

"Stop stalling. Tell me who he is," Val said and filled the glasses.

"He is the—" Rane deliberately took a sip of the champagne, letting the bubbles tickle her throat, ignoring Val's questions.

"Rane, we haven't toasted yet. And you're stalling. Come on, I'm dying." Val grabbed the glass away from her and held it out of her reach. "Tell me now, or I'm going to pour all the champagne down the drain."

Rane reached for the threatened bottle, but Val jerked it away from her and held it over the sink.

"Stop! I'll tell you," Rane paused and waited until Val completely straightened the bottle. "He isn't an employee. My boss introduced me to him this morning. He owns the company."

"No way! Did he remember you?"

"Yeah, and he mentioned that we'd met before and left it at that." She smiled and took her glass from Val's hand.

"You're kidding!"

Rane shook her head and Val joined in by taking a sip from her own glass.

"No, and you know what else I saw?" Rane grabbed the saved champagne bottle from the counter, ignored Val's open mouth, and sprinted to the family room.

"Rane! You're being mean. Do I have to call your mom? Remember, I'm three months older than you are."

Val followed her, carrying the bag of snacks.

"He has a great ass."

After saying the words, she dreamily sat down on the couch. Val joined her and it wasn't until they looked at each other, they busted out laughing together. Tears filled their eyes, causing them to laugh more, and they each swore they were going to pee their pants if they didn't stop. In between giggles and sips of champagne, the discussion turned to other parts of men's attributes, causing another round of loud laughter.

By the time their favorite movie, *The First Wives' Club*, ended, they'd depleted two mini bottles of champagne and a tray of cheese and crackers. Whenever either of them had something special to celebrate, this was their routine.

Movies and drinks.

Val opened a third mini bottle. "Are you going to ask Mr. Christmenn out?"

Almost choking on a spoonful of ice cream, Rane was shocked by Val's bluntness, which usually got her friend into trouble. "Are you kidding? I couldn't. He is my boss. Besides, it's in your book of rules. No dating your boss."

"I know it is, but he isn't."

Rane looked at Val who hit the play button on the remote control for the next movie, *Dirty Dancing*. "Yes, he is," she paused to think about it. Richard was her boss, Mr. Christmenn wasn't. "Okay, he isn't, but he is the owner."

"I don't have any rules about that. Any man with a nice ass is worth dating in my book. When can I visit? We could do lunch?"

"Yeah, right! What planet are you from? How would it look if my best friend comes to my office to check out the guy I've met twice and would love to have sex with? You bet, anytime."

Val slid her feet under her and tucked the throw blanket around her lap. "Fine. Be that way. I'll drop by unexpectedly. Now hand over that ice cream before you eat it all."

Rane smiled and gave up the half-gone pint of Dove Chocolate Ice Cream. She wouldn't want the odds on that threat. Val would do it.

The minute Patrick Swayze made his appearance, they each declared he was theirs. It was their game. Whoever said it first got to dream about him. When Baby and Johnny walked off together, they called it a night. Holding on tight to each other, laughing and tripping, they made it to the guest bedroom, arm-in-arm. Rane had to put Val to bed. She'd been the one who'd consumed most of the bottles.

"Johnny's mine for the night. You can have him next time."

Val's slurred words made her smile. Making sure she was covered with the quilt, Rane straightened up.

"Okay, you can have him. I'll have Mr. Christmenn tonight."

Not hearing a response, she turned off the light. They were like sisters through thick or thin. They'd each been married and divorced. Val's divorce had been far worse than hers. Rane had been there for her, and in turn, Val had been during her devastating breakup with David.

Val's advice about dating Mark had her thinking she might be able to pull it off, if she went about it slowly.

But how could she compete with all the women he most likely had falling all over him? She didn't want to be one of them. She wasn't a one-night stand type of girl.

Why would he even be interested in her?

In her semi-drunken state of mind, all Rane could focus on was her desire for him as she fell into her own bed.

She wanted to taste his lips on hers. She wanted him to kiss her.

Soon her sexual fantasy of Mark turned into a quirky dream.

Someone or something was knocking her down. Her ex-husband was standing next to her, laughing, and looking down at her. A knight dressed in shiny silver armor came out of nowhere to rescue her. When he lifted his visor, blue eyes sparkled back at her.

The next morning, she awoke tired and crabby, to find Val gone with only a note attached to an empty bottle of champagne.

"Best night ever. TTL. Thanks for letting Johnny be mine for the night. He gave me several orgasms."

The lightheartedness of the message changed her mood. Val could have him from now on; she'd found someone else to dream of. The metaphors from the night before were still very visible in her head.

Who was her knight, Mr. Christmenn? He did have blue eyes.

Did she need or want someone to save her? On the other hand, what did she need saving from?

Chapter Eight

The fading afternoon light made the fluorescent light brighter in the office. Rane hurried to finalize the memo she was working on, realizing it was later than she thought. Her phone dinged and saw a message from Val. "Remember we have a double date tonight. Don't be late." The emoji at the end was a wild-eyed smiley.

Shaking her head, she had to smile. Val had tricked her into saying yes, by agreeing to go shopping Saturday. She tagged the message with a thumb-up symbol.

Rane pressed 'save' and waited for her documents to print. She took pleasure in how her first two weeks had come and gone. She'd scheduled four meetings to tackle the departments that she'd found needed the most help. The reports she was printing emphasized her conclusions.

That's how she liked to work. Digging in until she found out how each department ticked and then dropped the bomb. The department heads were very open to the results and suggestions.

Checking the time, her watch showed it was almost five-thirty. Thor, the only dependable male in her life was going to be upset again.

He'd been giving her attitude since his dinners were served later than usual. He wasn't a cat you wanted to piss off. She'd found that out the hard way. When she'd forgotten to tell her neighbor, her cat sitter, to put out treats, he'd gone and chewed a hole in her favorite sweater. So, to pacify her finicky cat, she'd been leaving out more kitty treats than usual. He was just going to have to get used to her new schedule.

The printer spouted out the last of her ten copies and she headed out to deliver them. As she entered the hallway, the eerie quietness hit her. It was usually like this three-fourths of the time when she stayed late, with most of the office doors closed and only a few lights left on. She'd discovered not too many employees worked past five o'clock and had become accustomed to being alone when she did.

Mr. Christmenn's office was her first stop. As she walked to it, she wondered where he'd been because she hadn't caught a glimpse of his sexy body when he would stroll by her office.

She knew she shouldn't think of him that way, but she had to admit, she was very attracted to him. Whenever she could, she would steal a look at him, and her heart raced. She'd even gone so far as to send him an e-mail requesting to meet with him for a business lunch, but she had yet to receive a reply. So much for Val's advice, that would be the last time she took it from her.

"Ufff."

"Whoops."

Her surprised remark mixed with a male's, as their bodies collided. Then a slew of curse words echoed throughout the silence. Rane stepped back, struggling to stop her papers from falling, as she began to fall with them. Male hands quickly reached out to steady her and her scream stuck in her throat as she saw who she'd run into.

The one and only Mr. Christmenn.

Not again.

She couldn't believe her ill-fated luck. But was it?

After a second or two, the initial shock wore off and she noticed how close together they were standing.

Inches.

No, millimeters.

Her breasts almost touched his chest. Her hips were centimeters from his. If she raised her head a little, she'd be able to lock her lips on to his, for a delicious kiss.

A kiss?

What on earth was she thinking? She'd only kissed him in her dreams.

She needed to escape before her dreams became reality. He was her boss.

When she tried to put some distance between them, she found she couldn't. Mark still had his hands wrapped tightly around her arms and, surprisingly, she was gripping his.

"I'm so sorry. I didn't know anyone else was still here tonight. I was in a hurry. Thor is waiting for me. I saw...your light was on... but I thought you'd left already. I'm sorry. I wouldn't have come into your office if I'd known you were working late, too."

Rane stopped her jumbled apology as she recovered some of her composure at the same time. She regretfully loosened her grip on his arms and tried not to pay attention to the overwhelming urge to wrap her arms around him to take advantage of the fact he still held her.

The awkwardness thickened as they stood face-to-face.

"I'm okay. I'm not going to fall."

"You have an interesting way of making your presence known, Ms. Schoen," Mark stated and released his hold of her arms.

To cover up her embarrassment, Rane bent down to pick up her papers but felt him staring. Her palms became sweaty, and her heart raced. Her body tingled as ripples of excitement coursed through her.

Mark's curiosity got the better of him as he let his appreciative gaze devour Rane's body from her light blue oxford shirt right down to her feet. He focused on her bare feet. She wasn't wearing any shoes or nylons. Then he noticed all ten of her toes flaunted a deep purple polish. He felt his pulse quicken when he spotted a toe ring, one on each middle toe.

God in heaven, save him.

His fingers ached to caress each of her feet individually. He found feet highly sensual and hers were delicate and petite. Philip's earlier advice about going to see Alicia came back to him.

He continued to watch Rane gather her fallen papers, but her perfume overtook him, jolting his runaway desire even higher. He'd been in and out of the office so much he hadn't had the full impact of it until now. Ever since she'd started working, he'd get a whiff of her perfume at the oddest moments. The scent would grab hold of him and wouldn't let him think, not to mention the effect it had on his body.

It was the damnedest thing.

Maybe the government needed to patent its smell as a secret weapon. All they'd have to do was spray the intended criminals with her perfume and it would confuse and disorientate them as much as he was at this moment.

He took a couple of steps backward and took a second very candid look at the woman who could single-handedly take down men. He liked what he saw. She was a very attractive woman, confirming why he was attracted to her and explaining the reason his body was reacting the way it was. When he'd caught her from falling, her body had pressed seductively up against his and he wanted to pull her closer and lose himself in what he thought were very inviting lips.

Still lost in his appraisal of her, he watched as a strand of her light brown-blonde hair fell onto her face, hiding her beauty from his stare. She pushed the hair behind her ear, in an annoying sort of way. It fascinated him and disappointed him at the same time.

He'd wanted to be the one to brush it off her face. Now she stood staring at him, with her papers in complete disarray, her face sporting a little blush, and her blue eyes enlarged.

It surprised him he'd mistakenly thought her eyes had been green because they were bluer than blue. No, he'd been right, they were green. The light must have played a trick on him for a moment.

No, she had blue-green eyes.

What the heck?

He blinked several times because they'd gone back to blue. Her eye color had changed right before him. It was the most amazing thing he'd ever seen.

He'd read about eyes that changed colors in the classic fantasy series about *Pernese Dragons,* by Anne McCaffrey, and their riders. He'd read them over and over when he was younger, but to actually see someone's eyes change colors in person was truly remarkable.

"I'm glad to see you feel right at home." Mark glanced down at her feet to emphasize his words. He reeled in his out-of-control thoughts. Whoever Thor was, he was one lucky man.

———

Rane followed Mark's smiling blue gaze to her feet.

Her shoes. Damn it.

She'd taken them off as she usually did toward the end of the day and forgotten to put them back on when she'd left her office.

"I'm sorry, Mr. Christmenn. It won't happen again. If you will excuse me, I'll be on my way."

Turning quickly, she left his office, unknowingly leaving behind a tantalizing breeze of her perfume, and went straight back to her office to recover her shoes.

Stupid. Stupid. Stupid.

How could she have run around with no shoes on? Not too

bright in her book. To top it off, she'd been caught doing so by the president, which was even worse.

Rane shook her head; not the way to end her two weeks.

So far, she'd bumped into him twice. Not just simple innocent "excuse me" taps. No, they'd been extremely hard, body-smashing smacks. Not to mention that this time her breasts were still tingling from the contact. To her embarrassment, she'd also gotten a very good impression of what kind of package his trousers hid.

Fanning herself, she reached under her desk for her shoes as she imagined more details of his hidden anatomy.

Self-control.

Yeah, right.

It had gone out the door with her pride. How could she simply ignore Mark's sexy body? She couldn't, and that was her problem.

It had been odd having to look up to see his face, considering she was five foot six inches tall. She'd have actually fit perfectly in his arms, which would be to their advantage if they ever found themselves naked in bed.

Naked? In bed together? What was she thinking?

But that was her problem. She had to stop thinking, but she couldn't. His blue eyes, and hard body weren't easy to forget.

After she'd picked up her papers from the floor, she'd found Mark staring at her and sporting a smile with lips that would be able to do some extraordinary damage to another pair of lips. Like hers, if he had taken hers.

Well, she was convinced they'd be able to and wondered what it would be like to have those sensual lips kissing her.

However, the reality was that he was the owner of the company and ultimately her boss and almost certainly couldn't even fathom her as a woman. He probably thought she was a real klutz.

What did it matter what he thought? It wasn't as if she was going to go out with him.

Val was wrong. Mark was off limits.

He would be bad news all the way.

She wanted and liked her job. End of the daydream.

Rane hastily slipped on her shoes and continued delivering her memos, except the damn sexually frustrating episode wouldn't leave her brain. She shook her head again as the scene kept playing over and over in her mind. She had a job to do here and having a sexual affair with Mr. Hunk wasn't on the agenda and couldn't be.

Period.

The remaining thoughts of what Mr. Christmenn could or couldn't do vanished and she found herself back at her office. All she wanted to do was leave and do it as quickly as possible, but in her haste, she had almost forgotten her briefcase and had to go back for it. She then walked promptly and quietly to the elevators, not wanting another encounter with Mr. Christmenn, The Wall.

She laughed a little at the name she'd come up for him. It fit him. He never seemed to say anything, and he was as hard as a wall. Smiling to herself at her analogy, Rane glanced to the right.

His light was still on. He must still be in the building. She pushed the 'Down' button and it emitted a very loud beep as the doors opened.

"Good night, Ms. Schoen."

She groaned inwardly.

"Good night, Mr. Christmenn."

Making sure her tone was courteous, she stepped into the elevator, took one last look at his office, and wished the elevator doors would hurry up and close.

———

"Philip, go to the main parking level garage and make sure the woman who left the sixth floor gets safely to her car."

"Sure. Are we expecting a problem?"

"No," Mark said and added, "it's late."

He gave Philip no other explanation, hung up the phone, and waited, knowing what he requested would be done.

His lips curled in a deep smile as he recalled the identifiable beep from the elevator. The sounds had echoed in the quietness of the offices. He'd been anticipating it and when it did, he'd jumped at the chance to yell out to Rane.

What would have happened if he'd been out there waiting for her?

He could only imagine Rane's surprised expression. Her hair would've been covering one eye, and he would have been tempted to brush it aside for her.

Damn! What was he doing?

Mooning over a woman?

Yes, he was.

Anxiously, he waited for the return phone call from Philip.

What was wrong with him?

When the phone rang, he jumped like a nervous Nellie and hit the speaker button. "Hello."

"Everything went fine."

He relaxed back into his chair. "Did she see you?"

"No. I mean, I don't know. You didn't tell me to sneak around," Philip said.

Mark hit the armrest with his fist. "Damn it. You should've known."

"She's a real looker. Who is she?"

"Mind your own business," he said and began pacing around his office not sure why it mattered if Rane had seen Philip.

"Hey, man, it was a question. No need to snap. Are you still working? Or did you want me to bring the car around to the front?"

Mark heard a little chuckle at the end of the string of questions. Shit. Philip knew him better than anyone and wouldn't let this go until the real reason came out. "Yes, bring it out front in about an hour and a half. And call Ribbons to change our dinner reservation. Agent Nelson's flight has been delayed."

"Yes, Mr. Christmenn."

A robust laughter echoed through the speaker before the line disconnected. Philip would be fishing all night for an answer, but he wouldn't rise to the bait. This was something he had to figure out on his own.

Slipping off his suit coat, he loosened his tie as he drifted into his private bathroom to freshen up before his dinner meeting. The rooms off of his office could pass as an apartment, less a kitchen and dining room. More often than not, he used the bedroom here instead of going home. At times, it felt more like home than his house.

I'm following in my father's footsteps.

The realization hit him with disgust. It was another thing in his life he was going to have to change. Like father, like son, he kept a private residence off his office. It was common knowledge within the company that he used this private apartment most of the evenings when he was in town.

Apparently, Ms. Schoen being a new employee was unaware of his normal habit and needed to be informed. He made a mental note to have Mrs. Weber talk to her so there wouldn't be a repeat of tonight's episode.

As he stared in the mirror, he saw a man who'd seen too much in his forty-two years.

Where had the time gone?

Mark turned his head a little to the left and then to the right, watching the gray hairs catch the light. He frowned at the sight, however that only made the wrinkles more pronounced around his eyes and on his forehead.

He was getting old. When had that happened?

It was the fault of the damn picture and a girl's promise.

His mind drifted to that day so long ago, still crystal clear and etched in his memories. He'd been on his way to his family home on Marco Island for Spring Break, his senior year of college, when a teenage girl around thirteen had caught his attention as he waited at the gate. She'd been annoying in an odd sort of way. She'd asked her mother question after question, and the mother had been so patient.

His own mother had never had time for him, and to this day, she still didn't. Frustrated that he let any thoughts of his mother come to mind, he pushed away the painful memories.

Refocusing on the girl and her mother who had sat behind him in the waiting area. He had tried not to listen to their conversation but remembered smiling as he did. When he boarded the plane, his seat was next to the girl. He'd been tempted to ask for a different seat. He hadn't wanted anyone, child, man, or woman seated next to him after his unpleasant meeting with his father.

He had only wanted to get away for some fun in the sun and party time.

The girl had stared at him, a typical reaction he still received from females of all ages. Before the plane doors had even closed, the girl had asked him a string of questions.

The mirror now showed a man smiling, which softened the wrinkles, but had added different lines around his eyes.

The questions had ranged from, where are you going? Have you been to Disney World? Or Epcot? How many times have you been on a plane? Then she had shown him the damn picture.

The Epcot sphere, Spaceship Earth, with a figure of a girl on the left-hand side. She had informed him proudly that she'd hand-drawn it to give to her grandmother. It had been simply drawn and colored but yet very detailed.

He'd been captivated by what a gem she'd been on a couple of counts. She hadn't a clue who he was and didn't care. They'd laughed, talked, and he'd even helped her get to the next level on her Game Boy game. It had been as if they'd known each other forever and had made him wonder if that was what it was like to have had a sibling.

Toward the end of the flight, she'd asked if he was married. When he'd said 'no', she'd flat out told him that when she was old enough, she would marry him, and they'd be able to play games all night.

He'd been too shocked to laugh because she'd been so serious. Not wanting to hurt her feelings, he'd agreed to marry her when she was old enough, but not before she'd graduated from college and could prove to him she'd beaten the Mario Brothers game.

Her words rang clear and haunted his memories.

"Keep this picture to remember me. I'll meet you here in twenty years, and then we can get married."

She had pointed to the Spaceship Earth, and then tore the picture she'd drawn in half, giving him the half with the girl and added a boy to the half that she'd kept.

Now he watched his reflection as his smile faded and the light disappeared from his eyes. He splashed cold water on his face. That had been twenty years ago.

Mark stopped in mid-motion and stared at himself.

Twenty years ago.

Had it been that long?

Well, almost. The pre-arranged date was in a couple of months.

Subconsciously, he had held on to the promise he'd made all these years. But why?

In the beginning, he'd used it as an excuse for the reason he couldn't find a woman to marry. Now, he wasn't even sure if that was the real reason. He doubted the girl who would be an adult now would even show up. She could be married and have kids.

What if he did go?

He'd be going in blind since he'd never been able to track down her name or anything about her. Repeatedly over the years, Philip had stated there was nothing. It was as if she'd never had existed.

His phone alarm buzzed, bringing him back to the fact that he was old. He wasn't married and didn't have any prospects. Moreover, his plan to find a wife was going absolutely nowhere.

Instead of going out on a date, he was meeting Agent Nelson for dinner. Life kept on going like the Energizer bunny and didn't stop for anyone, not even the wealthy.

After brushing his teeth, he combed his hair, then straightened his tie.

"Not too bad," he thought.

Maybe a bit stuffy looking, but he was only meeting Agent Nelson. He sighed. Dating was going to have to wait again. Gathering up his suitcoat and collecting his papers, he made his way to the elevator.

For the first time in all the years he'd had his office here, the quietness of the building felt eerie. Why hadn't he noticed it before? The doors opened and he strolled into an empty elevator.

He inhaled a deep breath as he stood waiting for the doors to close. He was rewarded with Ms. Schoen's lingering perfume, a sweet, yet musky fragrance. It fit her in every sense of the way right down to her sexy feet. As he enjoyed the scent, images of what he'd like to do to them came to mind.

The doors opened too quickly for him, and he saw his limo at the curb.

Philip.

Always on time.

What would he do without him? Philip had proven himself not only as a best friend but also as a bodyguard over the last several months. He'd shown that during the Massaro raid.

Something he never wanted to test again.

"Good evening, Mr. Christmenn," the two security guards said in unison.

"Good evening, Larry. Good evening, Frank. See you tomorrow night," Mark said and strolled out the glass front doors. He stopped short and gaped in astonishment seeing Philip waited next to the passenger's open door.

"Sir, at your service."

"Philip? What are you doing?" His questions when unanswered. "I don't have time for this nonsense."

"Yes, sir," Philip said and grinned while still holding open the door.

Mark raised his eyebrows as he slid into the backseat of the limo. Philip took the front passenger seat. As soon as the car moved away from the curb, Philip broke the silence.

"I have one question, why after all these years are you interested in a—this woman?"

"Philip, I don't want to talk about it."

"You have your choice of women. They're constantly falling all over you. It makes my life hell as your bodyguard. Why her?"

He shifted positions in the seat. It was a question he'd been unable to answer. Philip took his job seriously. Did he know something about Rane? Over the years, he had protected him from angry ex-boyfriends of the many women he dated, blackmailers, scam artists and hired assassins.

"I don't want to talk about it. You're not my therapist."

"That's for sure. I'd love to know all your deep dark secrets. Remember the *date* is approaching fast."

"God damn it, Philip. You don't have to remind me. I'm over it. You've told me time after time there is no trace of the girl. I'm moving on, like you've told me so often to do."

Philip laughed.

Mark pressed the privacy window button, shutting out any more unwanted conversation, and locked it. Solitude was what he wanted. Peace and quiet. He hadn't been prepared to answer any of Philip's questions. By closing the window, he'd sent that message, knowing it would hold the other man at bay for a short time.

In the silence, Mark pondered why he'd had Philip check up on Ms. Schoen when she'd gone to the parking garage.

No, Rane Schoen.

No, Rane.

He liked the sound of just her first name. It rolled off his tongue with ease. It was an unusual name and had to be Scandinavian.

A lot of people who lived in Minnesota were a combination of Norwegian, Swedish, or German. His own bloodline was Swedish and French-Canadian. His father had told him it had been his own Swedish heritage that had encouraged him to find the perfect coffee blend.

That was what he, too, now sought. The supreme coffee flavor. He needed the right climate, the right intuition, and the right timing, which was everything, to pick the coffee beans.

The beans could be compared to women.

Once you picked them, you were treated to the ultimate outcome. However, for him, that's as far as he'd gotten. None had ever seemed perfect enough for his approval. That was the women, not the beans. The thought made him chuckle.

But yet, here he was thinking about how to get Ms. Schoen to go out on a date with him. It would be simple enough to get her phone number since she worked for him. He put his finger on the button to lower the window to ask Philip to get it for him, but his finger remained poised on the button.

Rane's confounded perfume was affecting him, the after-effect stimulating in an odd sort of way. The awareness that the delicate scent could still cause chaos to his emotions was disturbing.

It was weird how the effect of her fragrance on his senses was similar to the smell of coffee. They didn't smell the same, but he'd found the scent of freshly brewed coffee acted as an aphrodisiac. The company's research teams were very close to recreating the fragrance. He was hoping to market it as a special line of candles and other items.

His earlier urge to kiss Ms. Schoen when he had held her had been so strong it had caused him pain not to do it. She'd only topped the bottom of his chin, and he had found it quite tempting to lower his head. If he had, he would have been able to capture her lips. He thought he had sensed that she had wanted him to kiss her, too.

Stop.

She was an employee.

He never dated any of his female employees. It was a personal rule of his and he'd stuck to it over the years.

However, the more he thought about it, this was the first time he'd actually been tempted to kiss an employee. Not just any employee, but a very sexy one. He knew it wouldn't have been a simple friendly kiss, but a kiss that would have made her senseless with desire. He wanted to run his hands through her long, golden strands of hair. It had been calling out to him, *Touch me.*

Whoa. Slow down.

He shook his head to clear it. Hair that said, touch me?

"Get ahold of yourself," he muttered.

He was a grown man, not a naïve schoolboy. For God's sake, he'd seen hundreds of beautiful ladies before now.

Damn, but her eyes haunted him even now. He had seen them change colors as he'd stared into them. They had hypnotized him, not to mention he'd never seen anything like it in his life.

Air. Fresh air.

He needed air and pushed the button. The side windows went down, and he hoped the cool wind would help clear his confused thoughts.

What was wrong with him tonight?

It wasn't as if he'd never dated, or slept, with gorgeous women. He had a whole list of women, beginning with Jessica, the lingerie model. Then Monica, the Playboy Bunny, and, oh, could she make her furry tail do things.

And he couldn't forget Nicole, the actress. Her television show was becoming a huge success, but he'd never watched it. It was something about being a Cougar and having young men falling all over her. He understood firsthand why. She was every man's dream come true.

But Ms. Schoen was very beautiful and put the other women to shame; there was no doubt about it. He wondered how her assessments of the departments were coming along.

"Rules be damned," he muttered again aloud. "I'm going to ask her out."

The image of Rane standing with her papers in disarray, shoeless, with slightly blushed cheeks was very clear. Her navy-blue suit had fit her like a leather glove, but it hadn't said, "look at the body I have to show off." It had just been a very well-tailored suit. The skirt hadn't been long, nor had it been short. However, it had been short enough to have him, or should he say, men in general wondering what else the lady had to offer. It had been a tease. One he, on the other hand, considered to be in good taste.

The intercom between the front and the backseat rang.

"Yes, Philip," Mark said, as he unlocked the privacy window and his delightful thoughts of Rane vanished.

"Sir, I have confirmation Agent Nelson is at the front entrance waiting. We'll be arriving in about fifteen minutes. The casino is very packed tonight."

"I want to be dropped off at the front. Let Agent Nelson know where to meet me."

"But Sir, I'd recommend the private entrance."

"The front is okay," Mark said.

"I don't think—"

"I'll be fine. The front entrance it is."

"Yes, sir."

This time Mark left the window down, knowing Philip wouldn't dare ask any questions. Now was not the time with his pending meeting with Agent Nelson. He was mentally ready for any information Agent Nelson had to update him about, good, or bad. Thankfully, they'd been able to keep MAC Industries and his name out of any of the tabloid headlines. That, however, didn't mean it wasn't or couldn't happen yet.

Never let the business come second to anything.

His father's scolding words echoed through his mind. A vivid picture of his scowling face staring at him sent a chill down Mark's spine. His father would have been upset by allowing the threat of negative publicity to come this far.

His temper rose at the thought of the pathetic drug dealers attempting to get away with using his coffee bean business as a cover for smuggling illegal drugs into the United States. Not to mention his being shot. He placed his hand on his still sore chest, a reminder he was afraid would never leave him.

His blood boiled with hatred as he dwelled over the events from the last year. It had been a mid-September morning, starting out like any other day, until his BlackBerry flashed code one-one from the front gate. He had picked up the cordless house phone offhandedly, but before he'd been able to be connected, Philip ran in yelling, "Mark! Stay away from any windows."

In a matter of seconds, he found himself pushed out of the way and Philip positioned next to the sliding glass doors with his Glock thirty-eight pointed outside at some unseen target.

"Philip, what in the hell is going on?" He backed into the inner hallway, clear of any windows. Standing with his back pressed against a wall, Mark heard his goddamn beeper go off again. "Philip! Now!"

"The FBI is here. They have surrounded the property—"

The sound of a helicopter flying over the house cut off Philip's answers.

"Philip! What is happening?" Mark demanded more forcefully, feeling as if his world was crumbling down around him.

"Your life has been threatened by the drug cartel responsible for shipping the cocaine."

Philip backed up to face him with the gun still pointed out at something through the glass.

"Have you lost your mind? Who?"

"Remember the brick of cocaine we found a month ago in one of the coffee bean shipments?" Philip asked.

"Yes."

"When we turned it over to the police, they then handed it over to the FBI and they arrested a man by the name of Rudy Venezio. This particular shipment of cocaine was intended for Thomas Massaro. Do you know who that is?" Philip didn't wait for a reply. He kept scanning the backyard, watching for any type of movement, and then added, "The FBI has been trying to trap this man, Massaro, for years. Rudy Venezio is Massaro's grandson. The FBI received some information this morning that Massaro put a hit out on you."

Mark relaxed up against the wall in defeat, then calmly advanced over to the cordless phone and dialed fifty-seven and waited for Ron to answer.

"Mr. Christmenn, this is the front gate security. Please stay inside and away from any windows. Agent Nelson is on his way up to the house."

"Thank you, Ron."

Mark hung up as Philip came to stand next to him. They'd regarded each other with disgust, anger, and concern.

A rush of fresh air brought Mark back to the present as Philip opened the car door. He stepped out, letting the cool night air clear away the memories. Without looking over at Philip, he headed into the Mystic Lake Casino to face whatever new information the FBI had for him.

Chapter Nine

Thor voiced his annoyance with dinner being late again as Rane entered the house.

"Are you hungry, big boy?"

Meooowww, meeeowwe.

Thor rubbed up against her leg.

"Yeah, yeah I know, it's tuna night."

Taking a can out of the pantry, she used the electric can-opener, which had Thor jumping up onto the counter.

"Thor! Get down. Where are your manners?"

Instead of pushing him away, she snuggled up to him and continued to fill his dish as he snatched bites before she could set it down. Moving the dish to its place on the floor, he followed.

Checking the clock, she saw she only had about a half hour before Val arrived for their double dates. She had agreed to go out, for simply something to do on a Friday night. Val had met these guys through a dating service, not any of her clients or their friends. They were to have dinner at Mystic Lake Casino, which they had considered a safe place to meet. You didn't have to worry about getting drunk since the casino was located on the reservation with no drinking allowed, but wine was served at the restaurants. Connected to the casino was a huge hotel, which was convenient too, if it turned out you liked the guy, you could test the water. It also featured several restaurants, a mega bingo hall, and lots of gambling.

The casino was one of her and Val's favorite places to spend time looking for men. No, she corrected herself. It was Val's favorite place to pick up men and her favorite place to play slots. Val was a pro when it came to choosing men with money and was forever trying to get her to join in on the fun.

About fifteen minutes after feeding Thor, she heard the door open, then Val came inside.

"Hey, girlfriend, are you ready? You better be dressed in something sexy. And I mean sexy, and not one of your business suits. They definitely don't say you're available."

Smiling, she yelled, "I'm in the bedroom."

Patting her hair, Rane studied herself in the full-length mirror. She'd picked out a new pink spaghetti strap top, low-rise black jeans with a scarf belt, and a pair of high-heel sandals that showed off her newly pedicured toes. After appraising herself, she liked what she saw. David would never have let her out of the apartment dressed like this, but she could dress how she wanted to now.

It felt wonderful to show off her body. Would the good-looking Mr. Christmenn think she was sexy? Her body was still on fire from their run-in earlier at the office. She'd been so tempted to kiss him when he had looked at her. But his shocked expression when he spotted her bare feet probably meant he wasn't a foot man, had spoiled the moment.

She recalled an article in one of the *Cosmopolitan* magazines she'd recently read, stating that some men were turned off by looking at women's feet.

"Oh, well, his loss," she mumbled.

"Did you lose something?" Val asked as she entered her bedroom. "Oh my God, look at you. You look sensational. We won't have to waste any time re-dressing you tonight."

"Thanks. I'm trying. You look great, too." Val was dressed in a halter-top, one of the new spring fashion full skirts and, of course, she wore her signature high-heel shoes. "Is that a new top?"

"Ya, do you like it? It's a Karen Kane and I got it for seven bucks. Can you believe it?"

Val moved in front of Rane to look at her own reflection in the mirror.

"Do you ever pay full price for anything?"

"No," Val said and smiled. "Remember we can only stay till midnight. So, if you have to drag me away from my date, do it. I have an eight-a.m. court appointment. I know it's Saturday, but it was the only time my client could appear in between games."

"Another football player?"

"You know I can't tell you, but he does play Monday night this week."

They laughed at her hint and left the house arm-in-arm and in good spirits. As usual, Val was her chatty self while Rane drove. It was no wonder Val hardly ever lost a case. When she paused for a breath, Rane took the moment for herself.

"I ran into The Wall again."

"Get out of here! You're doing it on purpose. If you need a lawyer, I'm it for sure, you hear. I want to see this hunk."

"A lawyer?" Rane asked and merged into the turn lane to the casino.

"Yes, a lawyer."

"Why would I need one?

"Well, let's see. You've hit this man twice. You could've done some damage to, ah, to, ah—" Val cleared her throat and said in a very serious lawyer voice, "...to some parts of his body that would, or could, threaten his manhood."

She considered Val's comment for a moment and then laughed. "I did get a very good feel of what his, you know, was like today and it was packed."

This made Val erupt into laughter that was so infectious, she couldn't help herself but laugh, too. They composed themselves as they neared the parking valet. However, his interruption made them laugh harder as they both glanced at his groin at the same time. Ignoring his surprised expression, they quickly made their way inside to The Buffet Restaurant. It didn't take long for Val to spot their dates. After some polite introductions and conversation, they entered together.

For her, the dinner dragged on and on. She nodded here and there and spoke whenever Val kicked her under the table. She found the men boring, and her date kept whispering sexual innuendoes into her ear. They were sick and crude. She just wanted to slap the guy and walk out. But for Val's sake, she put on a smile and let herself indulge in images of Mark to make the time go by quicker.

The two of them would be lip-locked in a kiss. He would put his hand in her hair and pull her closer than they already were. His other hand would find its way to her butt, and he'd start inching her skirt up.

She blinked to clear away that picture.

No. They wouldn't have any clothes on. His lips would still be on hers while his hand would start a slow caress down her back and down her thigh—

"Ouch," Rane said. Her daydream ended when Val's foot found her leg once again. All three pairs of eyes turned to her. "I bit my tongue. Sorry, excuse me."

She stood and arched her eyebrows while she shook her head causing her hair to move from side to side. It was their signal that said, *Follow me*. Not waiting to see if Val had gotten her message, she headed straight to the bathrooms.

"What is your problem? Steve is really interested in you."

At least Val had waited until they had gotten inside before making a scene. It was so like her friend to get mad.

"Let's go home. No, Steve isn't my type. He is so vulgar. It was making me sick to my stomach. All he is looking for is sex.

Ken doesn't seem to be your type either, so why are we still here?"

"You're right. Sorry. Their profiles were great online, maybe too great. I guess money isn't everything," Val paused and added, "ya know, they are co-owners of their own car dealerships. We might've been able to get an exotic car cheap."

Rane shook her head in disbelief. "You're sick. You always look for something good. Let's just say goodbye. I think I still have some Chocolate Dove Ice Cream left at home."

"Fudge Chocolate?"

She nodded.

"Sounds better than getting an exotic car cheap."

Arm in arm, they returned to the table. Their dates weren't too pleased when Val announced they were leaving, but she was able to sweet-talk them into another possible date.

Before leaving the casino, they took a detour to play the quarter slots. Soon Val was down a hundred dollars, and she was up forty. Not needing any urging to leave when Val stated she'd lost enough they made their way to the exits. She handed the valet her ticket as a black limo arrived and when she turned to find Val, she collided into a man coming through the door.

"Excuse me. Sorry," Rane said.

"Ms. Schoen?"

A deep male voice made her head snap upward. She found herself staring into the pair of blue eyes that haunted her all evening. Mark Christmenn. Too stunned to answer, she heard him repeat her name but still she couldn't find her voice.

———

"Ms. Schoen? Ms. Schoen, are you okay?"

Mark stared at Rane. What was she doing here? She felt good in his arms, just like earlier in his office. He took in her sexy outfit, which was very different from the suits she wore to the office. He smiled.

Man, oh man alive, she looks good. I'm definitely in trouble, with a capital T.

Her extremely low-cut top displayed the swells of her breasts, and her tight jeans emphasized her narrow waist, and he knew firsthand just how small it was since he still held her.

He intensified his gaze as his eyes locked onto hers. There was a shocked recognition on her face., but his earlier suspicions were confirmed. Her eyes did change colors. They'd gone from blue to green and then back to blue.

He hadn't imagined it.

After an awkward silence, he released Rane when a woman who'd been standing off to the side asked, "And you are who?"

"Mark Christmenn," he stated as he turned to the woman who was clearly trying to protect Rane. "And you are...?"

"I'm Valerie Becker. Are you the same Mr. Christmenn who's the president of the company Rane works for?"

"Mr. Christmenn," Rane cut in, silencing her friend, "we were just leaving. I'll see you Monday."

Smiling, he watched as Rane pushed the openly gaping friend out the door to their waiting car, an eye-catching red Audi TT. For a split second, he almost ordered Philip to follow her, but they'd driven his lame limo, not his chick magnet Lamborghini, and he had Agent Nelson to contend with. With an inward groan, he continued toward the meeting place inside the casino.

"Mr. Christmenn, it's good to see you," Agent Nelson said.

"Oh yeah, right."

"Mr. Christmenn, Agent Nelson, we need to start moving. I have the security guards meeting us in the hallway," Philip stated.

"Which way?"

Mark knew from the tone of Philip's voice he meant business. Unexpectedly, Philip rushed him and grabbed his arm. Together, they began to walk briskly as a crowd of about fifty or more people moved aside slowly. He then saw six casino guards coming toward them. When they reached him and Philip, they formed a circle around him. Agent Nelson receded to the back of the group and Philip took the lead. They went through a corridor marked 'Emergency Exit Only'.

"I told you this wasn't a good idea. No more coming in the main entrance," Philip stated.

Mark didn't respond. He couldn't because he knew his best friend was right. They reached another set of doors and Philip escorted him through as the other guards cleared the area. He now stood in front of the restaurant, Ribbons.

"I'll take over from here. I have agents already stationed inside," Agent Nelson said.

Confused, Mark eyed Philip for an answer, but he only gave him a shrug. Leaving Philip at the entrance, he followed Agent Nelson inside to their table.

"We wanted to thank you again. The Bureau has been very successful in tracking down several dirty agents. Not to mention all the arrests of drug dealers."

"I'm glad to hear everything is falling into place for you," Mark said as they took their seats. He chose his words carefully. It was best not to say too much, something Philip had told him to do.

"There is one more thing that I need to fill you in on." Agent Nelson paused for a second and added, "Our intelligence has confirmed from a reliable informant that—"

"Spit it out," he demanded.

"We're not sure of the specifics. The agency is taking this very seriously. There's no other way to put this. There is a contract out on your life again."

"Another one, besides the two from earlier? Fuck. Massaro is a bastard. Fuck the mob!" He leaned back in the chair and closed his eyes. His temper was getting the better of him and he had to get it under control.

"No, only one more. Don't worry, we're very close to capturing the hit man."

"You have to do better than that." Philip took a seat at the table. "I will need more info, like where, when, and by whom."

"We can offer extra protection."

Agent Nelson's offer was like someone eating one piece of rice at a time. The discussion became heated for a time before Agent Nelson promised to get them any new information as quickly as possible. Philip protested, but Mark ignored him, letting him take on the agent.

He was so angry he wanted to hit something, anything. The news sickened him, but his recent brush with death had him knowing there was more to life than what he currently had. And seeing Ms. Schoen again had shown him there was.

By the time their dinner had arrived, the three of them had come to an understanding.

"I will give you twenty-four-seven protection," Agent Nelson said.

"That seems a little too late, doesn't it? If I hadn't rushed in and ushered Mr. Christmenn into one of the exits, who knows what could have happened," Philip stated.

"Mr. Christmenn, given what happened the last time, I needed to show you how real the threat is."

"Go on," Mark said tersely.

"There was a reason why I asked you to come here tonight. We leaked the info, and we got what we expected."

"And that was what?" Philip demanded.

"The leak worked. Our informant was able to confirm tonight was the night. Unknowingly, you changed the drop-off place, which worked in our favor, or should I say yours. We arrested a second hit man tonight at the other entrance."

"Agent Nelson, I don't appreciate being your guinea pig. It's my life you're playing with, damn it," Mark said disgustedly. "You are done fucking with me. Do you think this is a game?"

"No—"

"That's good," Mark said, cutting Agent Nelson off. "If and when you learn that there is to be another attempt on my life by the mob, I expect to be informed. Or I'll have your badge! Philip, we are leaving."

He stood quickly, almost knocking over the table. He felt Philip behind him as they exited the restaurant. He kept walking straight through the busy casino.

"Mark, stop."

"No."

"I said to stop," Philip yanked on his arm.

Mark turned and gave Philip his death stare.

"Shit, Mark! I can't protect you here."

"Think! There are probably more undercover police officers here than guests."

Philip, however, wouldn't let the conversation they'd had with Agent Nelson end. He continued ranting, not backing down, and they ended up having an intense argument while they strode through the casino causing people to stare at them.

Mark sent Philip a keep-your-mouth-shut glare, then barged through the glass doors to his waiting limo. "You're riding in the front, not in the back with me. I want some peace and quiet."

The silence during the ride home was a godsend. Tonight had proven one thing. He had to change his life. When was the last time he actually had fun or laughed?

As he entered his house, Mark felt immediately lonely. No one came to say hello. The atmosphere was all fake, specifically arranged by his house staff to his orders. All the lights had been turned on and Alexa was playing jazz music. A failed attempt at making a house seem like a home. Instead of enjoying the priceless artwork that hung on the walls as he passed by them or the ten thousand dollar per foot marble brick flooring, he frowned and went directly to his study.

Someone was trying to kill him again. What the hell?

All because he'd done the right thing by calling the police when they'd found narcotics in some of his shipments.

It wasn't his fault Massaro happened to be the grandson of some Mafia family. But here he was paying the consequences. He couldn't ask Rane or any woman to be part of his life right now. It wouldn't be fair.

At least that's what he told himself.

Was it fate that had him run into the woman who he couldn't stop thinking about having sex with till either of them was too tired to keep going?

He groaned as arousal for her came hard and fast. He wanted her right now in his arms. Wanted to bury his face in her hair and make love to her. Rane had surprised him again at the casino.

He poured himself a glass of brandy and enjoyed the burn of the golden liquid. He stared at the collection of dragons that decorated his study. Usually, they were able to calm him. However, tonight his pensive mood made them seem like they were all staring at him, telling him to go for it.

He allowed more visions of a naked Ms. Schoen to creep into his wandering mind as he sat. The image of her breasts filling out the low-cut top she'd been wearing had him shaking his head. He gulped a second swallow of brandy. The burn of alcohol didn't help. It only intensified his urge to run his mouth across the smooth skin of her neck and then lower to capture the sweet rewards she'd been showing off.

He drank the last of the brandy and knew he needed to find out more about Ms. Schoen. This insanity had to stop.

He slammed down his empty glass and took the half-filled decanter, strode to his private section of the house, and punched in his security code. After the death threat, he doubted he'd be able to sleep, but he had the brandy and thoughts of Rane to help.

As Rane drove away from the casino entrance, she glanced in the rearview mirror and saw Mark talking to another man, but his gaze was directed at her.

This was insane.

She half-listened to Val who demanded they go back. Mr. Christmenn was definitely going to think there was something mentally wrong with her.

She'd just left without a goodbye or anything.

Damn it, the gods were playing with her destiny. How many times was she going to run into the man?

"No smart ass comments?"

"I've been trying to get you to turn around for the last five minutes. Isn't that enough? You need to find a way to date that man. The way he held you was like telling the world you were his. I think he'd be wonderful in bed."

"Val, stop it. It was your rule, not mine. Now you're telling me to break it and date my *boss*."

"Rules were meant to be revised. It's not like they're laws, just guidelines. However, if you're not interested, I sure am. I'm going to stop by your office more often at lunchtime. I think I'm going to ask him out. Do you have his e-mail?"

Rane slammed on the brakes, yanked the steering wheel to the right, and moved the car to the side of the road. "No. No. No. He's off limits to you. If either of us is going to date him, it's gonna be me."

Val laughed, and Rane realized she'd been played. "That was mean."

"What? I didn't do anything."

With her blinker on, Rane maneuvered the car back onto the road, not sure why she'd gotten so mad at the thought of Val pursuing Mr. Christmenn. Val's snickers lasted until she reached her driveway.

"I'm not in the mood for ice cream after seeing how handsome your boss is. I'm going to head home. Remember I have an early court date."

"No problem. That means I get it all to myself."

Val got into her car and drove away smiling. Shaking her head, Rane went inside, and Thor came to greet her. Picking him up, she went to the refrigerator and took out the decadent ice cream and grabbed a spoon before heading to her bedroom.

"It's you and me tonight."

Thor meowed and began to purr as she sat him on the bed. Placing the container of ice cream on the nightstand, she undressed and put on her comfy robe. She snuggled up with Thor, who'd curled up beside her, then proceeded to devour what was left of the pint.

OMG, she'd agreed to date Mr. Christmenn.

Why had she'd gotten so mad at the thought of Val going after her boss? If Val had started dating him and they got tired of each other, it would've been awkward. She never dated anyone Val had dated. It was another of their rules, uh, *guidelines*.

She'd done it now.

There was no backing down on her commitment. She couldn't let Val get her greedy manicured hands on the best-looking man she'd seen in years. He was going to be hers first.

Damn Val's trickery.

She didn't even know if he was available. He could be married or engaged, for all she knew. Even if he was single and unattached, he was very wealthy and way out of her league.

"Oh my God, what am I going to do?"

Her sudden outburst caused Thor to perk his ears up and look at her.

Mr. Christmenn.

Mark.

She sighed and set the empty ice cream pint on the floor for Thor. "Okay, boy, it's your turn."

He jumped down and began licking the container. Her bed was empty again, like it had been lately.

Would Mr. Christmenn, no, would Mark be occupying it soon? He'd done a number on her already.

The spark of desire he'd created earlier at the office had exploded into full force want when he'd held her at the casino. Val had been right. When he'd stared into her eyes, she'd been lost. She'd felt his heartbeat when she'd placed her hand on his chest. Then the fuel that had ignited the flame into the burning need she was feeling had been the smell of Drakkar. It had her squirming as a very vivid image of Mark and her in bed, kissing, and having lazy sex, caused her to groan.

Monday seemed like eons away, but soon Mark wasn't going to know what hit him. Now that she'd made up her mind to go after him, The Wall.

The next morning, she found herself anxious, but didn't know why. She spent the late morning going grocery shopping and doing errands. When she returned home, she decided to tackle her special work projects.

"Done." Her outburst caused Thor to open his eyes, clearly annoyed she'd disturbed his nap.

"Hey, big boy, sorry."

She watched as Thor's eyes closed in indifference. Leaning back in the chair, she stared at the computer while she waited for the coveted report to finish printing after hours of working on the charts.

"I've done it."

This time, she made sure her outburst didn't interrupt Thor's nap again.

One report down. Time to celebrate. Which flavor to have, chocolate chip with pecans or turtle caramel swirl ice cream?

Decisions, decisions.

Her mouth watered at the thought of either. With the freezer open, she debated hard over the two choices. Closing her eyes, she reached inside and touched one of the containers. Opening her eyes, she was surprised to see the turtle caramel swirl had won. Taking it out and grabbing a spoon from the drawer, she went over to the couch. Her iPhone beeped, signaling a text message had come through. Without having to look, she knew it had to be from Val.

"My new man turned out to be a dud."

Rane smiled as she read Val's message. She didn't know how Val did it. They'd gone out last night. She'd had an early morning court appointment and still Val had been on another date tonight.

"Serves you right," she typed back.

"What about Tues for lunch?"

Leave it to Val to remind her about her own lunch date when she'd been trying to forget about it all weekend. Before she answered, another message flashed.

"What are you going to wear for your date?"

"It's not a date," Rane quickly typed and shoved a spoonful of ice cream into her mouth. Why did Val always have to turn things into a sexual encounter? Not about to let Val get away with changing the subject she typed another message. "It's a BUSI-NESS LUNCH date. And he hasn't even accepted."

Before she could correct her own misuse of the word date, her finger had hit 'send'. Damn.

The printer went quiet, drawing her attention back to the reports. She took the papers and stepped over to the table and laid them out. She'd just begun to sort them when she heard the unmistakable sound of another text on her phone.

Glancing over her shoulder, she contemplated ignoring it so she could focus on her task at hand, but curiosity got the better of her. Picking up her phone, she opened it and read.

"Make sure you get a good look at his hands."

Rane's eyebrows drew together. Hands? What was Val trying to get at? Afraid to ask, she pointed the conversation away from herself. "What was wrong with your date?"

As she hit send, a new message appeared.

"Measure the length of the middle finger to the wrist."

Rane gasped as yet another message came through.

"It's a sign as to how good he'll be in bed."

She gasped again and covered her mouth to quiet the sound. Thor meowed, clearly letting her know she'd disturbed him. Leave it to Val to come up with a sexual innuendo.

"I think you need to get laid," Rane pressed 'send' and quickly added a second text, "Not me."

She hit 'send' and typed a third text. "It is a lunch meeting."

However, even as she sent the messages, she couldn't help but recall his hands. He did have nice ones. And his fingers were long.

Another text arrived. "Doesn't mean you can't look. From what I saw, WOW! I'm going to bed. See ya at the mall. Night."

Smiling, Rane typed, "Manicure twelve-thirty. Night."

Clicking the phone off, she put it on the charger. The reports lay forgotten on the table. Val had her thinking once again about The Wall. Not that Mark had ever been far from her thoughts since their very first encounter the day of her interview.

The ice cream was half gone by the time she'd come up with a plan to make Mark go out with her. Nothing elaborate, just something simple. She was going to be straightforward and ask him for a business lunch.

No flirting.

No word games.

The last spoonful of ice cream made it to her mouth when her phone dinged.

What could Val want now? Didn't she say she was going to bed? Probably another sick idea.

Rane lifted the phone off the charger and an uneasy feeling came over her as the screen came to life. The message alert wasn't Val's name but someone with the letter D.

"Ro, Honey-Baby, I miss you."

White anger came over her as she opened the messages. The

screen went blurry for a second or two. There was only one person that had ever called her Honey-Baby.

David.

How had he gotten her new phone number? She'd blocked him from Facebook and her phone, or so she had thought. She hardly ever heard from him, usually only his accountant, to let her know her monthly deposits were being sent. She held her phone, staring at the words, unable to move.

"Ro, I want you back."

This second message prompted her out of her trance, and before a third message could come across her screen, she turned her phone off.

His words, *I want you back*, kept running through her mind. Her heart fluttered slightly at the thought. Not from the possibility of going back to him, but from what he'd do to get her back.

Tapping the screen, bringing the phone back online, it showed calming blue water and palm trees, so serene, so different from how she felt. She sat on the couch, holding her phone and an empty ice cream pint. Thor had joined her and was meowing.

What had just happened? Had she fallen asleep and had a nightmare?

No, she'd been awake the whole time the clock confirmed it.

Even if she hadn't been asleep, receiving a message from David was her worst nightmare coming true. Why had he contacted her, saying he wanted her back?

Her nerves were on edge, and she was afraid.

Even after all these years, would she fall into the same trap again?

He was so damn good looking it still tore at her heart to think about him. She'd given him everything only to have it thrown in her face.

Rane picked Thor up and went to bed, knowing deep down she was only putting off having to deal with David, but she needed time to figure out what to do.

Chapter Ten

Immediately after getting into his limo on Monday morning, Mark put up the privacy window. His home had felt like a jail all weekend with Philip fretting every time a car came near the house. He'd been worse than his childhood nannies by not letting him out of the gates.

At this moment, he had no passion to play darts ever again. All he wanted to do was take one of those fuckin' things and stick it into Philip. They'd played so much over the last couple of days, he never wanted to see the damn things again. To make matters worse, when they hadn't been engaged in a dart match, Philip only wanted to talk about how to secure his home, office building, and all his employees.

He and Philip had argued this morning because of their difference of opinion about going into the office. And Philip's mood had turned surly after breakfast. He hadn't wanted him to leave the safety of the grounds, saying he couldn't be protected with so many people around. Philip had finally given in when he'd agreed not to leave the MAC building.

To top off his morning, he had an ongoing headache, the one nagging him since the Massaro incident. Today it was persistent.

He was anxious to get to the office, grateful he'd have other people to talk to soon. As they neared the office, his mood became lighter. The thought of catching another whiff of Ms. Schoen's intoxicating perfume filled him with anticipation.

When they pulled up to the entrance, Mark hurried out of the car, not waiting for Philip. His mood elevated another degree as he entered the elevator. He hadn't been able to forget Ms. Schoen all weekend. He'd been like a man possessed, taking late-night swims in his private outdoor pool to cool his sexual fervor for her. His face tightened in regret as the doors closed. Her incredible fragrance had long since vanished, leaving only new aromas from the morning's previous passengers, none *hers*.

As he exited the elevator, Mark greeted Linda, then slyly glanced in the direction of Rane's office before continuing to his own. Her door had been open, but he hadn't been able to catch a glimpse of her. Without breaking stride, he grabbed the handful of messages Mrs. Weber held out and wandered to his desk. Then he picked up the phone, dialed extension five-seven-four, and ignored the stack of messages.

"Hello, this is Mr. Hansen."

"Mr. Hansen, I would like to see Ms. Schoen's personal file."

"Yes, Mr. Christmenn, I'll be there in about ten minutes."

"Fine. Thank you." Hanging up, he called out, "Mrs. Weber, come in here."

Mrs. Weber, who was nearly sixty-five, was the closest thing to a mother he'd known. She knew everything there was to know about the company business, his family, and his own private life. He could tell her anything and she wouldn't judge him but advise him knowing he'd listen. As a child, he wished she'd been his mother, and not the uncaring woman who raised him.

Sometimes he'd catch Mrs. Weber watching him with a certain longing look, as if she knew something he didn't and wanted to tell him but couldn't. It made him wonder about the possibility that she might truly be his mother.

It would've been like his father to do something as deceitful as to pass off his mistress' son as his wife's son. He'd known his father and Mrs. Weber had been seeing each other for years while his mother turned the other cheek, never saying anything. The affair had never lessened his opinion of Mrs. Weber, only of his father.

Maybe that was why he'd been an only child.

Could it be one of the many reasons why his mother had never wanted him around for very long, even to this day?

The day his father's will had been read, his mother had taken her inheritance and left the country. She rarely wrote, called, or came home to visit anymore. It was as if she had disowned him. He did, however, out of respect keep tabs on her in case she'd ever needed him. She was his mother, after all.

Or was she?

Damn it.

He wanted to know the truth.

Smiling at the possibility Mrs. Weber could actually be his mother, he waited for her to enter his office. She had received a huge trust for life in his father's will. No one had ever questioned it. His mother's reaction, however, had been unusual. She'd gotten up and left the room. He'd followed her, thinking she'd become sick or something, but she'd given him her usual pat on the head and with a fixed smile on her face. They'd returned to the room to find Mrs. Weber gone. The reading had continued as if nothing out of the ordinary had happened.

That had been eighteen years ago. Over the years, he'd even hired a handful of private investigators to find proof, one way or the other, of whether Mrs. Weber could be his biological mother. They'd always failed. He knew it would be simple to request a DNA test, but he wanted to find out the old-fashioned way. Someday, which wasn't today, he was going to just come out and ask her.

Mrs. Weber entered as usual, with her notepad in her hand, and took a seat in front of his desk. Some things never changed.

"Ms. Schoen has requested a business lunch for Tuesday," she announced. "Do you want me to schedule one in?"

He smiled broadly. "Tomorrow, yes, confirm it with her."

"But that will result in a conflict. You have a lunch scheduled with the company lawyers."

"Change it. They can wait. They only want a free meal," Mark said flatly.

"Yes, sir.

"Mr. Hansen will be arriving shortly. Bring him in when he does."

"Okay, Mr. Christmenn," she answered with assurance, and then asked, "Is there anything else?"

"Yes, please resend the memo about employees staying late. Apparently, Ms. Schoen isn't aware of my late-night habits here at the office."

"Oh my, did something happen?"

"Nothing other than running into each other. No harm done. And, yes, I was fully clothed." He smiled inwardly, wondering what would've happened if he hadn't been.

After she left, he continuously paced from one room to another as he waited for Mr. Hansen's arrival. The hand-drawn picture on his desk drew his attention, making him forget his original eagerness. He walked over to his desk, so he could see it.

The picture wasn't a masterpiece or worth millions, but it held memories beyond anything he'd ever thought possible. He had watched the girl from the plane painstakingly color it with colored pencils.

The frame was worth more than the paper inside. It greeted him every day when he sat at his desk, a constant reminder of the pending date. The sun had faded the Epcot park's big sphere, which was at the entrance. A stick figure of a girl was standing next to it and added in a child's handwriting in all large capital letters, the message at the top read, *Meet me in twenty years.*

Again, the nagging question arose; would she remember as has he had? He'd been twenty-two when she'd given it to him. She, on the other hand, could only have been around thirteen.

Which was too young to have known what she asked was inappropriate. Her marriage proposal had shocked him. It had been his first one, but over the years, many women had followed suit. The later ones were different. The young girl's had come from the heart. An innocent child, not a woman trying to obtain something.

He couldn't believe twenty years had gone by since that plane ride. His life sure hadn't turned out as he'd assumed it would. Lucy left him heartbroken at the tender age of eighteen. His father's death turned him into a man sooner than he had wanted. Then there'd been the many women who'd tried to seduce him for his fortune. And, if someone told him drug dealers would someday try to kill him, he would have laughed until his sides ached.

"Mr. Christmenn, Mr. Hansen is here to see you," Mrs. Weber announced over the intercom.

He set the picture down and gazed expectantly toward the door.

"John, come in and sit down," Mark said when the door opened. "I have some special projects coming up soon and I wanted to confirm Ms. Schoen will be able to handle them."

"Her references checked out so well, we offered her the job during her first interview."

Mark couldn't help but smile. It didn't surprise him she'd be good at what she did. "Great. The company is growing."

"Yes, it is. This is her first position with a company our size," John stated, then added, "However, she did come highly recommended from her previous employer. I can't believe some other Fortune Five Hundred Companies didn't know about her. I believe you'll find she'll be a welcome asset to the company."

John then held out the file to him. He took it and opened it.

"Thank you. I'll have Mrs. Weber return it when I'm finished."

He hardly noticed when John left, but waited to hear the door close before picking up the phone. "Philip, come to my office."

He didn't wait for a response. Mark simply hung up and studied Rane's resume and the HR's hiring papers in the folder.

Mrs. Weber announced that Philip was waiting from the door. Mark rose to his feet as she ushered him into his office.

"Thanks, Mrs. Weber," Mark said as she left.

He watched as Philip eyed him and then Mrs. Weber before taking a seat in a chair next to the couch. He strode over to the door, ignoring Mrs. Weber's unhappy look as he closed the door. Taking a seat on the couch, he placed Ms. Schoen's file on the table in front of them.

"Philip, I need you to check out this employee. I want a full history."

Not about to let Philip give him more attitude, he was about to say more, but stopped short when he saw Philip's eyebrows arched and a smile on his lips.

"Yes, I'm showing interest in an employee. I'm breaking all my own rules."

"How soon did you want this? I could have it for you in three weeks." Philip picked up the file and flipped through the papers casually.

Mark scowled at him. "Don't play games with me today, damn it. Your 'Mr. Scotty' attitude isn't going to work. You should know me better than that."

"From the look on your face, is one week a better time frame for you?"

Mark deepened his scowl and stood.

"Okay, okay, I need more dilithium crystals to get you your information by the end of the day."

"I'll give them to you in the ass if you don't wipe that grin off your face right now," Mark said and slammed his fist on the desk. "If I don't have the file by the end of the day, you won't have a dart partner for three months."

He got the response he wanted with that comment. Now the game had just ended. Smiling, he turned and saw Philip's grin disappear as fast as it had appeared. Mrs. Weber's knock stopped any more word games.

"I'll take this and leave," Philip waved the file in the air as he left.

"Sorry to interrupt, Mr. Christmenn..."

Thankful for her perfect timing, it was onto normal business. If time could stand still, it did that morning as he kept checking the clock. Even going to lunch hadn't given him the peace he'd wanted. Mark knew Mrs. Weber was beginning to suspect something was up. She asked if she could get him anything every time, he stepped in the doorway to see if Philip was coming yet.

He wanted that report now.

Patience wasn't one of his virtues. Even cursing Philip wasn't helping, so he swore that if he was even a minute late, he was going through with his earlier threat of not playing darts with him. To pass the time, he went over the charts Agent Nelson and Philip had designed for his protection. Beefing up security was easy, but keeping the press at bay was harder than he'd imagined.

"It's about damn time." He pushed aside the charts when Mrs. Weber announced Philip.

Mark watched as he strolled into the office as if there was no hurry in the papers he held in his hand. If Philip hadn't been his best friend, he'd have fired him on the spot for his cocky attitude.

The jerk was acting as if he had nothing to do but waste time.

Two could play this game.

Mark calmly waited for him to sit, not showing his friend the satisfaction of seeing he'd actually been waiting all day. Philip nonchalantly placed the coveted report on his lap and stared at him. Knowing Philip was good at reading him, Mark tried the best he could to guard his emotions. He clamped his jaw together and waited for Philip to break the silence first.

"I have the information you requested. Do you have time to go over my findings, or should I come back later?"

Philip's businesslike tone struck a nerve, but when he stood and began to leave tipped him over the edge. "Sit your ass down! You've advanced yourself to three months of no dart matches."

"Mark, come on. You know I was enjoying the moment. You wouldn't do that to me, now would you?" Philip was barely able to hide his smile and Mark saw a twinkle in his eyes as he handed the file to him. "Who would play darts with you if I don't?"

Ignoring the remark, knowing there was a truth to it he didn't want to admit, Mark opened the coveted file. Most of what he read he'd seen on her résumé. Nothing stood out. He turned the pages over in hopes of finding something, not really sure what that something was.

He hardly ever requested an investigation on a female employee. In fact, this had been a first. Rane's past was very clean. No bad information.

What the fuck?

He leaned forward and re-read the paragraphs he'd just read. She had an ex-husband that was a total asshole based on the information Philip had unearthed.

Slamming the file down on his desk, he stared at Philip. "Where is the ex-husband?"

"I'll have his report within the hour. I found out about him too late to be able to include much about him."

"Great, thanks. I just needed reassurance she is who she says she is." Mark paused for effect and added, "I'll be asking her out."

Seeing Philip's shocked expression was the reward he'd been waiting for, but before he could attack him with a mouthful of questions, Mark quickly changed the subject. "I've gone over the charts Agent Nelson gave us. Have you heard anything else from our friend?"

"Yes, he's given us ten full-time undercover agents. I'm using them mostly to protect the building and the employees. All info leads to something going down here." Philip slapped the desk hard and swore. "Damn it, Mark! I can't protect over a thousand people."

"Calm down. No one said *you* had to do it alone. Hire a whole damn army if you have to."

"This might be a joke to you, but for your information, your life is on the line here."

Neither said anything as they both took in the cold truth behind the words. Philip stood and began to pace. Mark broke the silence first this time.

"I'm sorry. I'm just so sick of this. What do you need me to do or not to do?"

Philip stopped his pacing, sat on the couch instead of the chair in front of his desk, and appeared to be choosing his words carefully. "I'm not sure. I'm out of my element here. The other week showed me how lax I'd become. I've gotten soft, man, and it scares me." He cleared his throat. "Maybe you should find a new bodyguard."

"Are you crazy? You're the best one I could have. We'll get through this together."

"Do I still have a dart partner?"

"That's still on the bargaining table. I should be ready to leave in about an hour, or when you have the other request completed. Bring the limo around to the front."

Mark watched Philip stand, nod and walk out of the office. Once he couldn't see him anymore, he reopened the file and concentrated on the information as he read.

Rane and her ex-husband, David Moore, had been high school sweethearts. She'd been a cheerleader and Homecoming Queen in her senior year of high school. David had been the captain of the football team. They'd dated all through high school and then got married the summer they graduated.

Where did Philip get this type of information?

It was way too personal for him to have gotten it from any normal agency.

He read on.

David had attended the University of Minnesota, majoring in medicine. Rane had attended the Minnesota School of Business for Fashion Merchandising. When she graduated, Rane had received a placement at one of the leading fashion companies. A couple of years later, David became a doctor and accepted a position at a hospital in California.

The next section of the report interestingly showed a handful of police reports indicating marital disturbances and also contained one picture of Rane with a swollen lip. Soon after that, they were divorced, ending ten years of marriage.

"What a piece of trash," Mark said aloud.

He saw she must have had a good lawyer even though it had taken almost two years before the divorce was finalized. The courts had awarded Rane a settlement of a monthly spousal maintenance fee for the next twenty years with guaranteed increases based on Dr. David Moore's income. She still had fifteen years left before the spousal payments would end.

Good for her. She'd taken the piece of scum to the cleaners.

The report went on to say that during the divorce she'd gone back to school. Three years later, she graduated from the University of Minnesota with a master's degree in marketing resource management.

There was more about her personal life, but nothing about any other men in her life. No live ins, no other marriages, and Philip had been able to confirm her ex had stayed in California.

No angry ex to worry about, nice.

Her bank account showed she was a pretty wealthy woman and didn't need to be working. That tidbit of information threw up several red flags.

What's she doing working here then?

———

Val's *"I told you so's,"* echoed in Rane's head as she drove to work Tuesday morning. She'd waited until the end of their Sunday monthly pedicures before sharing her unpleasant news about the texts from David. Val had totally flipped out, which hadn't been a surprise.

They'd ended up stopping at Starbucks to get Val a layered Latte and a Café Mocha for herself. One coffee drink led to two while they discussed what the messages could mean but hadn't been able to come up with any good reasons. Before calling it a night, Val made her promise she wouldn't talk to David via the phone or send any text messages or check out his Facebook page. To make it worse, Val had threatened to come over and melt all of her ice cream if she didn't keep her word.

The six text messages from David weighed heavily on her as she strode into her office. They were stuck in her head.

"Honey-Baby I want you back."

It kept playing over and over in her head. Even now, she was tempted to glance at her phone to see if she had another message from him. Val had been right to ignore them, but it didn't stop her from thinking about them.

What could he want?

He'd never personally contacted her, only through the lawyer.

Ignoring the nagging question, she took out the files she'd worked on at home from her briefcase when she reached her office. The last lingering thoughts of her dirtbag ex faded away. Setting her briefcase off to the side of her desk, she made her way toward the breakroom.

Today was the big day, her lunch meeting with Mark. No, Mr. Christmenn, she corrected herself. She needed to keep it professional at the office, no matter what Val said.

What would he say when it was time to discuss her findings?

Would he say "Nice job" when she told him his company was

sinking? Or, "Thanks for showing me I don't know how to run my companies?"

Yeah, she could see it now. "Thanks, but no thanks, you're fired."

It troubled her that this was the largest company that she'd had to reorganize, and she had nothing to compare her work to. So far, she'd found a few areas that needed very little refining or changing. Then other departments were so far gone it was going to take a lot of time and effort to get them back on track.

Vision.

That was the key.

She needed the employees, along with Mark, uh, Mr. Christmenn, to be able to envision success. To accomplish this mega project, she needed an early dose of caffeine. It was calling her, as it did every morning. She'd start with two cups of hot chocolate, then after ten o'clock, her *Coke*.

Routine. Routine.

She liked doing the same thing. It helped set the pace for the day. New plans began spinning through her mind as she pushed open the door to the breakroom.

Rane smiled at the other employees getting their own morning doses of caffeine. None of them acknowledged her or smiled back. Her stomach sank at their cold response. It made her realize that she wasn't going to make very many friends. As far as they were concerned, she was the enemy. An empty feeling came over her as she left the crowded room and returned to her office.

———

Mark hurried past a smiling Mrs. Weber and into his office. He groaned when he saw a very large note taped to his empty coffee pot.

"Your machine is broken. The new one won't be here until tomorrow afternoon. Let me know when you want your coffee."

Damn.

Today's special blend was French Vanilla made with Costa Rican beans and an added dash of cinnamon. It was a blend he'd hoped would do well this coming Christmas and he had been excited to taste it. He read the note a second time with growing dismay. It was signed with a very large happy face.

Great. Bad weekend and now this.

To make matters worse, he had to cancel his lunch with Rane to meet with Agent Nelson instead, to go over some new details. He hated having to break the lunch appointment with Rane.

Damn. Could the day get more unpleasant?

Mrs. Weber should've had a cup of coffee ready for him, but no. She'd just left a note.

Fucking shit.

Why was she giving him attitude? Had he done something to upset her?

Not taking the chance of making her angrier, he thought it best to go to the breakroom himself to walk off some steam. As he left his office, Mrs. Weber beamed at him with an angelic face.

"I can get my own coffee," Mark said as he strode past, knowing he was being rude, but damn it, he was the boss.

Coffee was his business. He wanted his damned cup of coffee when he came in.

He'd almost reached the breakroom doors when Rane's perfume hit him, and he smiled. He breathed in the intoxicating scent and spun around in anticipation. She had to be close, but he couldn't find her anywhere, and he eagerly pushed open the doors.

His stomach knotted as he scanned the room. There were only a couple of employees sitting at a table, but when they saw him, they got up and left. He ignored their reaction but found Rane's fragrance had lingered behind to taunt him. He smoothed down his suit coat and squared his shoulders, not allowing the scent to take over his ability to think clearly any more than it already was doing. It did, however, make him wonder if it was the perfume or the woman he was attracted to. He was beginning to think it was both.

The barista station was empty. Why?

It was a Special Blend Day.

Settling for a regular blend, he shoved coins into the coffee machine.

The sound of the door opening made him jump a little with excitement, and he turned slowly to see who had come in. His optimistic attitude didn't last.

It wasn't *her*.

Instead, it was the Manager of the Shipping Department, Danny.

"Good morning. How is the receiving project coming along with the overseas shipping problems?" Mark could see Danny was trying to recover from the shock of seeing him in the breakroom. It wasn't a daily occurrence. It wasn't even a weekly visit. It was a rarity to find him in the breakroom. He waited for what seemed an eternity before Danny was able to speak.

"Great, just great. I still have to clarify some problems and check out some of the responses that I've received. I think we have a meeting scheduled for Thursday morning. Did you want me to give you an update today?"

"No, Thursday will be fine. Please double-check with Mrs. Weber for my schedule. By the way, we have a new special blend coming out this week. Make sure to try it."

He grabbed the coffee cup from the vending machine, inwardly cursing as the hot cup burned his palm, then shot Danny a smile before opening the door.

Every so often, Mark caught whiffs of Rane's perfume as he strolled back to his office. If she came this way every morning, he'd have an excuse to see her. The mere thought of starting out each morning seeing Rane made him grin.

To hell with his coffeemaker, he thought.

He gazed at Mrs. Weber and saw her lips curl into a smile as he walked into his office. It was maddening the way she treated him as if he was a ten-year-old kid. But then again, it was nice to know someone did care about him. She was and always had been there for him.

"Just get me a coffeemaker fast and check to see why the barista station was empty this morning. We should have started testing the Christmas blend," he said and realized it had come out a little too rough.

"Ooo, I'll find out," Mrs. Weber replied and added, "by the way, I have the California plant holding on Line One."

"Send the call through."

Mark managed to say it nicely this time. Why was he so touchy lately?

———

Rane sat down at her desk still holding her cup of hot chocolate, and opened the top left desk drawer. She gathered a handful of Hershey's Kisses and unwrapped one of them, placed it into her mouth with the tip forward, and took a sip of the hot liquid.

Melted chocolate filled her mouth in a rush of absolute chocolate delight. Setting her cup down, she unwrapped a second kiss for a repeat.

Man, this was better than sex.

She should know. She hadn't been with a man in a very long time. One year, two months, twelve days, and eight hours, but who was counting?

As the second Hershey Kiss melted, she wondered if sex with Mr. Christmenn would be better than this aphrodisiac. Her eyes widened at the thought. Brushing the remaining kisses aside, she made herself concentrate on work and not on the owner of the company.

Rane immediately sent out e-mails to each of the department managers to set up meeting times, hoping this diversion would stop her train of thought from wandering again. She jumped a little when the phone rang.

"Hello, this is Ms. Schoen."

"Good morning, Rane, this is Richard. Mr. Christmenn asked me to meet with you today to go over the concluding stages of your information. He is unable to make the lunch appointment he had scheduled with you."

"Oh, thanks for letting me know. Would you like to come to my office, around two?" She struggled to keep her disappointment from her voice.

"Yes, that's fine. I'll see you at two."

Well, she now knew how hens felt having their eggs snatched from them. No lunch date with Mr. Wall. Upset, she stood and peered out the window.

Who was she trying to kid?

She was extremely annoyed. She'd built up this lunch as if it was to be a first date. It was her fault. The more she thought about it, the more she knew she'd been childish. Who in their right mind would ask out the owner of the company they worked for and think it would work out?

Val had been wrong. Rane knew she couldn't go through with the plan, no matter how attracted she was to Mark. He was out of her league, and she had to forget about his sexy body, his delicious lips, and, most of all, his package.

She concentrated even harder on her PowerPoint presentations and her disappointment faded. Time flew and her growling stomach let her know it was time for lunch. She picked up her purse to go to lunch alone.

She waited with annoyance for the stupid elevator, which always happened to be on the main level, no matter what time of day it was. She glanced at the stairwell, thinking it might be a better option at this point. At least it would give her a workout if she used them. With one foot poised, ready to move in its direction, the smell of Drakkar hit her.

Rane glanced over to her right, she couldn't help herself, knowing that it had to be him. She took in every detail, from Mark's navy-blue suit, his white starched shirt, to his red-striped tie.

Mmm, mmm, good enough to eat.

She shifted her eyes to his face and centered in on his lips; they looked to be firm and had a hint of a smile on them. Realizing she'd been staring, no, she corrected, *ogling* him again, she quickly glanced away.

"Going to lunch, Ms. Schoen?"

"Yes. Yes, I am."

Alone, courtesy of your canceling our date, she thought.

The doors opened, halting any more conversation for the moment.

Her earlier determination to forget Mark went unheeded. It was like being twelve again, all awkward and unsure of yourself. His nearness was overwhelming. She felt a tingle of excitement and glanced at his hands.

"After you," Mark said and motioned for her to enter. "Ms. Schoen, I'm sorry I had to cancel today's lunch. I'm sure Richard will enjoy your findings better than I would."

Entering first, she stood off to the side and waited for him to enter too. When he did and the doors closed, she continued their conversation. "Yes, but I wanted to touch base with you on a couple of things." Her words came out stiff. She needed to simply ask him out before she lost her nerve. It was the perfect setting. No one was around to hear him turn her down or witness her disgrace. Without any more thought, she blurted out, "I would still like to meet with you."

There. She'd done it. She'd asked him out.

"I'm free for lunch tomorrow."

"I am too," she said, feeling the heat rise to her cheeks.

"I'll have Mrs. Weber set up the time and place. She'll e-mail you. I have to go. Have a nice lunch."

Rane stared after his retreating figure unsure of what had just happened.

He'd actually accepted. She had a date with the owner.

Then, as if someone had let the air out of a balloon, she stopped short, flooded with disappointment. She hadn't really asked him out on a date; she'd said she would like to meet with him.

She hadn't said date.

Who was she trying to kid? He hadn't accepted her invite out on a date. He'd accepted a business lunch.

Holy cow, she was definitely rusty on the dating scene.

As Rane walked to Barnes & Noble for lunch, she texted Val, to let her know her lunch meeting had been changed to tomorrow.

Val's reply made her laugh. *Wednesdays are better sex days. U know, hump day.*

Rane couldn't think of a good reply, so she simply typed. *Talk 2 U later.*

She ate the soup of the day, chicken, and wild rice, and thought about all the men she'd dated. There weren't many. There'd been David, her first love. He'd been the only guy she'd dated during her high school years.

Nick, the truck driver, had come after the divorce and had lasted a full year. He'd been gone too much and was too crude for her taste.

Then there'd been the banker, Tim, who had promised her the world. She hadn't known he was married until Val had met him and his wife at her office. They'd been looking for a lawyer to write their living will.

Last, but not least, Kenny, the aspiring poet. A smile easily came across her face as she remembered him. He'd been so romantic and sweet. But he'd turned out to be a leach and had only wanted someone to support him so he could pursue his poetry.

Each one had been so different yet the same in one area.

They'd all turned out to be scum. She wanted the fairytale love ever after. She wanted children and a lifelong commitment. None of them could've given her that or had wanted to. And she wasn't willing to settle for anything less. The sex part had been simply okay in her book. The next man she dated was going to have to give her a resumé on his sexual prowess.

Grandma Greta was always telling her to be open-minded and someday her knight-in-shining-armor would appear. He'd make all her dreams come true. To this day, no man had made her feel that special. Her biological clock kept ticking and her knight had better show up soon.

I want the kind of sex that makes me see fireworks, or stars, or feel like I died and went to heaven.

Chapter Eleven

"**M**r. Christmenn, are you sure I can't get your coffee for you?" Mrs. Weber asked.

"No. Did you see any reports come through?" He wasn't expecting an answer. He was using small talk as a smoke screen. He'd found standing next to her desk gave him the best advantage point to see when Rane left her office.

"No, Mr. Christmenn."

"Oh, has the California plant called yet?"

"No, Mr. Christmenn. Did you want me to get them on the line for you?" She picked up the phone, ready to call them.

"No, I'll call them later. Did you send Ms. Schoen the e-mail reminder about lunch?" He saw her raise her eyebrows before answering.

"Yes, and she's confirmed the appointment. It's set for eleven forty-five, at Jack's. What time should I tell Philip to pick you up?"

"Eleven forty-five at Jack's. Thanks. No need to bother Philip. We'll walk." He caught a movement out of the corner of his eye. His prey was on the move. "Mrs. Weber, I'll be getting my coffee now."

He rushed away, ignoring the twinkle in the older woman's

eyes. Rane's perfume hit him like a speeding freight train as he headed down the hallway. There had to be something very wrong with him if perfume could make him behave like this. The scent began taking over his senses on impact and he struggled to get his emotions under control but failed.

All he could think about was *her*.

He had to find her now and was trailing after her like a dog in heat.

A vision of him attached to her leg doing the Humpty Dumpty had him second-guessing his uncontrollable actions. It was an absurd thought, but it didn't stop his ruttish behavior as he drew closer to his target. With every lungful of air, he took in, he was rewarded with her wonderful perfume. He pushed open the breakroom doors.

There she stood.

The ultimate prize.

A goddess, standing next to the coffee machine looking more enticing than he'd thought possible. She turned and smiled at him. Her face lit up like the morning sun. If he'd been a stick of butter, he would have melted right in his shoes. His knees weakened and he felt other parts of his body come to attention. One quick glance around the room told him they were alone.

"Good morning, Ms. Schoen," Mark said.

———

An awkward silence filled the room as Rane watched Mr. Christmenn move closer to her. She stood fixed in place, feeling his coiled power with each step he took toward her. When he stopped in front of her, she was overcome by his nearness, which felt closer than he really was. Blinking, she remembered to speak. "Hello."

Damn, did he have to smell so good this early in the morning? Was Drakkar the only cologne he wore?

She wanted to blame his cologne for the butterflies in her stomach but knew Mark was the major contributing factor. "I, um, I received the e-mail from your secretary about today's lunch. I believe you'll be very interested in some of the reports I'll be bringing with me".

"Yes, she mentioned you'd accepted."

Business?

Who wanted to discuss business when she had the world's sexiest man alive standing inches from her?

She took in his appearance, thinking he had a monopoly on virility. Today his dark green, single-breasted suit, white oxford shirt, with a yellow and green tie made his blue eyes bluer, if that was possible. Her palms grew sweaty and the cup she held almost slipped from her hand. "I haven't seen you in the breakroom before. Do you come here to get your morning coffee?"

Rane moved to the side to allow him to make his selection and deliberately studied his hand. Her heart began to hammer foolishly.

He had long fingers. Damn Val.

"I usually don't, but the coffeemaker in my office is broken. Mrs. Weber has ordered a new one," Mark said.

"Nice hands," she mumbled.

Shit.

Had she said nice hands aloud?

"What? Did you say something?"

"New Land is the brand of hot chocolate I buy. Does MAC have a line of hot chocolate?" she asked to cover up her slip, not even sure if that was a real brand.

"That's an interesting question. I'll have to look into that."

"If you need any tasters, I'm it. I haven't seen you in here since I've started with the company." She was now back on track and with any luck her slip didn't make him think she was an idiot.

"Do you come here every morning for your coffee?" He took

his now-filled paper coffee cup with the day's special blend of almond-chocolate.

"Yes and no." She laughed nervously. "What I mean is, yes, I come here every morning, but it's not for coffee. It's for hot chocolate. I have to admit I don't drink coffee."

Rane hoped her declaration didn't insult him. She winced, expecting a little backlash. Admitting to the president of the company that you don't like the product they made was pretty stupid.

"Did I hear you right? You do not drink coffee?"

He had emphasized each word. Crap. She couldn't tell if he was upset or not. "I-I enjoy the smell of coffee, but I don't like the taste. Sometimes I do have café mochas but have extra, extra chocolate added to cut the coffee taste."

She had done it again. Talk about putting your foot in your mouth. She decided it was time to back away to the door and make her escape before she inserted her other foot.

"Well, Ms. Schoen," Mark said, following her lead by heading to the door, "thanks for being so honest. I think we'll have to do something about your distaste for coffee."

"I promise to try one on the next Special Blend Day."

"Not everyone loves coffee at first," he replied. "Some people never acquire a taste for it and then again, some do. I hope you'll be one of those people who end up enjoying a good cup of coffee."

Arriving at the door, he held it open. "After you."

Their bodies almost touched causing Rane to stare into his eyes. "Sorry, excuse me."

She cleared the doorway, thankfully without spilling her hot chocolate or touching him.

"No, it's my fault. Just trying to be a gentleman."

"Mr. Christmenn, I hope I haven't insulted you. I didn't mean to if I did," she blurted, scarcely aware she'd spoken.

"I can't dislike or become mad at everyone who doesn't like coffee. Everyone has different likes and dislikes. I'll have to arrange for you to be included on the next tour of one of the coffee manufacturing plants." Mark slowed his walking pace. "You just missed the last one. It was about a week ago. Would you be interested in going on the next trip?"

"Yes, it sounds interesting. I'd like to learn more about the company."

Rane began to walk slower, seeing Mark was having trouble walking, talking, and holding his coffee at the same time. It was comical to watch and she hid her smile by sipping her hot chocolate.

"The company allows the employees to take a two-day trip to tour one of our plants. I feel it helps them understand the business better. One of the techniques used during the cupping evaluation is very interesting to watch. Do you know what cupping is?"

"No." Not wanting to seem ignorant, she added, "I've done some research into the coffee roasting process though."

"Excellent. I like it when an employee takes the initiative to find out about things they don't know. I've tried cupping several times and my findings are so different from my cupping specialists they've banned me from their room." Mark leaned in toward her and added in a husky murmur, "But between you and me, I think the employees just like having the days off and a chance to try all the new coffee blends."

As they stood staring at each other, Rane felt the urge to move closer. His breath mingled with hers.

Drakkar and Charlie mixed.

Time could have stopped for them. The sounds of people talking and phones ringing blended together in a sort of dull roar in her ears.

———

Mark broke the trance that had taken hold of him by stepping backward. He wanted nothing more than to kiss Rane and he couldn't in the middle of the busy office area. "Please excuse me, Ms. Schoen. I'll come by your office at eleven-thirty for lunch."

He forced himself to sound businesslike and gave her a weak smile. He turned away from her, walked toward the waiting Mrs. Weber, and noticed how she followed Rane's retreating form. She then refocused on him.

"Mr. Christmenn, Mr. Nelson is holding for you."

"Send it through." Keeping his eyes forward, he was tempted to look over his shoulder for one last glance of Rane himself. Picking up the phone, he listened intently, as all thoughts of the sexy Rane faded away.

"As per our conversation yesterday, Mr. Massaro had been jailed and is being charged with several crimes. Bond is being withheld. It seems even the bad guys have enemies," Mr. Nelson said.

"And this concerns me, why?"

"We are heading in the right direction. We've received intel that some of the mob members were relieved he has been arrested. They have stopped supporting him. Apparently, Massaro had been getting too sloppy and arrogant for the likes of them. Organized crime play by their own rules. They have their own limitations on what was right and wrong. I'm sorry to say the threat is still in effect. We've gotten some new leads, but we need you to be on high alert."

"Have you been in contact with Philip?"

"Yes, I spoke with him first."

"When is it going to end? I never signed on for all of this," Mark stated and sipped his coffee.

"We appreciate everything you've done but it takes time for things to work themselves out."

"I guess this is good news. Keep us informed if anything changes."

"For sure, Mr. Christmenn," Agent Nelson said.

Their conversation ended, and Mark stared at the phone. After all this time, he was close to getting his life back.

Life? What life?

He lifted the hand-drawn picture on his desk and studied it.

Why had he kept it all these years?

Because the girl had intrigued him. She hadn't seen him as a rich boy with everything. The girl had treated him as if she'd found a new friend but had never given him her full name, only a nickname. He knew it had started with the letter R and over the years, he'd been through every name book he could get his hands on, but the name still evaded him.

Mark sat back arduously in his chair to clear his mind. He rubbed his hand over his chin and mouth. A bad habit when he was frustrated. Suddenly an uncanny feeling came over him. An employee earlier had greeted Rane by calling her Ro on their walk back from the breakroom.

Ro.

Rane. Ro.

Ro. Rane.

Over and over, he said the names. Could it be a shortened version of Rane's name? But how could it? Her name was pronounced Rane not Rone. Ro, had a familiar sound to it. Could it be the nickname he'd been looking for all these years? The more he thought about the two names, Rane, and Ro, the more confused he became.

What were the chances Rane was the girl?

She couldn't be.

Maybe he only wanted it to be the name and wanted her to be the grownup version of the girl. It couldn't be that simple. Out of curiosity, he withdrew her personnel file and went over it yet again.

Nothing. He couldn't find any connection between Rane and the girl who'd hand-drawn the picture for him.

Did Rane look like the girl?

No, she wasn't anything like the girl he remembered. Rane was beautiful. No, she was stunning. There was no way Rane was the plain girl-next-door type.

All these years the picture had given him hope. Now as he stared at it, he saw it for what it had been. A childish promise, one that was never meant to happen. It saddened him as he let the old promise begin to fade.

He was ending it here and now.

Time to move on.

Rane didn't need to be the girl who had made him a promise to meet her twenty years ago for him to be interested in her. Damn it, if he wanted to ask her out, he was going to.

"Excuse me, Mr. Christmenn, it is eleven-fifteen," Mrs. Weber announced from the doorway.

He glanced at her and nodded. Before the twenty-year-old picture could make him change his mind, he laid it face down on his desk and left with a new conviction on life.

Again, the smell of Rane's perfume overtook him as he neared her office. Mark couldn't stop an image of the two of them locked in an embrace, naked and covered in sweat to be exact. He found himself in unfamiliar territory. No woman had ever made him want her as badly as Rane was doing. They hadn't ever kissed but yet his body was reacting as if they'd shared a night of hot and heavy sex.

Their glances met as he stood in the doorway to her office, blue eyes to blue eyes.

"I see you're ready to go." The tone of his voice had come out cool, not what he wanted, but he was trying to hide his growing desire for her. "You can leave the file. If I need to see something we discuss at lunch, you can show me when we return."

"Oh, okay, thanks. I was wondering if you really wanted to see the charts now or later."

Rane was relieved not to have to carry the file to lunch, but surprised because this was to be a business lunch, not a date, like Val had reminded her ten million times today.

"I thought we'd walk to the restaurant. It's a nice day. Is that all right with you?"

"That's great, I prefer to walk. Sometimes when you sit all day, it's nice to merely walk around. I've been trying to make sure I get out for lunch to do just that. I mean walk." She silently scolded herself. She was rambling and needed to stop as they waited for the elevator.

Thankfully, she was saved, and their conversation ended as soon as the door shut. But being in such close quarters with Mark made his cologne ten times stronger. The intoxicating aroma, all manly, was drowning her in its sexual aura.

She felt her better judgment diminishing. Not only could she smell him, but she also felt his body heat, and his breath on her hair. He stood behind her to the right and if she leaned back and turned, she'd fit very nicely into his arms.

As if her body had a will of its own, she felt herself gravitating toward him, wanting the comfort of his embrace. The opening of the door cleared her mind from doing something so irrational that she quickly stepped out as if she'd been freed from jail. She made sure there was plenty of empty space between them as they continued on their way.

"Good afternoon, Mr. Christmenn. Good afternoon, Ms. Schoen," Karen called out as they passed her desk.

"Karen, if you see Philip, please have him call Mrs. Weber," Mark stated.

"Yes, Mr. Christmenn," Karen said.

Once safely out of earshot, Rane asked, "Is she always that happy?"

He turned and smiled at her, which softened his face, making him appear sexier than he already was and caused her heart to skip a beat.

"Ms. Schoen, may I call you Rane?"

"Yes of course."

"Are you always this straightforward?"

"I am. Sometimes it gets me into trouble. My mother was always able to tell when I wasn't telling the truth. Oh my, I didn't mean I make a habit of lying."

His teasing laughter had her searching for a plausible explanation.

"My ex-husband would never allow me to play poker. He said I would lose my shirt."

Val was going to kill her. Dating rule Number Two: Never talk about your ex until the third date because by then they'll be hooked. Then again, this wasn't a date. She was having a conversation with her top boss.

But she couldn't undo what she'd said. It had just come out. What was she going to do? All she could do was pray it would work to her advantage.

"Well, I'd have to agree one hundred percent with your ex-husband. How long were you married?"

"Eleven years. We were high school sweet—"

"Sorry," he said, interrupting her, "we need to walk straight ahead about two blocks. High school sweethearts? How special. Please continue."

More personal questions?

Val would say that was a good sign. She let her level of confidence climb up a step, finding it easy to talk to Mark. But the conversation was put on hold as they maneuvered in and out of people.

As they did, Rane noticed most of the women would take a second look at Mark or try to gain his attention. He, on the other hand, simply ignored them by keeping his eyes focused straight ahead.

When the crowd thinned, she continued. "I was a cheerleader. He was the captain of the football team. Everyone expected us to get married, so we did. What about you, Mr. Christmenn? I know you're not married." She saw his eyebrows raise up slightly. "It states it in the company's annual report. But why?"

She held her breath, hoping she hadn't overstepped the line and wondered if he would keep going or pull back.

"Rane, please call me Mark," he paused, beamed at her, and added, "I've never found the right woman. Yet."

The unspoken implication sent waves of excitement through her. Had he just made a pass at her? Or had he only made an overall statement? Not chancing eye contact with him, she stayed attentive to the crowd of people in front of her.

"It can't be that hard to find a woman." Realizing how her comment might have come across she added, "I'm sorry. That was very impolite of me."

"It's okay," he said with a little snicker. "No harm done. Now more about you. Eleven years. That was a long time to be married. If you don't mind me asking, what happened?"

A red streetlight halted their progress for a moment. When it turned green, Mark placed his hand on her elbow and guided her down over the curb. She cleared her throat as his hand left her elbow and she pretended not to be affected by his electrifying touch. Her skin tingled and she felt a tide of sexual excitement course through her.

"Mark, I don't mind if you don't mind me asking questions in return."

She noted that her voice had sounded shallow but saw him give her a smile and a nod of affirmation. Sharing what had caused her divorce wasn't something she did. Taking a deep breath and releasing it gave her courage to do it. "He, my ex, came home from accepting his first appointment at a clinic in California, and said he wanted a divorce. He'd found someone else. Nine months later I was single."

In unison, they sidestepped a man talking on a cell phone.

"That was harsh."

"Yeah, but I'm over it. Now it's my turn. I Googled you and found your name linked to several high-profile women. How come none of them ever became Mrs. Christmenn?"

"You Googled me?"

"Yes, I wanted to find out all I could about your company. I like to be prepared," she said but didn't tell him the real reason, which had been to find out if he was currently seeing anyone.

"I guess I should Google myself. Did you find anything interesting?"

"I'm glad you find this amusing. Nothing seems to be private anymore. I found that your company is sound. It's highly rated, and investors are itching for you to go public."

"Wow. Modern technology. I've had talks with the board about going public, but it was behind closed doors. Anything else?"

"I did find a blog that mentioned you, and let's say it was *very* interesting," Rane said and smiled.

"A blog?"

"Yes, a blog. Do you mean you didn't know?" She watched as he shook his head. "You know you should have someone watching these things for you. Apparently, some of your past, ah, let's say dates, have started a website to ease their pain. They say you only go out with a woman three times and then you send them packing. Is that true?"

His rich baritone laughter caused several heads to turn. "Here I've been trying not to have my name linked to any one woman and they think I'm being insensitive. Very interesting."

"I don't think they found it funny. Why only three dates?"

"I thought I was being kind. I never wanted to leave the impression I was seriously looking or interested in any woman I casually dated."

"Oh, I see," she said, but not really understanding his male logic. If a man of Mark's influence were to ask her out three times, she, too, would think they might have a chance of some sort of a long-term relationship.

"The restaurant is ahead to the left. Do you think I was unfair to the women?"

"If you told them upfront of your intentions, then no. What exactly are you looking for in a woman?"

She couldn't believe she was having this type of conversation with him. Val would be so proud of her. Her last question had been more for her benefit to gain some insight into what he wanted in a woman and to see if she would fit the bill for him.

"What am I looking for in a woman? That's a really good question. I've dated many women. Each had different things to offer but none ever met my expectations. Why? Are you going to try to be a matchmaker?"

"I could be. We could add it to my job description. My friend, Val, you met her the other night, knows a lot of single women."

He laughed and then she joined in as they entered the restaurant. The hostess greeted them and led them to a table.

Calmly, after taking a seat, she placed her napkin on her lap to hide her shaking hands from him. She told herself it was now or never.

"I'd be lying if I said I didn't find you attractive, Mark. I've never had a relationship with my boss or the president of the company where I've worked, so this would be a first. Is this a business lunch or are we on a lunch date?"

She waited, elated by her new objectives and boldness. The expression on his face was priceless. It was a mixture of surprise and delight.

"Rane, I'm wounded." He placed his right hand over his heart. "I'm not a playboy. Those women gave you the wrong impression. I like to keep my business separate from my private life. But things can change. Would you be offended if I told you I wanted to get to know you better?"

"I can see you don't like to play cat and mouse games. You won this round," Rane replied and wiped the sweat off her hands on the napkin.

From that point, their lunch took on a different tone. They each now knew where the other stood. They laughed more and talked about things two people wouldn't normally disclose about each other. She wasn't the employee, and he wasn't the owner of the company she worked for.

———

Mark found the conversation flowed easily and he was enjoying himself more than he had in years. On paper, she'd been perfect, and in person, she was an angel. When they had finished their lunch, he decided he wanted to spend more time with her. "Would you care to have lunch with me again, tomorrow?"

"Of course, I enjoyed our lunch. But I do have to ask, will we be discussing business or our personal lives again?"

He heard the flirtatiousness in her voice. For a split second he knew he shouldn't have asked, but her answer had been a good sign. Could she be reading his mind? She'd beaten him to the punch.

"I prefer to leave business at the office."

She laughed and he noticed her eye color had become a deeper blue. He stood and pulled out her chair. They took their time walking down Nicolette Mall as the lunch hustle and bustle thinned. He liked the way she matched his steps and how she was unaware of the looks she was receiving from the men.

Karen greeted them in her same cheerful voice from earlier as they came into the lobby. He and Rane looked at each other, holding in a laugh. As they waited for the elevators, several other employees joined them. When it arrived, they entered and had to stand very close to each other. A couple of times their fingers touched, sending tiny shocks through him.

Neither of them said a word. He was glad she hadn't tried to keep up their conversation with so many people able to witness their exchange. The doors opened at the sixth floor, and they got off the elevator together.

"Ms. Schoen, be prepared for both, tomorrow at lunch. I'll have Mrs. Weber e-mail you with the time."

"Thank you, Mr. Christmenn. I'll be waiting." She walked toward her office.

Mark stayed rooted in place and watched her, admiring the sway of her hips. The ding of the elevator made him realize that he was still standing in the middle of the hallway and hadn't moved. He quickly turned and moved over to Linda's desk, to pick up any messages. As he did, he caught Mrs. Weber watching him out of the corner of his eye and noticed a huge smile on her face.

Dumping the pile of messages on Mrs. Weber's desk, he paused for a second. "Mind your own business. You're not my mother."

He cringed at the amount of sarcasm he had used. Not wanting to discuss his actions or answer any of her questions yet, he walked into his office. About an hour later, after he'd had some time to understand his actions himself, he called her into his office.

She arrived as usual with a pen and paper in hand.

"Mrs. Weber, please call in to make a lunch reservation for tomorrow at Jack's for two people. Send Ms. Schoen an e-mail to confirm the time. Come to think of it, arrange lunch reservations for every day this week for two. But don't send out e-mails to her for those. Send only an e-mail about tomorrow's lunch. Do you have any questions?"

Closing her notepad, she looked at him. "Mr. Christmenn, are you sure you know what you're doing? Getting involved with an employee is not a very good idea."

He met her gaze and didn't reply.

"You should know better than anyone how that works out. Now, don't try to tell me its business. I have two eyes. Do you want me to return your new coffeemaker?"

"I hear the concern in your voice but I'm a big boy. She fascinates me. I can't pinpoint what it is yet but I'm going to find out soon. Keep me informed if the employees start to talk. I don't want it to affect what Ms. Schoen needs to do as part of her job."

"I'm just going to caution you this once. I'll do my best to nip things in the bud, if I hear any rumblings," she said and stood.

"Thank you."

"Don't thank me yet. This could go south quickly."

Mark pressed his lips together and nodded. She turned away from him and left. He didn't need or want the gossip to start. He wanted to shield their relationship.

Relationship? Did they have one?

———

Rane sat down at her desk and looked at her phone, which she had ignored the entire time during lunch. There were four texts from Val.

"Tell me what is going on."

"Did U check his hands?"

"Don't play hard to get."

"If you don't call me in the next five minutes it will have to wait. I have court in a few."

Each one made her smile. The entire afternoon had her head spinning. The fact that she had another lunch date with Mark was unreal. Checking the time from Val's last message, she saw their conversation would have to wait.

She was kind of glad Val wasn't available. It gave her more time to go over what had happened, since she was unclear how to describe it to Val.

It seemed more confusing as she thought about it than when it had transpired. Val was going to kill her. She'd flirted, which Val wasn't going to believe, and then Mark had asked personal questions.

No, they were very personal questions. Ones, a person would ask on a first date, not on a business lunch. But Mark had told her not to bring her reports.

Had she had her first date with him?

It seemed like it.

Why had she simply answered his questions without hesitation? She had talked about David too.

Oh, for heaven's sake, Val wasn't going to like that.

All she'd been doing was following Mark's lead, which had led to her asking him some personal questions.

No, she had asked him stupid questions. Which, she realized now, he'd never given her any straight answers to.

Rane covered her face with her hands at what she'd done next. She had admitted she was attracted to him. It had slipped out. He'd been so easy to talk too, and she'd gotten lost in the moment.

And then she had agreed to go to lunch with him again.

Stupid?

Talk about putting yourself out in left field, she'd done it with no one's help. Except, he hadn't ignored her, he'd actually flirted back.

What had he said about her?

That she was straightforward with her opinions, and he liked that in a person. If she was going to get a real date out of all this, she needed a new plan of attack for tomorrow's lunch. This opened a completely new assortment of problems she hadn't foreseen.

Where did one take a man who's probably eaten at all the five-star restaurants in town or seen and done everything?

A movie?

No, that was too lame.

To a bar?

No, too much competition and it would be loud.

To dinner?

No, stupid. Dinner would be too much like their lunch.

Frustrated, Rane found she couldn't come up with anything special. What was she going to do?

———

The next morning, Mark once again stood at Mrs. Weber's desk.

"Mr. Christmenn, would you like me to call you when she leaves her office? At this rate you'll have the employees talking sooner than you want."

"You're right. I'll head to the breakroom now. Tomorrow, you can call me."

He left her desk and proceeded down the hallway. Today when he entered the breakroom there were no employees in the room. He made his selection and was reaching for it when he caught a movement out of the corner of his eye.

She had entered the room. He tried to stay calm and stood as she approached him.

Surprisingly the level of anticipation increased when he turned to look at her. He was drawn to her like the most coveted high-grown coffee beans. She was dressed in navy blue slacks, a white blouse, and again a belt emphasizing her narrow waist. He watched as she pushed her hair behind one ear.

"Good morning, Ms. Schoen."

"Mr. Christmenn, good morning."

She stopped next to him, and he inhaled. Forgetting where he was, he gazed into her eyes. She smiled, and it was as if a cloudy day had been pushed away allowing the heavens to open up with sunshine. One of the machines beeped, breaking their trance.

He stepped out of her way, allowing her access to the vending machine. "I Googled myself last night. What I found was very interesting, but I wasn't able to find the site you had told me about."

"I could show you if you want me to. Maybe before lunch you could—"

Rane stopped as several other employees came into the break-room, the moment was lost to say what she had wanted to ask. The employees' shocked reactions became apparent. Some tried to ignore him, while others greeted him, and some simply left without getting anything. To ease the climbing tension, he saw Rane pick up her cup of hot chocolate and headed toward the door. He followed and held it open for her as they exited.

"Do all the employees act like that when they see you? Am I the only one who isn't afraid to talk to you?"

Her questions took him by surprise, and he almost spilled his coffee when he heard her laugh.

"From your dumbfounded expression, I take that as a yes. I don't understand. You are a man who just so happens to be the president and owner of the company. Your lack of interaction with your employees is obvious. They seem to treat you like some sort of God."

"A god? Now you're being mean, I think."

"No, I'm not. I can't remember my Ancient Greek history, but you could pass for one. Maybe like Zeus or Apollo. I do recall a fountain in Greece that had these statues. Val and I went there to recuperate from our divorces. Did you model for one of them?"

"Are you flirting with me?"

"I could be. Will it get me fired?"

"You really are something else. Maybe I'm a fire-breathing dragon and that is why my employees avoid me."

Mark watched as Rane shrugged her shoulders. "If the shoe fits. Or should I say, if the scales fit?"

He chuckled at her dry humor. "You're right, that's one of the reasons you were hired. I need to have my employees be able to talk to me without being frightened. I am not formidable. It's how they picture me."

"Just from my observation, the women find you too attractive to talk to. The men are simply too nervous to approach you. Yeah, I can see why they do," she stated.

As they neared the lobby, he had to find out why she wasn't. "Why aren't you afraid of me?"

"Mr. Christmenn, tell me why would I be? You're just a man who happens to own this company. Should I be afraid of you?"

"No, you shouldn't be. You've made your point. I've never viewed it that way. To me, employees are people. I'll have to think about what you've said. I'll see you later for lunch. Mrs. Weber should've sent you an e-mail with the time."

"Okay, I'll look for it. I'll be ready when you arrive." She walked away from him.

He hadn't intended to end their conversation so abruptly, but he needed some space. She was too intoxicating. He couldn't concentrate on anything but her.

He wanted to kiss her.

And run his hands through her hair.

—————

Safely back in her office, she couldn't believe she had told him he looked like a Greek God. Val had told her last night to stay on point. Like that was going to happen after getting whiffs of his cologne.

Bringing her computer to life, she opened Word and began typing a list on how to interact with Mark. Mr. Adams hadn't mentioned she was to improve the relationship between the employees and Mark. But, seeing the employees' reaction to Mark's presence in the breakroom, she needed to somehow improve his relationships with them.

As the morning flew by, her appointed time had arrived, and her phone buzzed.

"Ms. Schoen, Mr. Christmenn is leaving his office and heading your way," Linda said.

"Thank you. I owe you."

She had asked Linda earlier to ring her when he was on his

way to her office. Standing, she smoothed down her slacks and tucked in her shirt at the waist, before grabbing her purse. When he came to her door, she was ready to go.

"You're ready?"

"I told you, I would be."

"Great. Should we walk again, or should I have Philip meet us downstairs with the limo?"

"Walking is fine. Thanks for asking."

The elevator was full as they entered, and once again Mark's presence caused all conversation to stop. She gave him a look that should have prompted him to say something. He shook his head, and his lips were pursed into a thin line. Clearly, the whole situation was causing him displeasure.

She bit her lip to stifle her grin. It wasn't until they stepped out into the fresh air that Mark broke the silence.

"Rane."

"Mark."

They both said each other's names at the same time.

"I'd like to go to lunch with you for the rest of this week and," he paused, then quickly added, "and I don't want to discuss business. I only want to get to know you better. And you'd-you'd said you found me attractive."

"I don't know what to say. I was out of place to say that to you. I'd be apprehensive about dating or seeing someone that works with me. It goes against my work ethics," she said.

Seeing the disappointment on his face, it wasn't what she wanted. She had been trying to tease him. Touching his hand, she added, "There's always a first for everything. I'd like that very much. That is, going to lunch. I mean having lunch and getting to know you better."

"Great. Now that you've agreed, who is Thor? Should I be worried about him?"

Rane laughed so hard tears came to her eyes. "He is my cat."

"Your cat? You mean to tell me I've lost sleep over a cat?"

They laughed together at his misunderstanding. When they arrived at their destination, the same restaurant as the day before, they found the waiting area crowded. Mark caught the hostess' attention and was about to move forward when she called out to greet them.

"Mr. Christmenn, your table is ready. Please follow me."

Suddenly several cameras went off, leaving a show of flashing colors. All eyes turned to stare at them as they made their way through the crowd.

Chapter Twelve

The commotion their entrance had made hadn't worn off by the time the waiter had finished taking his and Rane's order. Acting as if he was ignoring the commotion, Mark tried to be casual. "The weather held up for our walk."

"How do you do it? All this?"

"I don't see anything. What are you talking about?"

"Nice," she said, laughing. "I noticed it yesterday and again today. People just stop and stare. Doesn't it bother you when they act like this? I'd be intimidated. No, I am intimidated."

"I'm so used to the staring and the photographers following me. It's nothing except when they get out of hand."

"Why are they so interested in you? I know it sure isn't me. Do they know something I don't?"

"I'm sorry. It's the damn tabloids. They've made me popular. I don't think of myself as famous. I tune them out, but I didn't think how it might affect you." He pushed his chair away from the table and took out his cell phone. "I'm going to call Philip to come pick us up. We can go someplace else to eat. A fast-food drive through might be our only option."

"No, no, it's really okay."

"If, you're sure?" Seeing her nod, he pocketed his phone. "I thought it would be safe to come here. Did you know I own Jake's?"

"Really? I've heard about this restaurant, but I hadn't eaten here until yesterday. I believe it's been written up twice in the *Minnesota Monthly*."

"You're correct. Those articles were great for business. I try to hire new and upcoming chefs. I let them create their own style of cuisine. So far, so good. Each one of my restaurants is different, but of course, it's a requirement they all serve my coffees. It helps promote the new blends."

"I didn't realize you'd gone that far to secure the success of the blends. The chefs must love you. I mean, to have a boss who allows them to be creative," Rane said.

"Sometimes I do need to step in, but overall, my chefs are acquiring quite a reputation."

The noise from the front grew louder. Mark glanced over her shoulder. The crowd had become bigger. He reached into his pocket again for his phone, ready to place a call if necessary.

"The interior is nice. I like all the wildlife pictures. It's so Minnesotan."

"Thanks. I'm so sorry about the commotion. Someone must've seen us yesterday and somehow found out I was coming again today. Things like this happen a lot, getting ambushed, I mean. The press tries to see if I'm meeting someone important or famous. I usually arrive through the back entrances to avoid trouble," he said.

Lifting his glass of water to take a drink, he wondered if all this attention was because of the pending Massaro trial. Had the local newspapers pieced together his involvement? Philip was going to be so mad.

"Wow, to be a part of the rich and famous. Are you on the top ten most eligible bachelors list?"

"Funny you should ask that. In fact, I am. I moved up to the number seventh position a few months ago. I'm surprised that didn't come up when you Googled me."

Seeing her eyebrows raise, he wondered just how much she knew about him. It was refreshing to find someone who didn't know him. He was actually number three on the eligible bachelor list. He hadn't lied, he'd simply stretched the truth to test her. The new list came out last week and he had moved up four notches.

She was passing every test with flying colors, which was gaining his approval.

"I'm impressed. If you look me up, I'm not listed."

"Nice, you're quick. I'll have to talk to the manager, so this doesn't happen again. It's good for business, but I don't want or need the attention. Come to think of it, maybe I'll have to purchase another restaurant."

Rane laughed. "Sure, why not purchase another one? You could start collecting them."

"I just might. I already own five. The new one would be safe for a while until they found out I own that one, too."

He laughed along with her. Not wanting to ruin their time together, he again glanced toward the waiting area. It was now crowded to the point no customers could come in and there was an occasional flash lighting up the dining room.

Someone was going to pay dearly for this screw up. He forced himself to relax when he saw Rane fidget with her napkin. He gently placed his hand on top of hers and absentmindedly rubbed his thumb across her smooth skin, not caring if anyone saw them. "Are you sure you don't want to leave now?"

"Is this what it feels like to be a movie star? Do you think I'm dressed okay? Is my hair in place? I think I forgot to put on lipstick before leaving the office. Do you think they noticed?"

Her sense of humor and smile eased his uncertainties. Mark slid his hand away from hers, leaned back, and laughed. It was time for him to enjoy her company and he became oblivious to the several flashes that went off.

———

Glad she'd been able to tease Mark about the unwanted attention, Rane observed how remarkable the change in him was when he laughed. It eased the lines on his forehead. In that instant, as she stared at him, an image of a boy she'd met on an airplane when she was twelve, came to mind. She had thought any guy who didn't have pimples was a hunk.

Mark most definitely didn't have any acne. His face was clean-shaven.

Another thing she remembered about the boy was he'd been so nice to her during the flight, she had proposed to him. She bit her lip to hide her mischievous smile, at the thought and realized Mark was responding to her attempt of humor over all the cameras on them.

"You look fantastic. Every man here is wishing they were the one sitting across from you."

His grin, which showed off straight white teeth, caught her off guard. Her stomach did a flip from the sexual attraction she was experiencing. Reminding herself to breathe, she did before she replied. "Yeah, right. Are you trying to earn brownie points?"

"Who me? Did I get any?"

She shook her head and used her napkin to hide her smile by wiping her mouth. "On a more serious note, it's really okay. You'll have to decide what's best. All this attention has caught me off guard, that's all. Besides, you still owe me your answer. What are you looking for in a woman?"

He smiled but didn't reply.

"I'm not going to tell you one more thing about myself until you spill your guts."

She replaced her napkin on her lap, folded her hands in front of her and waited.

"Rane, you're absolutely amazing. I was hoping you wouldn't remember."

She tilted her head to the side, cleared her throat and waited.

"Okay, okay, you win," he said and threw up his hands, showing defeat.

———

Mark observed the stubborn tilt of her chin and her rigid shoulders. Still Rane said nothing.

"Wow, you're tough. I'm getting your message loud and clear. Here it is. My truthful answer. I've been waiting for the right woman all my life." It was an understatement. He'd been waiting the last twenty years. As the words rambled through his mind, they seemed foolish. "I want to find someone who wants me for who I am, not what I am. You see, half the women I meet want to go out with me because of what I am. The other half want my money. They see dollar signs. Like winning the lottery. They want what I have. All the money, homes, and fame. That's what draws them to me. Not me as a person."

The waiter arrived with lunch, halting their conversation. This gave him a minute to look closely at Rane. Usually, he could tell by her facial expression what she was thinking, but not this time. She was holding in her emotions.

Once the waiter had left, she picked up her knife and cut into the grilled chicken breast she had ordered. "Can't you find yourself a rich woman? She wouldn't be looking for those things."

"You're wrong. They want more. They're never satisfied. I'm old-fashioned. I want love. I've found rich women are usually only looking for a good time."

"By a good time, do you mean sex?"

He nodded, quickly shoving a French-fry into his mouth.

"I've found that in the men I've dated, too. They're looking for one thing, and if you don't give out, they're gone. No phone calls, no goodbyes, and you're left with a bag full of their items to donate to charity. Not to mention the big letdown, an empty bed, and a bunch of emotional stress."

"Don't put me in that category. I never leave anything behind." He saw her eyebrows raise and a sparkle appeared in her eyes. "Okay, I'm not a saint. If the women are willing, why would I turn down a night of sex and the lost pair of boxers?"

"Oh right. Ahh, huh, I got your number. You're an active healthy male."

"And you're not an active healthy single woman?" He half expected her not to answer, thinking he'd crossed the line. But his gut told him to push forward. "Are you saying you don't enjoy sex?"

"No. I mean, yes, I do. I simply don't offer it to every man I meet. Absolutely never on the first date. Or the second."

Forgetting about his lunch, he placed his elbows on the table and leaned in toward her. "I've heard about women who only give out on the third date."

Mark laughed as her blue eyes widened in astonishment. He felt so comfortable talking to her, it was strange. He hadn't felt this at ease with a female since the girl on the plane. "It's not as easy as you think. It's been hard over the years to distance myself from the women I take to social functions. I've been very cautious not to lead any of them on in any way because most of them turn out to be cunning little bitches. Some have actually used blackmail to snare me."

"By the way, sex is never an option on the third date either. I think that's sad. You should try what my friend, Val, does. She's joined several dating apps. She does very well. Have you tried that yet?"

Her attempt to hide her smile by sipping her *Coke* didn't work. "Very funny. Do I swipe right or left? Would my bio read, rich, single, white male, looking for love. It would probably cause the site to crash."

Rane burst out laughing, which caused more flashes to go off.

"Don't forget to add, famous Top Ten eligible bachelor willing and able for a good time."

He loved her clever bantering and wished they were alone and not in a crowded restaurant. The urge to kiss her was overwhelming, instead he reached across the table and took ahold of her hand.

———

His simple action of touching her hand had sent pounding currents through her. She was glad when the conversation changed tones as Mark talked about how his family companies were founded by his father and grandfather. It gave her time to regain her spiraling emotions.

"I didn't know your grandfather helped build the empire."

"He did. I never had the chance to meet him. He died a couple of years before I was born. With both the founding family members dead, I've been so careful over the years to make it stronger. I don't want to lose what my family created," Mark said.

"How are you going to pass on your legacy if you don't marry and have children? I think you should check out the dating apps."

"Perhaps I will. It might help. I want to settle down, marry, and have children someday. No one has come along yet that I've wanted to share my life with or give my love to."

"Maybe try some of the personal dating services. They help professionals who don't have time to date. They go over the applicants and set up lunch dates."

"Like what we are doing? I will if you will. I'll even pay the fees for you."

If he did, she'd be the first person to apply. Rane shook her head and smiled. He returned her smile which was some sort of a challenge. "Nice of you to offer, but I'll stick to the old-fashioned way of finding a husband."

"Then it's settled. We both try the old-fashioned way. Now,

that you've gotten the lowdown on the wealthy Mr. Christmenn's pathetic love life, it's my turn."

"Not yet. You sure know how to keep a woman interested. I fully understand now why the women want to be close to you. You have a soft spot deep down under that manly ego. Are you always this genuine with all the women? Or is this one of your pick-up techniques?" She watched as a look of innocence came over his face. The softened appearance made him a hundred percent more handsome than he already was. It caused her heart to stop beating for a full second. "My grandma warned me about men like you. Am I to understand there is no special woman in your life right now?"

"You're correct. No one has come close to stealing my heart."

His pretend sadness had her laughing.

"Is that why you have your bodyguard around most of the time? To protect you from the person who might try to take your heart?"

"He might be my driver and bodyguard but most of all he is my best friend. He's the only person I'd trust with my life."

"Well, Mark, what is the big question you want to ask? I'll warn you that you can ask, but I'm not going to guarantee that I'll answer it. Plus, beware, I will come back with a set of my own questions for you to answer."

The waiter appeared and cleared away their empty dishes and they paused their conversation. Once the table had been cleaned and the waiter had left, Mark spoke. "Excuse me, I need to talk to the manager. We'll continue my line of questioning then."

She grinned and heard him mutter that if he had to call Philip, he was going to be very pissed as he walked away. She didn't want to be either of them at this point.

Going over what he wanted in a woman, the tally worked in her favor. Her heart already felt lost to him, and she didn't have anything else to lose. She might as well go all the way and really go out on a date with him. If she did, there'd be no turning back from this point.

She'd fallen for him in one afternoon.

Was she crazy?

Did she just want to see if Val was right about the finger thing because she knew how long his middle finger was? The mere thought of knowing how long it was had her squirming in her chair.

She had to lower her head, not wanting Mark to see the desire written on her face as he took his seat across from her.

"The problem is taken care of for the moment. Now where were we? Oh, right, do your eyes turn colors?"

His ability to go from one topic to a new one in a heartbeat was weird. There was no emotional connection to his words. It caught her off guard. "What kind of question is that?"

"The one I've been dying to ask you."

"I see. Not what I was expecting you'd ask, but I've been told they do. I guess it depends on my mood. I've never personally seen it happen."

"I knew it. It's amazing when they do. I've seen them change to a green color for just a couple of seconds. Next question."

She sat back carelessly in the chair, enjoying the moment but stopped suddenly when her bare foot contacted his ankle. He unfolded his arms, lifted the tablecloth, and looked beneath it.

"Do you usually take your shoes off whenever you feel like it? Or is it a shoe aversion?"

Knowing he was referring to the other night when she had run into him in his office, she slipped her shoes back on under the table. "No, to both questions."

"It's all right. I like a woman who feels comfortable anywhere she goes."

"I said my apologies that night."

"Yes, you did. I'm not looking for one now. I'm wondering if it's a habit and if I need to add something to the employees' hand-book," he said.

"It is a very bad habit. I can't believe we're discussing my feet." She shook her head and continued. "The minute I get home at night my shoes are off. Or for that matter, anyplace I can."

Just talking about the incident brought up feelings she thought she had safely concealed. She could still recall Mark's chest pressed to hers and the muscles in his hand on her arm when their bodies had collided.

Thankfully, their dessert arrived, and she decided to change the topic to their childhood.

"My grandma lives in Florida. I spent many summer vacations and spring breaks with her because my dad had died when I was young. Being a single parent was hard on my mom."

"I'm sorry about your dad. Like I said, I never knew my grand-parents. I was sent away to private schools, which made it almost impossible to make real friends growing up."

"That is really sad. I can't imagine not having Val around all these years. We are like glue. We have stuck together through thick and thin problems."

"I met Philip-"

He didn't get to finish because the manager came over. "Mr. Christmenn, I am sorry the crowd out front ruined your lunch. I'll be better prepared the next time. I hope your cherry cobbler was to your liking."

"It was, thank you."

"If you are ready to leave, the front entrance has been cleared for you and your guest."

"We'll be leaving in a couple of minutes," Mark stated.

The manager nodded and left.

"I'm ready when you are. I think Mr. Adams is going to ques-tion me on how long my lunches are."

"If he does, you let me know."

Mark stood and like the day before, he came over and pulled her chair out for her.

"The coast is clear," he said and together they left the restaurant from the front door.

He kept looking behind them for any signs of journalists with cameras. They briskly walked to the office with minimal conversation. When they reached the MAC building, Mark's bodyguard, Philip, was waiting for them along with several people with cameras.

"Mr. Christmenn, over here," Philip said, waving to them.

All of a sudden, four security guards rushed out to escort them into the building. In all the madness, Mark trapped Rane in the safety of his arms, securing her against his side. He didn't release her until they stood in front of Karen's desk. The guards had formed a human shield in front of the doors, not allowing anyone inside.

"Go to your office, Rane. You'll be safe there. I'll give you a call later," Mark stated.

Rane didn't question him or hesitate. As she left, she glanced around and saw a lot of people she didn't know and only a few employees. Their looks said it all. She and Mark appeared to be a couple returning from an afternoon of sex.

———

Stunned, Rane waited in the quietness of her office.

Was her face going to be plastered all over the tabloid covers in the morning or worse, all over the Internet?

How could she have been so naïve as to not have thought that dating a man of his notability wasn't going to have consequences?

Her mom was going to die of shame, when and if she saw the pictures.

Then rational thinking took over. Maybe she was taking this

too far. Her imagination had taken her ten steps out of whack before.

Nothing is going to happen. Everything is going to be fine.

But her sense of calm didn't last long. Every time she heard the elevator beep, she glanced toward her door with the silent expectation that Mark would come to see her. She wanted to know what was going on. She didn't like being kept in the dark.

She texted Val. *"You can't believe what happened during my lunch today. The paparazzi came. They took pics of us."*

"I can't find any breaking news."

"Very funny. I'm freaked out." Rane sat at her desk, still waiting for Mark.

Another text message alert pinged her phone. *"If you're on a cover of a magazine, I want an autographed copy."*

Rane laughed aloud at Val's message. Leave it to her friend to make the situation less troubling than it was. Even with the tension-breaking text, she found herself unable to concentrate on the Purchasing Department report on the screen in front of her. After an hour of redoing page after page of numbers, she decided to send Mark an e-mail letting him know she'd keep her lunches open. Once she hit the 'send' button, she was able to calm down enough to work on the report.

She was surprised when she heard Linda calling out good-night to the employees and glanced at the computer's clock to confirm the time. It was much later than she'd thought, and Mr. Long Finger hadn't interrupted her thoughts too many times.

She admired the completed PowerPoint report and saved the file. It had come out much better than she'd thought considering her mind had been elsewhere. Mr. Adams was going to be impressed, which was what she'd wanted to accomplish. As she laid everything out for the meeting on the table, Mark slipped into her thoughts again. He hadn't stopped by to talk to her or confirm her e-mail.

Was he having second thoughts? Could the media have

destroyed any chance she might have had and that was why he'd dismissed her so insensitively? He said he protected himself from unwanted attention. Was she the cause of today's ordeal?

Her new inner self took over and she decided to take drastic measures. She'd stop by his office on her way out. Simple, but direct, that's what she taught people to do.

She knew it worked, so what was holding her back?

David.

That one word caused old demons to surface. His abusive voice echoed in her head. At last count, she had twenty-five Facebook messages and eighteen text messages. They haunted her every time she checked her phone.

No. She wasn't going to allow him to ruin her chances with Mark.

Brushing aside her David problem in one sweep, she dwelled on her Mark problem. Her plan had to work. If it didn't, she'd have to resort to some of Val's tactics. Adamant the plan she'd set in motion would work, she finished and finalized everything for the meeting.

The meeting.

How stupid. She couldn't have lunch with Mark tomorrow. She had her meeting. Talk about having a blonde moment.

She was going to have to stop by his office and tell him she had to cancel tomorrow's lunch date. Looking at her phone, she saw it was after seven. Leaving her office with her briefcase and purse, she came out into a very quiet reception area. Not sure if Mark had left, she moved around Mrs. Weber's empty desk. A dim light peeked through his half-closed door.

There was no turning back now.

Moving with optimism, she stood at his door and pushed it a little. She saw him bent over, holding his head in his hand, looking at some papers at his desk. He seemed to be deep in thought. Before she lost her nerve, she knocked.

"Mr. Christmenn, I sent you an e-mail, about lunch tomorrow but I'm—"

The force of her knock caused the door to open further. He raised his head, and his blue eyes pierced the distance between them as if none existed. Without saying a word, he stood. He placed one hand in his pants pocket, brushed at his wayward hair with the other, and sauntered toward her.

She moistened her lips.

Oh my God, what a walk.

It was almost as good as Richard Gere's in the movie, *An Officer, and a Gentleman.*

Mark had abandoned his suit coat and had unbuttoned a handful of buttons on his dress shirt, exposing his chest hair. The dress shirtsleeves were rolled up past his elbows showing his extremely bulky biceps.

Mmmm, mmmm. Eye candy for sure. She felt her heart pounding. Her breath caught in her throat as she tried to talk.

"I see you have your shoes on tonight," Mark said.

Even though she knew she did, she glanced downward briefly. When she looked up in a trance-like state, he came to her. Stopping a couple of feet in front of her.

"Yes, I still want to have lunch with you."

Her mouth went dry at his softly spoken words. She couldn't say anything or swallow. His cologne, along with his masculine body standing less than a foot from her, was affecting her in ways she wasn't prepared for, yet her body was inflamed by desire.

If falling in love was this invigorating, she'd definitely never experienced it before. When she'd fallen for David, it had been slow and comforting.

However, Mark was... Her mind went blank. She searched for words, but none came. Another tiny gasp escaped from her as his hand reached out to her.

Was he going to kiss her?

No, he couldn't. He just couldn't.

She'd forgotten to pop a breath mint in her mouth. It was Rule Number One for kissing. Always carry breath mints in your pocket in case.

———

Mark gazed into Rane's eyes very closely. They were changing to a greenish color. He wondered what mood she was in to have them do that and was tempted to ask. He watched them change again as he brushed some hair from her face.

"I promise tomorrow's lunch will be a lot quieter. I had Mrs. Weber make a reservation at one of my other restaurants and Philip will be driving us. They will know how to handle my coming to dine properly."

"I've never had to deal with the press or photographers before. It was surreal. I don't like getting my picture taken. Am I, are we going to be on some magazine cover?"

"No," Mark snickered. Philip had informed him earlier they'd paid tens of thousands of dollars to make sure. She and her identity would be safe for the time being.

"Good. My mother would have killed me. She reads those things weekly."

"You'll live another day. Your identity hasn't been disclosed." Her laughter caused his heart to falter. His emotions were racing out of control. He was so close to her it wouldn't take much to pull her into his arms and press his mouth to hers. "Rane, would you consider going out on a date with me?"

Mark waited for her reply and watched hungrily as her tongue moistened her top lip before it ran slowly over her bottom lip. Her apparent nervous act aroused him more than he'd expected. He forced himself not to enfold her into his arms and capture her now glistening lips.

"I need to leave. Thor is waiting. Where would we go?"

"Anywhere you want. I could arrange something for this weekend. Was that a yes?"

What was he doing? A weekend, not just one day?

It was insane but what the heck.

———

Rane shifted her stance a little backward, to put some much-needed space between the two of them. The real reason she'd stopped in to talk to him forgotten. She couldn't help but sneak glances at his open shirt. His dark chest hairs called to her. She found the way they moved with every breath he took very erotic. She swallowed hard as a delicious shudder heated her body. Her hands ached to touch him.

"This weekend? I'll need to check my employee handbook to see if it's against company policy. I don't want to lose my job. You never know what the boss might think."

"If there is anything in the employees' handbook, I'll have Mrs. Wallen or Mr. Hansen rewrite the policy immediately." Mark laughed and added, "I don't think the boss will mind. You think about it tonight. I'll want your answer tomorrow."

"I better get going. You seem to have a lot to do before you can go home," she said, and slowly backed away.

"I'm not going home. I'm going to spend the night here."

"You're doing an all-nighter?" She felt her cheeks burn and knew she was blushing. Wrong choice of words. She hoped her discomfort wasn't visible.

"I do them a lot. My office is also an apartment. Didn't you know?"

"No, I got the memo that you work late most nights."

She studied his office with interest, half-wondering where the bedroom was located. Should she break her own rule of not giving out on the first date?

"My apology, no one has mentioned it before now. This is why I'm here late most of the nights. Would you like a tour?"

"Ah, yeah. It never occurred to me you'd have something like that here." Rane marveled at his luxurious office and the fact there were other rooms attached to it. She set her briefcase and purse on a chair by his desk.

How convenient for a bachelor.

Was she falling for a man who said one thing but meant another? Was it why he was still single?

He wandered to a door to the right, which was ajar. In a flamboyant manner he pushed it open all the way. "This is the entertainment room."

"Oh, my. It's very convenient. Sorry, I mean it's handy, no, appropriate for you to have a room. I'm giving up. It looks nice."

"It's a perk, being the president and all."

"Right."

Mark motioned for her to come closer. Her feet moved of their own accord. She saw a huge plasma television on the far wall and a pool table in the middle of the room. Once inside, there were other doors.

"If you'd like, I could fix you a cocktail or maybe a glass of wine?"

"No, thanks, I need to drive home."

What was she supposed to do?

Was his offer a veiled invitation to spend the night, but was she ready? Would she ever be?

"Welcome to my home away from home."

The playing of the *Pink Panther* theme song interrupted their conversation.

"Sorry, that's my ringtone for Val," Rane said. Slipping her phone out of her pocket, she turned away from Mark for some privacy.

Tapping 'accept', she didn't give Val a chance to say anything. "I'll call you later. Bye."

Then she pressed 'end call' and put the phone on silent before slipping it back into her pocket. As she refocused her attention back to Mark, the sexually intoxicating mood had vanished.

Reality had taken over.

"Sorry, about that. This place looks lovely. I'm sure it's nothing compared to your home but for emergencies, it's great. I'll think about your offer for a weekend getaway. I better get going."

Even though the moment was lost, she was having a hard time ignoring him. She knew any spur of the moment sex wasn't the best thing to do. Taking a step backward, she attempted to leave.

"Wait. Rane, we are both adults. My offers don't come lightly."

That was not what she wanted to hear. She stopped as he came to her. His body filled any and all the empty space between them. Then he gathered her into his arms.

"I've wanted to kiss you since I first met you."

"I can't lie. I've thought about it too."

Her approval, had him leaning in and gently, but firmly, his lips touched hers. The kiss didn't surprise her. She wanted it and opened her lips. Their tongues met. The excitement sent sparks of pleasure through her, and she wrapped her arms around his hard body. Slowly, she glided her hands over his broad shoulders.

For a brief second, their tongues paused and then they danced with each other again.

A vibration from her pocket broke into the moment. Releasing his lips, she lowered her head. "Sorry."

The vibrations stopped and she gazed up at Mark.

"Your eyes are very green."

"Are they?" The air around them was so sexually electrified, she knew if he kissed her again, they would stay that color and she wouldn't be able to leave. If her eyes were green, it meant she was aroused. He had sparked the flame of her desire. "I really have to go home."

"If you must. Don't forget, you owe me an answer this time."

He released her and without replying, she picked up her brief-case and purse and left his office. In a trance, she drifted into the waiting elevator. She saw he had followed her and gave her a smile as the doors closed. It brought her out of her dazed state. Lifting a hand to her lips, she wished she could bring back his electrifying kiss.

How could she have allowed him to kiss her? He was the owner of the company, not just an employee.

With her body still trembling from the unleashed desire, she slowly made her way to her car. She wasn't sure how she was going to drive home in her condition. Rane sat with her hand poised on the ignition, sorely tempted to go back upstairs to his office, but her fingers turned the key.

Tonight was not the night.

Chapter Thirteen

M ark stared at the doors and watched the elevator's numbers light up until they reached one, the main lobby. He felt very placated and grinned as he returned to his office alone and sat at his desk.

It pleased him that she'd refused his invite to spend the night. But it irritated him at the same time. Her unanticipated response made his eyebrows draw together as he fought to remember the last time a woman had turned down the chance to spend a night with him.

Just when he thought he was beginning to understand Rane, she threw him a curve. And it was a big one. He hadn't planned to kiss her yet, but the silkiness of her hair as it'd slipped through his fingers had done him in.

Damn.

Double damn and triple damn.

The kiss had teased him. He wanted more. He wanted to make love to her.

What was he thinking?

Man alive, he was in trouble if a first kiss could affect him as this one had.

Fuck. He needed a cold shower.

Unsuccessful in cooling his still-heated body, he directed his thoughts to their lunches together. He'd enjoyed listening and observing her. When she let down her guard, he found her to be smart, intelligent, and sophisticated. She was exactly what he was looking for in a woman. He found it refreshing to be with someone who could be so natural.

Not able to postpone the inevitable, he reached for the phone and called Philip. It rang more times than he thought it should have.

"Yes, Mr. Christmenn?"

"Come to my office."

"I'll be there in a few minutes," Philip replied.

"Make it so."

Pushing the button to disconnect, Mark then left his desk and went into the entertainment room. He sat on the couch and waited for Philip. He let his head fall back and closed his eyes in another attempt to cool his rising desire. He tried to focus on the paparazzi and the chaos they had put on during his lunch.

They'd really pissed him off. Their surprise appearance angered him the most. Who could have tipped them off? It had been years since the paparazzi had gotten the better of him like they had today. His anger rose as he remembered when the damn cameras had gone off in the main lobby. He had instinctively moved Rane to shield her, knowing firsthand how much damage a picture could be to a person.

"Mark, what's wrong?"

He opened his eyes. The concern he saw on Philip's face was genuine, but he ignored it.

"I asked Ms. Schoen out on a date, and then I kissed her."

Philip's uncontrollable laughter caused Mark to frown. "For Christ's sake, stop it. I don't find this funny. I really like her."

That was all it took for Philip to cease his laughing, but he saw a smile.

"Are you sure that was a good idea?"

"Which one, the kiss, or asking her out?"

"Either." Philip began laughing again.

"Oh hell, I don't know. I mean, it doesn't matter, it's done. This is serious. Damn it!"

"This wasn't our plan. I just had to pay a hefty sum for the very damaging photos. My threat still stands. If you ever do anything so foolish as to leave the building without security, I will handcuff you to your desk."

"I know that if word gets out, I'm involved with someone, whether it was true or not, all hell will break loose with the media." Mark knew Philip's threat was real. He didn't know which would be worse, the tabloids or being handcuffed to his desk.

"Right. Remember I'm here to protect you. You have to take that seriously. Plus, the hit man is still at large and if I'm going to help Agent Nelson nail this guy, the two of you better start cooperating. Asking out a woman isn't a huge problem. Where would you want to go? You know I need more than twenty-four hours to set up the security, if you want to go anyplace but dinner."

"I know. I want to invite her to my house." He watched Philip's smile disappear to be replaced by shock.

"Your, your house? You never invite anyone there."

"I know. I don't want the mobs and the chaos that usually goes on whenever I go out. She experienced that today. Rest assured, the paparazzi will be on my tail from now on."

"You were fucking stupid for leaving with no protection."

Philip did laps around the pool table. Their friendship had developed over the last seventeen years, from bodyguard to friend. Without him, he'd probably be broke or dead by now. Philip being ex-military had saved them on many occasions.

"I know that now."

"As long as we are on the same page from now on, that's all

that matters. You know, usually people go to dinner or a play on their first date. Don't you know anything about dating?"

Philip's annoying humor made Mark sit up straighter. "Didn't you hear me? I said I really like her."

"You're thinking with your dick. You've never brought a woman to your home."

Mark knew he was right again. "I know I am. This whole Massaro thing has me rethinking my life."

"If you were looking for sex, why didn't you say something? Are you sure I can't arrange a nice simple dinner?"

"Why is everyone so quick to give me advice about dating? Besides, what the hell do you know about dating? I've never seen you with a woman. Maybe you should find one. All I know is that I want to get to know Rane better. I can't do that if I'm in the public's eye with her. And it's not about sex."

His justifications sounded weak to his ears. What was the real reason he was attracted to her?

Philip joined him on the couch. They sat staring at each other. The tension was as thick as fog. Mark waited in silence for him to say something.

"If this is what you want, let me know when this date will occur. I'll make sure it will be as private as I can arrange. And my love life or lack of it isn't any of your business."

Mark raised his eyebrows at Philip's comment. Had he struck a sore spot with him? Was it his fault Philip hadn't found anyone? He sighed, another problem to add to his list. "Exactly how much money *did* you have to fork out to pay off the paparazzi?"

"More than normal. They know something is up with her. You should've gone to a different restaurant today."

Mark turned to look at Philip.

"Don't look at me like that! You know I'm right, Mark. Should I set up security for her to stop any pending trouble?"

"Yeah, do it, twenty-four/seven." He stood and ran his hand along the pool table's edge. Should he be involving a woman in his life right now? Remembering how she felt in his arms, the answer was yes. "Any word yet if the reporters have figured out our involvement in the arrest of Massaro?"

"Only one newspaper has pieced it together. I had to make a deal with *Star-Tribune*. You will be giving them an exclusive interview once it does break, in exchange for them keeping it quiet. Plus, they will let us know the minute any little tidbit arises."

"What about the person or persons involved with hijacking my shipments and how they came to be an employee?"

"According to Agent Nelson, the employee-no, ex-employee is not cooperating. I haven't been able to dig up anything on him either. All my contacts have come up with nothing too," Philip stated.

"I need to know how the drugs got into my plants and why they picked my company."

"I'm working on it."

Silence once again filled the room. Mark went to the bar and poured himself a bourbon. "I'd offer you one, but you're still on the clock."

"If that was the case, I'd never get to drink. I'll take a raincheck. If there isn't anything else, I better get someone over to her house." Philip stood.

"Fine, just get it done." His stomach growled, reminding him he needed to eat something.

"Is that breaking news? Do you want me to pick up dinner?"

"Sushi would be great."

"I hope this works out with you and this woman. You need to forget about the damn picture," Philip said.

"Only time will tell."

He saw Philip give him a weird look before snickering as he walked out of his office. Mark waited a second time for the sound of the elevator ding before he went back to his desk. Picking up the picture in question, he stared at it.

Why had he believed so heavily in this promise from a girl so long ago? Should he go to Epcot to see if the now adult woman would be there waiting for him? Would he even recognize her to know it was her, or would she know it was him?

The three questions nagged at him. No matter how hard he tried to forget the promise.

Did he want reality or possibility?

Reality won by a landslide tonight.

Setting the picture back down with some regret, he recalled the feel of Rane's lips opening to his kiss. He ran his hand through his hair, what was wrong with him? Now all he could think about was how much he wanted her.

When Rane had stared at him after the damn phone interruption, her eyes had been green and had stayed that way. Could green mean she had been feeling desire?

He smiled at his theory.

How green could they get? As dark as a forest green? He wanted the chance to find out.

Waiting for Philip's return with dinner, he poured himself a second bourbon and sat on the couch. He let his thoughts go to Rane. She was something he hadn't hoped to find. Her blue then green eye color were unique and the way her face lit up when she smiled was genuine. She had fit right into his arms when he had kissed her. Closing his eyes, he reimagined her sweet-tasting lips on his.

———

Rane arrived home safely, unsure how, but she'd done it. She decided after she'd fed Thor that a hot steamy bubble bath would relax the pent-up sexual tension Mark had created. With the steam rising from the tub, she sat on its edge waiting for it to fill.

What if Val's phone call hadn't interrupted them? Would she be lying naked next to him right now?

On the other hand, would they have made scandalous love on

top of his desk? On second thought, maybe they would have had sex on top of the pool table. She smiled at an image of them on the green velvet making love.

When he had touched her hair, it had sent electric jolts through each single strand. She took those strands of hair and stroked them. A faint scent of Drakkar was released. She moaned as it made her stomach turn upside down.

The rising water brought her back to the present. She slipped into the hot water, laid her head back, and let her eyes close. The lit candles emitted aromas that were supposed to help her relax.

She lay perfectly still as the water gently lapped at her breasts. Soon she was imagining the water was Mark's strong fingers caressing her breasts, rolling her hardened nipple between his fingers. She pushed her hips a little, as his other hand slid lower, all the while his tongue lapped at her breasts.

Startled, she sat up, splashing water everywhere. She opened her eyes to make sure she was alone. No other person was in the bathroom, only Thor who lay on the rug next to the tub. She released a sigh at how real the images were and laid back again.

What was happening to her?

Every inch of her body cried out for Mark's touch. He'd asked her to stay. Maybe she should get in her car and drive back to the office.

No.

That would give him the wrong impression.

What would Val do? She'd have—wrong, she wasn't Val.

Val was probably enjoying a night of steamy sex with her new hotty. Which was probably the reason she'd called and interrupted her and Mark's kiss. To tell her about some delightful, handsome, and magnificent male she was having dinner.

She was the opposite of Val. Taking things slow and easy was her way. Always the safe route.

Wrong again. She had thought about Mark's invitation to stay. That would not have been slow and safe.

Unable to enjoy her attempt at a relaxing bath, she got out hastily and toweled off.

But Mark wouldn't leave her thoughts.

She could see him walking. Then standing in front of her. And those tempting chest hairs, revealed by his unbutton shirt.

He wouldn't leave her thoughts. She slipped on her nightshirt over her head. As the silky fabric slid down over her body, it became Mark's hands caressing her heated skin. She gasped aloud, as the fabric brushed the hairs between her legs.

Thor meowed.

"Sorry boy. Did I interrupt your nap?"

She lifted him into her arms, annoyed she couldn't keep Mark out of her thoughts. Making her way into the kitchen, she set Thor down on the floor.

"Mommy's going to have some ice cream, do you want some treats too?"

Thor's reply was to meow and rub up against her calves.

"I thought you'd want some too." Taking a handful from his treat jar, she laid them on the floor next to him. Then she grabbed a pint of mocha caramel ice cream from the freezer. "Come on to bed when you're done."

As if he understood, his tail swished from side to side. Turning off the lights, she went to the bedroom and climbed into bed still clutching the ice cream container. Not taking the time to crawl under the blankets, she leaned back and began to shove spoonsful of the rich creamy brown ice cream into her mouth.

With each spoonful her mind wandered back to Mark. She found it surprising how much she enjoyed talking to him at lunch. Sometimes it felt like he knew what she was thinking or going to say.

It was uncanny. Their conversations hadn't centered on him or what he wanted. He'd acted genuinely interested in what she said.

That had been more than David had done. He was still texting her. She now had over thirty-five messages on her phone from him.

She shoved an extra-large spoonful of ice cream into her mouth.

He could go to hell. She wasn't about to give into him.

During their divorce, she'd thought a lot about what she'd ever seen in him. It was the same then as it was now. He'd said all the right things at all the right times. Now more than ever she realized David had used her as a thing that would be able to give him what he wanted.

In high school after every football game, they'd have sex in the backseat of his black Trans Am. She'd thought it had been what was expected of her. She never liked doing it in the car. It had been so cramped, awkward, and unsatisfying to her.

Then after they'd been married, living off campus, he would stay out late saying he was studying. The grim fact, as she found out later, was he'd been out seeing other women.

Angry tears came to her eyes as she realized she'd given him everything.

It made her sick thinking about what she'd done for him. Instead of spending her money on clothes, vacations, or things for their little condominium, she'd saved the money. For what? So, they'd be able to pay for his graduate school.

He hadn't allowed her to spend any money on fun things, but he had. He had never worked a day of their marriage to help with the bills. In the summers, he'd spend her money at the bars and go out with his friends rather than find a summer job. He'd been allowed to spend money on whatever he wanted and grew accustomed to the lifestyle she'd provided for him. She'd never questioned him because she had trusted him. He'd promised her when he became a doctor, they'd have everything.

She'd been devastated the day he had left her. Even now, as she went over these things, she realized she had never loved

David. She didn't know what true love was and only dreamed about finding the right man.

If Mark was the man for her, she was going to give it all she could, and if he wasn't, she'd learn by her mistake.

Thor jumped onto the bed signaling it was time to turn out the lights. Realizing she'd eaten the entire pint of ice cream, she set the empty container on the nightstand and turned off the lights. Crawling under the blankets, Rane patted the spot next to her and Thor laid down in it. As she stroked him, she played out just how she was going to get Mark to make love to her.

––––––––

Halfway into her morning drive to work, Rane realized she hadn't told Mark she couldn't have lunch with him. It had been the main reason she'd gone to his office to see him.

Who was she trying to kid?

She'd gone to see him because she'd wanted to, no needed to.

When she'd seen him with his shirt open and sleeves rolled up, she'd forgotten everything. He had been so handsome standing behind his desk, she had tried not to assess his features.

That had failed too.

His deliberate but sexy walk had been her undoing, which had led to her letting him kiss her. She had taken control and even now there had been a dreamy intimacy when their lips had touched.

Her ice cream coma before going to bed hadn't worked either. Rane knew she couldn't trust herself to be in his presence without wanting a second kiss. Her only solution was to e-mail him about having to cancel their lunch.

Traffic wasn't on her side, and she hit red light after red light. As she waited for the last one to turn green she remembered a weird dream she'd had last night. A knight had come to her rescue again.

Not quite sure why she needed rescuing, but he'd been there

to save her, from what, she couldn't remember. This time there'd been some sort of dinosaur looking creature talking to the knight. No, to her knight, in shining armor. The large, winged creature had cat-like eyes that sparkled like emerald stones. She'd heard the knight talking but couldn't find herself anywhere in the dream even though she heard herself answer him. She told the knight she would die without him as if he was the core of her existence.

Beeepppp, beeppp.

A car behind her honked and she saw the light was green. She didn't have time to dwell on her dream, Mark, or the creature and shoved them into the very back of her mind. She had her first presentation to concentrate on.

Inside the MAC building when she reached the sixth floor, instead of going to her office she went straight to the breakroom for her morning dose of hot chocolate. Before making the turn to go to her office, she glanced toward Mark's office.

Seeing his door was open, she sat at her desk and typed a regret e-mail to him. "Mr. Christmenn, I'm sorry I have to cancel our lunch this afternoon. Please let me know when we can reschedule it. Ms. Schoen."

Once she hit send, she saw she only had a few minutes before her nine o'clock meeting. Snatching a couple of Hershey kisses from her desk drawer, she put them into her pocket. Then went to the table and gathered the packets she had bundled up last night. There was one for each person. With the stack of papers tucked under her arm and her cup of hot chocolate in her hand. She yanked open the door and backed out, trying to close it with her foot.

"Let me help."

"Mark, Mr. Christmenn, what are you doing—"

When she took a step backward, her foot encountered another foot. She jerked forward and bumped into Mark's outstretched arm. Her files slid out from under her arm and spilled all over the floor in front of her.

As she viewed all her hard work in a jumbled mess, she felt her hot chocolate stinging her hand and a brown stain down the front of her blouse. "Ohhhh, no. Oh, crap."

Rane turned her head and frowned at Mark. She tried to back up again, but this time his hard, stone like body stopped her. His hand was immediately on her elbow to prevent her from falling. She felt her cheeks burn from humiliation and anger. About to give him a piece of her mind, she stopped short when she saw other employees were staring at them. To make matters worse, her body was overheated, and it wasn't because of the spilled hot chocolate.

"Are you all right, Ms. Schoen?"

"Yes, Mr. Christmenn. I think you should release my elbow. We have become the center of attention."

Instantly he did so and retreated a step. Rane stared at all the files scattered on the floor and wiped at the stain on her blouse. This was not something she could fix in a minute or two, but somehow, she'd have to. Without saying another word, she bent down and began picking up her papers.

"Let me help you," Mark stated.

"That's okay. I got this. You've made me late to my meeting and look at my blouse. So much for first impressions."

"Mrs. Weber!"

Mark bellowed so loud she looked up at him. When he bent down to help, he said in a quieter tone, "I'm sorry, Rane."

She ignored him and he stood. As she continued to gather her mess by herself, she saw his shiny shoes move away as other hands began picking up the papers.

"Thank you so much," she said.

As the very formidable Mrs. Weber appeared, Rane noticed Mark was standing with his hands clasped behind his back. "Mrs. Weber, call Macy's and have someone deliver a white blouse. Ms. Schoen a size six?"

Even though Mark's tone had been demanding, Rane nodded. How had he known what size shirt she wore?

"Have them deliver it right away. Ms. Schoen is late for a meeting."

"Yes, Mr. Christmenn," Mrs. Weber replied and hastened away.

"Jessica, Roger, Kathy, please stay and help Ms. Schoen reorganize her reports," Mark said.

"Yes, Mr. Christmenn," they responded in unison.

A tiny smile tweaked at the corners of her lips, despite the seriousness of the situation. She felt as if she was in the military. All that was missing was "sir" instead of Mr. Christmenn.

"Ms. Schoen, please accept my apology. I'll go ahead to your meeting and give them a pep talk. This should give you some time to prepare your papers and for the new blouse to arrive. I should be able to stall them for about forty-five minutes at the max. Will that be enough time?"

"Yes, Mr. Christmenn."

Damn it, now she was saying it.

She closed her eyes for a moment to clear her thoughts. "No need for an apology. It was my fault. I wasn't expecting anyone to be outside my office door. I didn't look."

"Which boardroom is your meeting in?"

"Boardroom C," she said.

"Forty-five minutes, Ms. Schoen. Mrs. Weber, if you need me, I'll be in Boardroom C."

After making it clear to everyone within shouting distant of his intentions, he walked away.

"Hi, I'm Jessica," a woman with shoulder-length brown hair said and pointed to the office next to the receptionist's desk. "Let's take these papers into the conference room right over there."

Roger, the other employee who'd she met before, was one step ahead of them and had already taken everything into the vacant office. Rane took a quick glance over her shoulder and watched Mark turn the corner toward the boardroom.

———

Mark proceeded to Boardroom C flexing his left hand. It felt like it was on fire. He took a deep breath. Then he caught the smell of her perfume. She wasn't even close by, and he could still smell it. He lifted his hand to his nose and sniffed. The scent was on his hand, but it was too late. The damage had already been done. His body was betraying him.

Damn.

Was he that hard up? How long had it been since he'd had sex?

Maybe Philip had been right again. All he needed was a night of sex.

Was that the reason he felt so attracted to Rane? Because he only wanted to make love to her?

That was insane. Why would he think that, after telling Philip he liked her?

He slowed his walk and shoved his hands into his pockets. This was not the time to think about Rane and how he'd like to make love to her. He was about to walk into a room of his employees.

Thankfully, there wasn't anyone in the hallway, he had to pull himself together. This is not the time to think about having sex.

Think.

That was his problem. He was thinking too much about other things. He needed to come up with something to talk about for an hour. He was the king of the spur-of-the-moment speeches.

Concentrate.

Mark took a deep breath, which happened to be the wrong thing to do at the moment. He got another whiff of Rane's perfume. With as much self-control as a teenager, he stepped over to the conference room door and opened it.

"Good morning, ladies and gentlemen."

He saw a stunned group of employees as he closed the door. This was going to be interesting, to say the least, as he walked up to the podium.

———

Rane frantically instructed Jessica and Roger to place all the papers on the table. "Please separate all the like papers into piles. Once we have them sorted, we can collate them again."

"No problem, Ms. Schoen. Are you sure you're alright? Did you get burned?" Jessica asked.

"I'm not burned. My hand is okay, and it only splattered my blouse. I'm fine, just a little shaken. I didn't even see Mr. Christmenn behind me. I don't know how it happened." Rane shook her head. "I was closing the door, and then he was there. I feel so stupid. Look at my blouse! Look at my papers."

What she couldn't say was no, she wasn't fine. Her body was on fire. She wanted to have sex with the owner of the company.

For God's sake, how many times did she have to bump into him? Every time she did, she became more and more aware of his physique.

"Don't worry, Ms. Schoen. We'll get everything in order for you," Roger said.

"Thank you. You're all so very kind."

"Excuse me, Ms. Schoen. The blouse has arrived. I have it here."

Rane looked up and Mrs. Weber was at the door holding a package. "Already? That was quick. Thank you so much. I'll be back in a couple of minutes. Excuse me."

She took the package from Mrs. Weber and headed toward the bathrooms.

"Ms. Schoen, Mr. Christmenn has a private restroom. I don't think he'll mind if you use it to change. As you enter his office, it's to the left," Mrs. Weber stated.

Confused, Rane hesitated for a moment.

"Go on, you had best hurry. If Mr. Christmenn said forty-five minutes, then that is what he means."

"Right. Thank you. To the left in his office," Rane replied.

Mrs. Weber nodded.

Hurrying down the hall to Mark's office, she checked her phone for the time, nine-twenty-six. She had about fifteen minutes to change and get to the boardroom. When she entered his office, scenes from last night vividly replayed in her mind. She saw him standing in front of her declaring he wanted to kiss her and telling him she did to.

She brushed the images away and glanced around the room until she found the door. Opening it slowly, it revealed a bathroom-no his bathroom.

Was this the bathroom they might've used last night if she had stayed? Would they have come in here after making love to shower?

Stop thinking about him, she told herself.

Noting it was neat, like one you'd find in a hotel room, it only had a shower, a toilet, and a vanity. Off to the side was a separate area for changing, plus a closet. That door was open, and she couldn't resist peeking and did, but felt guilty.

It was his closet.

There were an array of dress shirts, suits, and a dark blue bathrobe hung on a hook. She reached in and smelled the robe. A manly, musky, and clean scent was her reward.

Would he have offered her his robe? Would she ever find out?

Rane moved away, tempted to investigate his clothes further, until she eyed the vanity, displaying an assortment of personal care items and a bottle of Drakkar cologne. She picked it up and slowly raised it to her nose. She inhaled deeply and closed her eyes. It didn't take long for the smell to overtake her senses and images of Mark.

It brought her back to the first night she'd bumped into him in his office. Their bodies hitting each other, her breasts touching his chest, and his arms enfolding her. The memory of his muscles and the power his arms held, were very clear.

She heard a noise outside in Mark's office. It spurred her forward to her task at hand, changing her shirt. Quickly, unbuttoning her soiled blouse, she noticed another door behind her. Ripping off the price tag on the new blouse, she slipped it on and tucked it into the waist band of her skirt.

Checking her phone, she saw she still had eleven minutes. Turning the knob on the other door, it opened. She looked inside and saw it was a bedroom.

His bedroom.

Her mind imagined an image of Mark naked laying on the bed.

Shaking her head, to refocus her thoughts, didn't work. A second image of her joining him on the bed materialized.

Damn it, she had a job to do.

Forcing the door shut, the daydream faded. She picked up her stained blouse, turned off the lights, leaving his bathroom, and all the 'what if's, behind.

Her rescue team, along with Mrs. Weber, were finished by the time she returned.

"We have them all sorted, Ms. Schoen," Jessica announced.

"I can't thank you enough. I owe you all coffees or lunch. They look great," Rane said.

"Glad we could help," Roger stated and handed her the pile of her reports.

"You all are life savers. Thanks again." With the papers secured in her arms, she headed down the hall. As she approached Boardroom C, she took a breath clearing her mind. Shifting the stack of papers, she placed her hand on the door handle and pushed down with confidence.

When she entered, Mark looked over at her and nodded.

"I'd like to thank you all for this opportunity to speak to you this morning. It has given me a chance to share with you my outlook on the company for the upcoming year. As you can see, Ms. Schoen has arrived. She'll be taking over the meeting. Let's give her a warm welcome."

Everyone clapped as she proceeded to the front of the room.

"Good morning and thank you for the warm welcome. Thank you, Mr. Christmenn, for the introduction. I'm sorry I was unable to hear your speech. I have been told you could part certain waters with your inspirational talks"

The forced smile on his face was replaced with a smirk. Rane watched him move to an empty chair and sat down instead of leaving.

Great.

It was one thing to have him present but to have the man you yearned to see naked watching your every move and hanging on your every word was another thing. Could he be mentally undressing her, as she had done to him minutes ago in his bathroom?

"It seems Mr. Christmenn has decided to stay. I don't want anyone to become nervous. You see, this is a learning meeting. Apparently, Mr. Christmenn needs to learn something today and that is why he has chosen to stay." She had to stop talking as laughter broke out, but it quickly stopped. "As my first instruction I want you to treat him as any other fellow employee this morning. I have seen a lot of you around the office in the last couple of weeks. I have also met with some of you about your positions."

The facial expressions she saw on the group of employees were those of caution. This was the normal type of reaction she received. She knew some of them thought they might be losing their jobs. She proceeded with care, picked up the files, and moseyed around the tables as she continued to talk.

"I'm handing out an outline of some of the items I found in your departments. Let us look at the second packet. It is a *Get to Know Someone in Your Department* test. The paper has a list of seven food items on it. What I need for each of you to do is to find two or more fellow employees, from this room only, that like each of the foods listed."

Pausing for a moment, she debated whether she should give Mark the papers too. He was the reason she had been late, and he had chosen to stay, so he had now become part of the group. Placing a paper and packet in front of him, she avoided eye contact. By doing this, she noted most everyone was reading the outline and not the second packet as instructed. She raised her voice a tone louder to gain back their attention.

"Second, find two or more fellow employees, again from this room only, that dislike the same foods listed. Now, I can see from your faces this might seem odd, but the exercise will begin in a minute. Please hold up your packet."

Hands went up in the air. Once everyone had raised their packets, she went to the front of the room. "Great, everyone passes the first step. To complete this task, I am going to let you all take a twenty-five minute break."

The room became loud with the employees beginning to act on her announcement. She caught Mark's surprised look from the corner of her eye. He seemed to want to interrupt, but she didn't give him the opportunity too.

"I need everyone's attention." Rane waited for the talking to cease. "Thank you. I have a few more instructions, so listen carefully. During the break, you can choose to leave the room, go to the breakroom for snacks, or use the restrooms. However, if the list isn't completed by the time you return, you will be asked to leave the room."

Moans and groans erupted, and for a third time she had to talk louder. "Please, can I have everyone's attention."

The room quieted down.

"Let me repeat, if the test isn't completed, you will be asked to leave this room. Are there any questions?" Hearing and seeing no one raise their hand, she continued. "One last thing, after the twenty-five minute break is over, the door will be locked. What does this mean? You need to return on time. My phone says nine fifty-nine. I will start the break at ten o'clock and set the timer."

Rane halted for a second before excusing the group of thirty-eight employees and pushed start on the timer. She sat and watched the reactions of the employees trying to handle this set of problems. It was her 'never fail' test. She observed everyone and took notes as most of the employees left the room, including Mark.

Chapter Fourteen

M ark stood and promptly left the boardroom with all the other employees. He almost ran to his office, not sure he'd be able to make the deadline.

"Mrs. Weber, cancel all my appointments for the day."

"Is there another problem?"

"No." Mark went to his desk, considered the mess of papers laying there and frowned. What was he doing? He hadn't even planned on attending Rane's meeting. But somehow, he had become part of it and picked up his pen.

"When should I reschedule your four meetings, Mr. Christmenn?" Mrs. Weber asked from the doorway.

"Tomorrow or Monday," Mark said and eyed his watch. Fifteen minutes. He couldn't be late, or the doors would be locked. "What fruits do you like?"

"Excuse me, what?"

"I need to know what fruits you like and dislike," Mark said.

"This is odd. I don't like strawberries and blueberries, but I love oranges and cherries."

He opened the packet, and was about to mark down her reply,

but remembered Rane had said to ask only people in the room. "Damn it, I have to go."

"I'll check your calendar. But, Mr. Christmenn, you have Mr. —"

"It doesn't matter. I'm in a hurry. If you need me, I'll be in Boardroom C."

"Boardroom C," Mrs. Weber repeated then smiled.

"I'm unavailable for the rest of the day. Only, and I mean only if a real emergency arises, should I be interrupted."

"Yes, sir."

He practically ran down the hall and had to slow because other employees were rushing too. Once inside, Mark saw almost everyone had made it back in time. He worked the room with expertise and filled out the form with names. The room was a buzz of activity with only five minutes left. The excitement was contagious. He felt pride in the fact Rane had been able to do this to the employees.

What did she have planned next?

He saw her at the podium. She glanced at her phone and scanned the room. Their eyes met. Rane approached him with her eyebrows lifted and wearing a tight smile.

"Mr. Christmenn, is there a problem? Can I help you?"

"No. No, problem. I'd like to attend the rest of your meeting today. Of course, that is, if it's all right with you?"

He knew she wouldn't, and couldn't, say no. Her look of surprise made him smile.

"Yes, of course, Mr. Christmenn. I hope you have completed the form, otherwise I will have to ask you to leave," Rane said and walked toward the doors.

Her audacity was refreshing. No employee had ever talked to him like that. He took a seat at one of the front tables.

"Mr. Christmenn, mind if I join you?"

Looking up, he saw Richard standing next to him. "My all means. This is really exciting. Did you complete the form too?"

"I did and I see you have too," Richard said and sat.

"I found myself talking to some of the employees for the first time. This was good for me," he said and checked his watch.

Three minutes before the time of reckoning would be here.

———

Rane moved away from Mark. She doubted he'd been able to finish the assignment like he had said. Should she prove a point by calling the president out? No, but she'd have to change the program just in case.

Crap.

She couldn't believe her stroke of bad luck today. A stained blouse. Late to her first official meeting. Now he, Mark, wanted to stay for her presentation.

Why? She'd given him the opportunity to exit with grace and he hadn't taken it. What were his intentions, to observe her as an employee or a woman?

She hoped it was because he was interested in her.

Not about to let his presence unsettle her, she decided to use him so the employees could get to know him better. They probably would hesitate at first, but that would work to her advantage.

Making her way to the doors, she glanced at her phone. It was almost time with two minutes to go. Her last count, she was short five employees. The ratio was better than she'd expected.

Advancing slowly toward the door, the room quieted without her having to do anything. It was what always happened at this point.

Stunned silence.

With her hand on the door handle, the only sounds she heard were people moving nervously. Rane started her final countdown in her mind.

Five. Four. Three. Two. One. Zero.

Only one of the missing five employees made it inside in time. The sound of the clicking of the lock echoed throughout the room.

"Wait. Let me in."

The voice from the other side of the door shattered through the quiet room. Gasps filled the air as she simply turned away from the door. Like bees buzzing, the sound grew louder as she approached the front of the room. "I'm going to take roll call to see which of your fellow team members are missing in action."

During the roll call, the repeated rattle of the door handle caused another round of whispers.

It has begun.

"Welcome back," she said above the shaking of the door handle. "How many of you have completed your test?"

Some hands raised quickly and others rather slowly. Rane strolled around the tables and checked each of the tests.

The first test she found uncompleted, she asked that employee to leave the room. The employee hesitantly stood, took a momentary glance at Mr. Christmenn and Mr. Adams, and walked out. Finding ten more uncompleted tests, she also asked each of those employees to leave.

Once the door closed behind the last person, Rane addressed the remaining group still in the room. "As you can see, following through with an assignment is very important when you're instructed to do something. How many of you could have done what I just did?"

She stared at a mixture of stunned, annoyed, and angry faces. A couple of hands rose into the air.

"Good, I'm glad to see we have some leaders in our group. If one piece of the instruction is not completed, look what has happened. We now have fifteen members of our team missing. The team members that ignored the time schedule might have had a completed test. However, they were late so their input couldn't be used. The team members that didn't feel it was important enough to complete the work also weren't able to contribute to the end result. Mr. Adams, will you please invite our other team members to rejoin the meeting?"

Rane waited for the group to reenter and sit. She walked to the podium and casually glanced in Mark's direction. Surprised beyond belief when he winked at her. That was not office protocol, but she lowered her head to hide her smile.

The room buzzed again with conversation. She heard several mean comments.

"That was wrong."

"Who does she think she is?"

"In front of him."

None of their angry words surprised her. Rane breathed in deeply. Time to face the pack of wolves.

She stood with her hands clasped behind her back. "What did we learn from our exercise this morning?"

Pausing, she allowed the question to sink in. But no one spoke.

"That once a department has created a team it's very important that all the team members work together. Let me repeat that last statement. All team members need to work together. You cannot rely on others to do your work for you."

Rane spent the next hour going over the results and effects when things weren't done correctly and in sequential or methodical order. It had been tough, but she was able to have them come around and start working together in smaller teams.

The latter part of the hour before lunch, she instructed the teams to share the information they'd discovered from their tests. The results were entertaining with rounds of laughter about Mark's dislike for broccoli. The groups had loosened up and weren't as intimidated by him as before.

She felt the vibration from the alarm on her phone, signaling it was close to lunchtime. "I hate to interrupt all the reasons why Mr. Christmenn hates broccoli but it's time to break for lunch. You'll have one hour and fifteen minutes. See you at one-fifteen. You're excused."

A few hands raised.

"Do you have a question?"

"Are the doors going to be locked this time?"

Laughter erupted and she saw smiles. They were catching on. "The doors will remain unlocked and open. But do try to be back on time. You never know what you'll miss."

More laughter came from the group, and she noticed the look of approval on Mark's face. The room emptied quickly, and she cleaned up her papers and arranged the handouts for the afternoon.

"Rane, did you want to go to lunch?" Mr. Adams asked.

"That would be—"

"Ms. Schoen and I have already planned to have lunch today," Mark said.

"No problem, Mr. Christmenn. Will you be attending the afternoon session?" Mr. Adams asked.

"Yes, I need to see what other surprises Ms. Schoen has in store for us. She did a wonderful job this morning."

"Yes, she did. Have a nice lunch. See you in about an hour."

Richard excused himself, leaving Mark and her alone in the room. The only thing separating them was a table.

"No one cancels lunch with me." Mark proceeded to smile at her. It wasn't just a smile; it was one that made her heart flutter.

She couldn't resist its power and she smiled back. "If you're ready, let's go. We'll have to eat in the cafeteria. I can't be late to my own meeting a second time. You never know when the boss is going to show up."

"I know what you mean."

Laughing, they left the conference room and took the stairs instead of the elevators. Mark almost ran into her when she stopped a few steps before the landing and turned.

"Why are you lagging behind? Aren't you hungry?"

"I am. Just admiring the way, you walk and how your skirt hugs every curve. You look good in high heels. Do you work out?"

"Sometimes," she said and held on to the railing for support. If he wasn't the president of the company and he was simply a man she was interested in, she'd have kissed him by now. But he wasn't and she had to handle their actions carefully, even if he didn't. "Is this in the employee handbook, flirting with female employees?"

"Probably not."

He came down to the step she was on and brushed back a few strands of her hair from her face.

"Oh."

She breathed in and waited for him to kiss her, but he didn't. He stepped around her and took her hand into his.

"Come on, if we had more time, I'd take you up on that offer your face is showing me."

Rane let him lead her down the rest of the stairs. Regretfully, he had to release her hand to push open the door. As she passed him, he whispered, "Later I promise to kiss you till you melt in my arms."

God help me, I just wet my panties.

Almost embarrassed by her body's reaction because of his suggestion, she forced herself to rein in her sexual desires. She didn't know if she'd be able to wait until tonight for him to kiss her. At this rate, she was liable to jump him at the next opportunity and to heck with being coy.

Not trusting herself to say anything, she followed him, tight lipped.

A long line of people greeted them as they rounded the corner. Her senses returned and she noticed quite a few of the employees turning to stare at them. "Have you ever been to the cafeteria before?"

"Let's say I've thought about it, but I've never made it down here myself. Usually, I have Mrs. Weber bring me something to eat," he said.

Rane noticed the employees' reactions to seeing Mark and saw he was ready to run. She touched his arm in an attempt to have him focus on her.

"I expected your answer to be something like that. Again, you are creating a scene with your presence. Good thing these are friendly faces, and I don't see any cameras."

"That's for sure. Friendly territory here."

"I think you need to eat with your employees more often. It wouldn't hurt you to be more accessible to them."

"I guess I could try." Mark ran his fingers through his hair.

"You guess?" She raised her eyebrows in what she hoped was an 'I don't believe you, sort of way.'

"I usually don't—"

"No, no, no, I'm going to have Mrs. Weber schedule you to dine in once a week." She poked her finger into his shoulder and added, "And make you come down here yourself to get your own lunch."

Rane couldn't keep a straight face when she saw his look of absolute disbelief. She lost her battle, her composure, and laughed, which caused more employees to glance their way. The line moved forward.

"This is our in-house barista, a *Professional Chef of Coffee*. They are trained in the craft of coffee preparation and customer service skills," Mark said.

"I've read about the baristas in my research of the company, and I know that MAC has a reputation for its educational programs."

"Yes, we do."

She watched the man with interest. He moved from machine to machine in a manner that was almost dance-like. The machines made hissing and gushing noises. The employees waiting for their orders were excited as they took away their coveted drink. The heady alluring coffee aroma almost made her want to try the day's special.

She saw the barista wave excitedly at Mark and he in turn

placed his closed fingers in front of his puckered lips and kissed them in a salute.

"That is Antonio. He's been working for me since he was twenty-one. On a trip to Italy, my clients took me to a local coffee shop. Unbeknownst to the barista, his young apprentice had prepared a special *macchiato* for me. The blend had a marvelous taste, one I'd never tasted before. I was so impressed with it, with him, I sponsored him to come to the United States to work for me."

"Wasn't he at Jake's the other day?"

"Yes. When he's in a creative mood, he comes here to try out new blends. Mrs. Weber raves about them. Now I know why the line was so long. Did you want to try one?"

"No, not today," she said, shaking her head.

"I will get you to try coffee in the near future, be assured of that."

"We'll see about that. I can be very stubborn."

With their trays filled with delicious-looking food, they headed to the cashier who dropped Mark's change twice. Rane smiled at the lady and led him away.

Choosing not to sit inside, she proceeded to the outside eating area where there were plenty of vacant umbrella tables. Thankfully, the weather had turned warmer, and they could enjoy the outside air. Opting for one closest to the pond, she sat down with her back to the other employees and Mark followed suit. She hoped if the employees only saw their backs that they wouldn't recognize Mark. From their table the view was awesome with a pond to the right, surrounded by a grassy hill that was home to a couple of white swans.

"This is rather nice. Makes you want to have a picnic," he said. "I helped design this area. I was even here for the opening but forgot all about the pond. Now I understand why Mrs. Weber comes down here for lunch every day."

Mark's statements didn't surprise her. She'd already guessed he didn't leave his office much. He didn't have to.

"I swear I'm going to have a chat with her. You have two legs and two arms. There is no reason you can't come down here."

"Okay, okay, you win. I'll see if I can make it work."

"I will check up on you, I promise." She smiled and began eating her lunch. Not sure what to talk about, she decided on a safe subject, coffee. "The entire coffee process is interesting. How do the barista—"

"Will you be giving me your answer to my proposed date? You said you'd let me know."

"A date?" Stunned, she repeated, "A real date. Not a lunch date?"

"Yes, what about like, I don't know, a movie?"

"Oh, right, like you go to the movies regularly. When was the last time you went to see one?"

"I went to the opening premier of *Top Gun:* Maverick, in Los Angeles, during Covid."

"See what I mean. That's not going to a movie. You were probably dressed in a tuxedo and sipping champagne as you watched it."

"As a matter of fact, I was." He drank some water.

"You've got to be kidding. I was joking around. That's not going to a movie. To me, going to a movie is paying ten bucks for the afternoon matinee, ordering a butter-loaded bucket of popcorn, and sitting in a crowded theater."

"I did that once too, a long time ago."

"It's tough to envision you as an everyday guy. I've seen first-hand what *your* out of the office is like," she said shaking her head.

"I don't know if I can afford the ten bucks. We might have to go Dutch."

"That's fine. I'd prefer to pay my own way. Which theater would we go to? Do you like plain or buttered popcorn?"

"We wouldn't really go to a movie theater. I'm asking if you'd come to my house to watch a movie?"

"Your house?" She set down her fork and looked at him.

"Yea, my house. We can make our own popcorn. You can add as much butter as you want. I have a popcorn machine that looks like a wagon. You'd love it." Mark cleared his throat, before he continued. "You see, Philip would need more time to arrange everything if we actually went to a theater. And I haven't told him yet that I was planning on our date for this evening."

"Arrange? What would he need to organize? It's only a theater."

"Remember what happened yesterday at the restaurant and in front of the building? That would be nothing compared to us going to a public movie theater. It would be easier if you came over to my house."

"Oh, sorry I didn't think about *your* problem. How are you able to do anything?" She took a bite of her turkey sandwich.

Why is the public so interested in him?

She could understand why women were, but the public?

It didn't make sense. She might have to ask Val.

"That's part of the fun, trying to cheat them out of finding me." Mark pushed his tray of half-eaten food away.

"What type of movies do you like? I'm a romance and comedy type of girl," she said, still not committing to anything.

"I think we should stick to a comedy. Was that a, yes?"

"It was, but I'm not sure why I have agreed. What movie channels do you have?"

"Movie channels?"

"Yeah, like through your cable subscription. Isn't that how we are going to watch a movie? You know, like Netflix or Paramount Plus. Don't you watch television either?"

"Sometimes. I don't have much time to relax and do nothing but when I do, Philip sets it up," Mark stated.

"Okay, why don't you have Philip arrange a movie for us to watch at your house," she said and laughed.

"That would work. I will let him that is our plan for tonight." He reached for his cell phone.

"Is he going to watch the movie with us, too?"

Setting his phone down, he turned toward. "No, he won't be a third wheel."

Seeing Mark take out his phone, she took hers out and checked the time. Twelve-fifty-eight. "We need to go back inside. Remember, we can't be late."

He took both their trays and they back to the double-glass doors. A handful of employees glanced at them. She chose to ignore them this time, however when they stepped inside the cafeteria, it suddenly became quiet. Immediately, she saw Mark's body posture change. He was putting up barriers and almost dropped their trays before setting them on the rack. Like yesterday, she was in uncharted territory. Not sure what to do, she followed Mark across the room.

"Mr. Christmenn. Ms. Schoen. How was your lunch?"

She turned and found Mr. Adams had come to their rescue. His question ended the eerie silence and halted their progress.

"It was tasty, thank you. Ms. Schoen and I discussed some of her intake on this morning's meeting," Mark replied.

The three of them moved through the cafeteria. The employees now ignored them, and she saw Mark was beginning to relax again.

"What was Antonio's creation today?" he asked.

"It's a mocha—"

Mr. Adams stopped as his name was announced over the loudspeaker for a phone call. He excused himself and left her and Mark alone by the elevators. The elevator arrived empty and no one else joined them. The instant the doors closed, Mark hit the stop button and turned to face her.

Rane glanced around, nervously at first, and stared at him not sure why he'd pressed the button. He held her gaze relentlessly. If he was hunting his prey, she was it. The sexual tension inside the elevator was so high, she wondered if the alarms would go off. She made the first move, by turning to face him, and moistened her lips. Their closeness was a drug, luring her to him. Or was it his cologne that was intoxicating her?

"Your eyes are changing color."

"They are?"

Unaware she had replied, she held her breath.

He moved even closer to her and put his hands on her shoulders. Knots formed in her stomach as he drew her closer.

Time ceased.

"Are you going to kiss me?"

"Yes."

He leaned down and kissed her on the lips. It ended too quickly, and she wondered if he had or not, but she was breathless. All her thoughts of reasoning was gone as she stared into his eyes.

"I've wanted to do that all morning. Ever since last night, I've wanted a second taste," Mark said. He slid his hands down her arms and rested them on her hips. "Have you ever made love in an elevator?"

"No. Make love in an elevator? Right now?"

"It can be very exciting."

His husky tone sent shivers down her spine. The thought of them half undressed in the elevator shocked and enthralled her at the same time.

Her meeting be damned!

She let go of her hesitations, forgetting they were in a public place, in the middle of the day, and ran her hands up his chest to his neck. Her actions gave him permission and he captured her lips again. This time she knew he was kissing her. His warm lips were soft but searching as they claimed hers. She moved in, so their bodies touched. He slid his hand down lower to the end of her skirt and pulled.

"Is everything okay in there, Mr. Christmenn?"

A loud voice asked through a speaker on the wall, and they moved apart. She looked up at Mark. He shook his head and closed his eyes.

"Yes, I must have bumped the button. Sorry, I'll release it."

He kept his back to the camera, shielding her from any prying eyes, allowing her to adjust her skirt. She took one small step backward and smoothed her hair.

"I forgot about them. It's another thing I'll have to take care of. Are you ready?"

Mark gave her a boyish grin and she nodded, hoping whoever had been watching hadn't seen much. He pivoted, still not giving the spying eyes a chance to see her and reset the button.

She couldn't think of anything to say. His kiss had turned her gut inside out. The elevator began to move and then stopped on the next floor, saving her as several people got in. She moved further back while Mark positioned himself by the buttons, putting as much space as she could between them. When the doors opened again, Mark stepped out and placed his hands on the door waiting for her to exit. But she shook her head, and he released the doors.

She rode the elevator up to the top floor and then down to the sixth floor dazed. This time when the doors opened on her floor, she exited, more in control of her emotions. Last night's kiss she had anticipated and been able to control, but today's kisses had her confused. She was shocked at how eager she'd been to act on his suggestion of making love in the elevator.

Wow, she didn't think she'd be able to ride in an elevator ever again without remembering what she'd almost done. She was convinced he was either a very persistent male or a full-fledged ladies' man.

Rane smiled, hoping he was the first one. She imagined Mark dressed in a seventeenth-century costume and bowing to her in a flamboyant fashion.

He had the talk, the actions, and certainly the money to be a player. He also had her right where she thought he wanted her, guessing. However, it didn't really matter at this point because she was ready to do whatever he wanted. Falling this hard, this soon, for a man she'd just met, had to be a good sign not a bad one.

Right?

Checking her phone for the time, she saw she had a few minutes to text Val before heading to the boardroom and went to her office. Closing the door, she leaned against it. What had she almost done?

Typing as fast as she could, she sent Val a text. *"Have you ever had sex in an elevator."*

Val replied, *"Four times."* With several halo smiling emojis.

Maybe it was time to follow Val's example. She decided to shed her old-fashioned ways and to be more adventurous. If the opportunity arose again, she'd take Mark up on his offer and see how exciting and special elevators could be. Sometimes she wondered if Val made things up and typed. *"Is that a club, too? Like the mile high?"*

"No. Make sure it has mirrors. LOL"

Rane smiled. Mirrors? Of course, Val would say that, but she did have a good point. Checking her clothing, she made sure there was no telltale sign she'd made out in the elevator with the company's president. However, images of her and Mark pressed up against mirrored walls of an elevator, wouldn't go away. Damn Val and her suggestive comment.

Opening the office door, she headed back to the boardroom. When she entered, she found it nearly filled. She moved in between people chatting and made her way to the front with a little clearer mind.

"It looks like they're learning to follow directions better."

Rane felt Mark's presence behind her. "Yes, I see. Mr. Christmenn, please take your seat. The afternoon session has started."

She dismissed him with her cool tone in an effort to hide her desire to cozy up to him. He had to learn that she was doing a job, and his actions could cross a line that neither of them would know the consequences of.

"Right, sorry."

Mark gave her a slow, secretive smile that had her blushing. Willing herself not to react, she watched him walk away wishing they could be someplace else at this moment.

Damn, he could strut.

She went to the podium, knowing it was time to do her job. "I hope everyone enjoyed their lunches. This afternoon I want you to break into groups with six people in them. Once everyone has found a group, I'll give you the assignment."

The room became loud with raised voices filled with energy and enthusiasm. Observing the progress as she went from group to group, Rane found herself delighted with the success. Mark and Richard had both integrated themselves with the employees. Some of the employees were shy at first about having to talk in front of Mark but they soon got over their initial fears. He was such a people person that soon the employees were fighting over who was to be his next partner.

Several times during the session, Rane became conscious of Mark watching her. She'd look up from whatever she'd been doing, and their eyes would lock. He would grin at her mischievously and then turn his attention back to the task.

She groaned inwardly as butterflies formed in the pit of her stomach each time.

Don't flash those baby blues at me.

Not needing any kind of distraction, she went against her better judgement and stole another look at him. Her feelings for him puzzled her. Quickly, she averted her gaze away from Mark, not wanting anyone in the room to catch her staring at him.

Soon her phone vibrated, indicating that the time was up for the last assignment. Rane excused herself from the current group of employees she'd been working with. Her heart warmed to see she'd been successful, and she was so proud of everyone. They were doing such a wonderful job.

"May I have your attention please?" She waited for the room to quiet down before she continued. "I'd like to thank all of you for attending today. It was nice to see how well everyone participated. If there is one thing you walk away with today, I hope you've learned it's very important for everyone to implement what you've accomplished today into your everyday work habits."

Rane scanned the room and saw nodding and smiling. "Sometimes it takes a shock to the system for all the parts to work together. I'll be meeting every two weeks with your department to go over new items and solve some of the items we've had to defer from this meeting. As a treat for all your hard work today, I'm dismissing everyone early. Have a nice afternoon."

This time the employees broke out in excitement and chatter. She watched as Mark methodically said goodbye to each employee at the door. He'd made a huge progress today. She'd to have to tell him. His newfound involvement with his employees was a step in the right direction.

The room emptied until only Richard, Mark, and she remained.

"I think it went exceedingly well. Mr. Christmenn, I'm glad you were able to stay and participate. It gave the employees new insight into what the company is and what you expect from them," Richard said and then added, "Rane, let's meet in the morning to go over your recap before our other meeting?"

"I'm not sure if I'll have everything ready by tomorrow morning, but I should be able to give you a verbal update instead of one in writing. It will take me a couple of days to write the full report," she said and refused to look at Mark. He knew why she wouldn't be able to have the report done.

"That's fine," Richard said. "I better get going. I need to finish some paperwork too before I meet my wife at six for dinner. She hates it when I'm late."

"I enjoyed today, Ms. Schoen. I'll have to make it a point to be included in all the department meetings. Richard, I hope you have a nice dinner with your wife," Mark stated.

"I will. Rane, again, great job. Mr. Christmenn, I'll talk to you tomorrow."

"Yea, have a great night," Rane said.

Richard nodded and headed out the door. Rane watched his retreating figure with mounting anticipation. She was about to be alone with Mark.

When the door shut, Mark moved to stand next to her, leaving only enough space so that if she leaned in toward him, he'd be able to pull her close and kiss her.

And that's exactly what he did.

Rane couldn't resist, she didn't want to. Kissing him was a temptation that she wanted to give in to. She put her hand on his shoulder for a second, before running it up to the nape of his neck to deepen the kiss. Mark pulled her closer, so their bodies were one.

———

Mark sensed her surrender to the moment. He held her closer, and their bodies moved until a table stopped them. He ran his hand down over the curve of her hips and inched her skirt upward until he felt the silkiness of her panties. Using his thumb and finger, he pulled away the material, and was rewarded with the warmth and smoothness of her skin. Releasing her lips, he gazed into her green eyes before placing small kisses on her jawline and then to her neck. She tilted her head allowing him to continue his explorations.

With his fingers ready to find her other soft lips, a rattling sound at the door had them jerking away from each other. His temper flared. This was the third time something had interrupted their moment. First it had been Rane's phone last night and today the security guards in the elevator.

The rattling continued, but this time at one of the other doors. Mark shifted in an attempt to shield Rane from whomever dared enter. But the doors never opened. He focused on Rane and saw she had an amused look on her face.

"The door locks automatically, remember," she said.

"You think that was funny."

"Yes, I think our timing is all off. I do offer a class on that subject, too."

He wrapped his arms around her again, so she was pressed against him, and gently brushed his lips over hers. "Do you offer private lessons?"

"I'd have to check my employee handbook. I don't think I can moonlight. It might be against company policy."

"Again, that stupid handbook. What did you do, memorize it?"

She smiled and ruffled his hair.

"How soon can you be ready to leave?" Mark asked.

"Give me an hour?"

"An hour it is."

"Will I be following you in my car?" She moved away from him and started clearing the tables of papers and supplies.

Her question puzzled him. "I hadn't thought about how we are going to do things. We'll have to plan better next time. What would you like to do?"

"Val says a woman should always drive herself to a date, so I'll drive my car. I'll stop by your office when I've finished with my report."

"Sounds good. You have one hour and not a minute more," Mark was tempted to kiss her again but thought better of it. Shoving his hands into his pockets, he walked toward the door and waited for her. The fact they were going to spend an evening together felt like winning the lottery.

Chapter Fifteen

Rane became nervous as she gathered up her items from the table and the podium. What was she thinking of doing, hooking up with the owner of the company she worked for?

Yup, she had agreed to go out on a date with him. Not just a date but to his house. Stealing a glance in Mark's direction, she frowned.

What about Thor? Damn it, he should be her number one priority, not having sex.

She made her way toward the door, that Mark held open and tried her best not to touch him. They continued walking in the direction of her office as if nothing had happened.

How was he able to turn his desire on and off like a light switch while she was still burning up inside from their kisses?

They stopped in front of her office.

"One hour." He walked away.

His commands were just that, commands. Heaven forbid if a person didn't do what he said. Setting her stuff down, she picked up her purse and headed to the restroom. She saw Linda had left for the day. Then she noticed most everyone else had too. Checking her phone for the time, she saw it was after five.

Entering the restroom, she stood in front of the sink and waited for her stomach to calm down. She had a date in less than an hour. What was she going to do?

Call Val.

Tapping Val's number, she waited for her to answer.

"Hello girlie, what's up?"

"I have a date. Things happened and I said yes. It's tonight with you know who."

"I'm so proud of you. Do you have your emergency kit like I taught you?"

"Yes, I'm in the restroom now," Rane stated.

"Good. Freshen up and I mean all parts of your body. I hope you have a great time." Val laughed.

"Stop that. We're seeing a movie. Well, we're not going to a theater, but watching one at his house. And I will need you to feed Thor."

"You're definitely going to need the kit tonight. You know the rule. All first dates require a call in."

Rane shook her head. Usually, she had to call Val to check in on her. She wasn't going to let Val interrupt them again, so she made a mental note to call her when they arrived at his house.

"I'll stop and visit with Thor. He loves me. Did you do it?"

"Do what?"

"You know, in the elevator."

"No, but I think we might've if security hadn't interrupted us."

"Oh, my Gawd, Rane! You have some explaining to do, girlfriend."

"First things first. We can talk more tomorrow. You're more than welcome to spend the night at my house if you want. I think there is still a pint of coffee chocolate ice cream. Thor will love the company. Thanks for being there for me. I have to hurry. I'll text you to let you know I'm fine."

They said goodbye and Rane dug into her purse and found her emergency kit. She took out a mini toothbrush, sample makeup giveaways, toothpaste, an extra pair of thong panties, a condom, and her vintage perfume, *Charlie*.

Combing her hair and then quickly brushing her teeth, she dabbed on some blush and freshened up her lipstick. Last, she sprayed on a little perfume. Pushing the baggie with the undies aside, she couldn't help but grin. They would be for the morning, if she did decide to have sex and spend the night. She remembered when Val suggested including them in her emergency kit, thinking she'd never have the opportunity to use them.

Studying her reflection, Rane saw she'd done well. She could be damn attractive, even if Val hated her business suits. Tucking a wayward strand of hair behind her ear, she decided she was one hundred percent ready for anything that might happen tonight.

With her emergency kit repacked and tucked inside her purse, she remembered all the reports waiting for her to complete. Would she be able to concentrate on them, knowing in minutes Mark would be coming to get her? The answer was simple, no.

When she reached her office, she left all the papers from the meeting lying on the table and retrieved her briefcase. Closing the door, she went to Mark's office.

Once again, they were the only ones left on their section of the floor. Everyone else had left, taking advantage of the extra time off. His door was open, and she saw him standing in front of his desk with his back to the door. He had one hand on his hip with his suit coat pushed back.

Sweet heaven, he had a nice ass.

Her already elevated emotions intensified, and immediately imagined running her hands over both his muscular butt cheeks.

"Hello."

Mark turned and gave her a huge smile, but then it disappeared.

"Is everything all right?" she asked.

"Sorry. It's just you're so beautiful. I see you're ready to leave?"

"I'm not sure if we should do this." She shifted from one foot to the other. "You don't know me very well, and I don't know you that well. Maybe, we should give ourselves a couple more weeks before we go out with each other."

What was she doing? A minute before, she was thinking of having sex and spending the night at his house. Why was she doubting herself?

She watched as he closed his briefcase, picked it up, and walked to her. When he was within an arm's length of her, he stopped and set his briefcase down against the doorframe. Then he took hers from her hands and set it next to his.

He took a strand of her hair and gently moved it to the side, hooking it around her ear. "Isn't that what dates are all about, getting to know each other better? I feel I've known you forever. You'll have your own car and can leave at any time. Please don't back out now."

Her self-confidence pushed forward. She was very attracted to him and wanted to see what could become of the two of them dating. The panties in her emergency kit would have to wait to be used. "A movie it is, but that's all. I need to work tomorrow, at least to make some attempt to complete that report for Richard."

"Dates during the week are sometimes tiring when you have to get up early for work the next day. I'll agree to those terms. Philip is waiting for us by your car. Shall we go?"

Rane nodded, relieved that Mark didn't expect her to stay the night. She'd be able to see how things were going before she committed herself to the next step. Neither spoke much on the way down to the parking garage. The sexual tension in the elevator felt electrifying. Again, images of them pressed up against the mirrors made her swallow hard and clear her throat. She was grateful when the doors opened, and she could breathe without having to smell Drakkar.

As Mark had indicated, Philip and the limo were waiting next to her car. Philip stood by the limo, with his hand poised on the door handle. Instead of going to the limo, Mark followed her to her Audi TT Coupe. She pressed unlock on the key fob and he opened the driver's side door. She slid into the seat, put her foot on the clutch and a hand on the stick shift.

"A four-on-the-floor. Nice."

"Oh yeah, I like the way it slides into gear." She felt her cheeks begin to burn." I mean—"

"No worries. I can tell you're nervous. I used to drive a stick shift in college. It's unusual to find a woman who can drive one. Philip will keep you in sight at all times. If a light stops you, we'll pull over to wait. It should take about thirty minutes to get to my house."

"Okay, I'll be right behind you."

"Here's my cell phone number if you need anything." He handed her his business card with the number handwritten on the backside and closed the door.

From her side mirror, she watched Mark get into the limo. She looked at herself in the visor mirror for a moment. Her cheeks had returned to normal, but her eyes were turning green.

Why had she indicated she wouldn't stay the night? Would she be able to deny Mark even though her body clearly wanted him to make love to her?

The questions went unanswered as she flipped up the sun visor. Putting the car into reverse and then into drive, she followed the limo's red taillights through the streets. They brightened and signaled a right turn on to Calhoun Parkway.

Mark lived by the lakes.

This couldn't be happening. The huge old mansions around Lake Calhoun and Lake Harriet had always fascinated her. She and Val would cruise the parkway and gaze at the homes, making up stories about the people who lived in them. These homes were part of an era long gone by. She'd read older couples, and young entrepreneurs were snatching up the vintage homes when they were for sale.

The brake lights went on again, then the blinker, and the limo turned into a driveway protected by two enormous stone dragon sculptures sitting on each side of the gate. With a gasp, Rane recognized this driveway. It'd held her interest over the years. The winged creatures at the front gate intrigued her. She'd never understood why someone would use dragons instead of the typical lions. The pair gave you the impression they were ready to take flight to kill anything that tried to get past them. They'd often made her wonder what or whom they were protecting.

With curiosity, she watched as a man advanced from a hidden guardhouse and approached the limo. The man who was wearing a belt with what looked to be guns in it, nodded and with a hand signal, opened the gate. Rane followed the limo past them and the guard. As her car cleared the gate, the ornate metal doors closed behind her, sealing off any escape on her behalf. There was no turning back now but that didn't stop her from having second thoughts.

You're nothing. I never loved you. You were just an easy fuck.

David's parting words to her the day he'd signed the divorce papers ending their marriage played in her mind.

Tears welled up in her eyes.

Could that be why her past lovers always left her after a couple nights of lovemaking? Had they, too, found her sexually lacking? What if Mark found her to be inadequate in bed?

No, he wouldn't find her to be. Mark was somehow different.

She was just having pre-sex jitters. Everything was going to be fine. Besides, this was just a date. She was not going to end up in bed with him.

The circular driveway led them up to the front door. The limo stopped. Rane stared apprehensively at the house she'd never been able to see from the road. Sometimes in the winter when the tall hedges were bare, she'd gotten glimpses of the roof of the house, but it had always been mostly well hidden from any passing cars or persons. Now she could see why it had been so well protected.

It was a damn mansion. About four stories high and a football field long.

On my god, I don't belong here.

Leave, her mind screamed. This was a mistake. *Forget about your feelings for him. He isn't the man for you.* She had to tell Mark she couldn't stay.

Her car door opened and there he stood. "Rane, welcome to my home."

"I can't. This is wrong, Mark."

"Take your foot off the clutch, put your car in neutral, and apply the parking brake. Please come inside."

"You're my boss. I should leave. I can't—"

"Take my hand. It's okay. I don't bite. I'm at your service, Madame."

She closed her eyes, refusing to look at his outstretched hand. She played out several outcomes and the one that she went inside with him won. Turning her car off and securing the parking brake, she took his hand.

"I'm warning you that sometimes I do bite, when the mood strikes me."

To her shock and delight, he lifted her hand to his lips and kissed the inside of her wrist. The millisecond his lips touched her skin, every inch of her body felt the kiss as it burned its way up her arm, down to the pit of her stomach, and lower.

"What other services do you perform?"

He leaned in closer to her and whispered. "What other services do you desire?"

She felt it again, the deep burning need, and glanced up at Mark to see if he was affected by the same electrifying feeling. But she couldn't tell. His expression was well guarded. She looked away first, not wanting him to see how his touch had aroused her and grabbed her purse from her car before he shut the door.

Mark cleared his throat to cover up his laughter when he saw Rane's face turn a lovely shade of pink.

He could think of a lot of services he'd love to perform for her. He would start with stripping her naked, then covering her with kisses, starting at her toes and ending with a soul-searching kiss on her lips. Or after making love to her, taking a long shower. He'd so enjoy running a bar of soap over her body. On the other hand, feeding her grapes, and drinking champagne while they floated naked in his pool.

All of those ideas were going to have to wait for another time. Slow and easy was his plan, not fast and furious.

She walked next to him quietly. Her nervousness was very apparent. Somehow, he needed to assure her things would be okay. As they approached the massive double-wood doors, he placed his right hand lightly in the small of her back. "Shall we go inside?"

He was poised with his hand on the handle ready to push the door open and told himself to get ahold of his emotions. He'd caught Rane staring at him from the corner of his eye and saw the desire on her face. At first, he'd been stunned by his own body's reaction. All he'd done was touch her and every nerve in his body came alive. He wanted her so bad he felt as if he didn't take her now, he'd explode. But he wasn't a sex-crazed teenager going through puberty and forced his carnal craving to a controllable level.

"I suppose so," she said and nodded.

With her consent, he pushed the door open and together they stepped inside. The smell of freshly popped popcorn greeted them. He hoped that was a sign to her that he hadn't just invited her over to have sex.

"Would you like a tour of my home first before the movie?"

"That would be great. Uh, you have a very lovely house."

"Thank you. You can set your purse down on the table here if you like. Then we can begin by going over to the room on the right."

He was about to touch her again but dropped his hand, not knowing if he could handle another round of sexual tension without acting on it. Instead of risking the contact, he moved to the left and held his hand out, offering her entrance into the first room.

"This is my ballroom."

With a flick of his hand, light flooded into the room. Open-mouthed, she stood in the doorway, and he smiled.

"You have a ballroom?"

"The ever-straightforward Ms. Schoen. Yes, I do. Maybe I should start hosting parties."

His heart swelled with pride as her face reflected the beauty of the room he'd designed. It wasn't every day someone gave him a compliment and really meant it. Tonight was going to be interesting for sure.

———

Rane couldn't contain her excitement. It was the most magnificent room she'd seen in her life.

"Oh my gosh! It's just like in the old days, like in *Gone with the Wind*."

He smirked but said nothing.

She counted one, two, three, four, five chandeliers on the ceiling that had been raised to give the room more height. Turning her head, she saw that the left and right-side walls were entirely mirrored from the ceiling to the floor.

Straight ahead at the far end of the room, floor-to-ceiling glass doors led to the patio. Half spinning, Rane faced back to the front of the room again and saw that the left corner had a raised stage set up with all the equipment needed for a band, no, make that an orchestra.

As she took everything in, the room became magically alive in her mind. She saw images of tables laden with food, people dancing, and heard the music and laughter. It made her wonder what it would be like to waltz around the room in Mark's arms.

"Oh my. Wow," she exclaimed as the chandeliers came on one by one.

Once all of them were lit, the room was even more elegant than before. The lights illuminated the ceiling to reveal paintings of dragons adorning the ceiling. Each dragon was elaborately painted and had either a man or woman nearby. They seemed to be alive with their wings and long, curved tails, their claw-like feet, and diamond-shaped eyes.

One particular dragon caught her attention. It appeared to stare at her. The creature was so mesmerizing she couldn't look away. Her trance, however, was shattered with the sound of Mark's voice.

"I don't use this room very often."

"What a shame."

She tore her gaze away from the alluring dragon and looked at Mark. His expression remained the same.

"Would you like to go inside?"

She gave him an enormous smile and stepped into the magnificent room. It was right out of a storybook. Timidly, she examined the room from left to right until she reached the middle.

I'm a princess.

Impishly, she twirled and twirled, then stopped suddenly. Dizzy, she found Mark standing in the doorway watching her with a bemused grin on his face. Feeling her cheeks beginning to heat up, she walked toward the glass doors.

"What's outside?"

"You can take a look."

As she peered through the glass, she thought she could make

out a garden with rose bushes and more large hedges. She was about to turn away when the darkness started to reveal its secrets as lights came on. A circular fountain suddenly lit up in red lights. In the center of the fountain stood a large stone dragon with water flowing from its mouth into a pond below. The red lights added to the illusion that the dragon was spitting fire from its mouth.

Turning her attention away from the fountain, Rane spotted benches lining a walkway lined with bushes and flowers to give privacy to whomever wanted or needed it.

"Is that Lover's Lane?"

Suddenly Mark was at her side and his deep laughter was music to her ears.

"I guess you could call it that. I've heard many stories of relationships starting and ending out there." He swooped into a bow, as they did in the royal courts, and asked, "Shall we continue with the tour?"

"Yes, sir."

She held out her arm as an invitation for him to escort her out. He took it into his and they sauntered out together. When they reached the doorway, she couldn't help but take one last look before he turned out the lights.

"The living room," he announced when they reached the next door, and he pushed it open.

Rane looked into the room. It, too, reminded her of an old nostalgic time, a room called a parlor. The room featured a huge brick fireplace with an exquisite antique wood mantel, two couches, and seven oversized chairs.

Mark only allowed her a peek before moving on to the next room. This turned out to be the library. Again, he only permitted a quick view before closing the etched-glass French doors. They moved to the next room where he held open the door and tapped the light switch.

"This is my office. You are welcome to enter," he said with a wave of his hand.

The room was decorated in very heavy and large mahogany furniture. One piece stood out, a beautiful wood desk, which was set off to the right side. A wall of books lined the opposite side of the room. Shelves covered the wall behind the desk. They held numerous dragon figurines that varied in size, shape, and texture made from glass, crystal, wood, and porcelain.

"So, am I to understand that I'm seeing a part of you not too many people know about? I'm sure Mrs. Weber wouldn't approve of your mess." She waved her hands out over the papers and files scattered across the top of the desk.

"Only my true friends are allowed in here and that's not many. Mrs. Weber has threatened on occasions to come over whenever I complain I can't find a certain document."

"I thought so."

Rane laughed. Her earlier misgivings were fast disappearing the more time she spent with him. If this date had been all about getting her into bed, he had a weird way of doing it. He was treating her like someone he wanted to share things with.

"When I do entertain, this room is locked with a special alarm separate from all the other alarms. I can't have my secret coffee blends fall into the wrong hands."

"No, that would be very bad for the company. What's with all the dragons? You have a very extensive collection. I noticed them at the front gate and in the ballroom. Aren't they supposed to be vicious and cruel? How long have you collected them? Did you know that some dragons are supposed to—? Oh, sorry, of course you know all about dragons. I have collections of dolphins."

She realized she was rambling and stopped. Mark had come up to stand next to her. He didn't even have to touch her, for her to feel his magnetism. The confines of the small room had her thinking what it would be like to make love among the beautiful creatures. They had an aura of sexuality about them.

"So many questions. Yes, I enjoy dragons. They've interested me since I was a boy. Don't you like my stone dragons out front?"

"I do. I do. They are a bit scary but . . . weird and wonderful at the same time."

"I like that analogy. Thank you. I've read all the books I can find about dragons. Most people don't understand them. They think of them as fairytale creatures, but scientists have found some bones that could be from a dragon." Mark stepped over to the wall housing the figurines and took one down from the shelf. "If you were to study them, you would see they are powerful yet gentle beings. Some are funny looking, some are cute, and some are scary. The main reason I enjoy them is they're amazingly mysterious."

He replaced the dragon and walked back to her.

"They remind me of you."

His comment took her breath away. She remained silent, unable to come up with anything to say.

"Shall we carry on?" Mark didn't wait for her reply and took her hand. "This is the way to my private quarters."

"Private in as...?"

"As in most of the house is for show," he said and led her down a hallway.

"That's a shame. Every room is beautiful. Is this your family home?"

"Yes, I added on the back section a few years after my father passed away. My mom and I didn't get along. She doesn't live here anymore. I guess it was too much for her."

As they came to the end of the hallway a pair of closed doors greeted them. He kept his grip tight on her hand and with his other, he punched in a code on the security pad. A loud click sounded as the lock released and the doors opened on their own.

"My home."

When she crossed over the threshold, she saw a room that any teen would die to have. There were two large couches, a pool table, a foosball table, three pinball machines, and three rows of theater-style chairs. These leather ones were oversized and faced an immense flat screen television.

His own mini movie theater.

"What is the going rate for your movie tickets?"

Feeling somewhat overwhelmed, Rane didn't know what to do. She felt overdressed. Who watched a movie in a business suit?

"A six pack," he said and motioned for her to enter.

"Do you take IOU's? I don't have any beer with me."

"I guess I could, for a cost. Just so you know I do charge interest."

"I think I can handle anything you might request." She laughed and moved into the room. Straight ahead was a pair of double-glass doors leading out to what appeared to be another patio, and to the right was a staircase.

"This is where I live and spend my time when I'm not at my office apartment. The stairs lead up to the master bedroom. As you can see, I have all I need right here. The other parts of the house-hold no interest to me."

Still holding his hand, he stopped and took ahold of her other hand, so she faced him. Her heart began to flutter wildly. Their eyes locked and she saw he made no attempt to hide the desire she saw in his. Ignoring all her wishy-washy thoughts and doubts, she took command of the moment.

"Mark—"

"Let me talk. I'm so glad you're here with me. I want you to know that I haven't allowed many people into this section of the house."

He was opening up to her as if they were a couple. Rane took a breath and inhaled.

Drakkar. Damn his cologne.

She stood frozen as all of her senses came alive. Waiting in anticipation for him to kiss her, his breath mingled with hers first, making her lips tingle. She felt his hand caress her arm softly and this time when she looked up to his face, he was boldly staring at her. It was arousing.

As eager as a summer storm, she moved her arms to encircle

his neck and ran her fingers through his hair. The thick, smooth strands tickled her fingers like tiny feathers. Rane inhaled and held her breath waiting for his lips to take hers.

———

Mark leaned forward not touching her lips but poised his centimeters away.

"Rane?"

When he saw her imperceptible nod, he framed her face with his hands and claimed her lips. Using his thumb, he stroked her jaw line, before deepening the kiss. He drew her closer and felt her heartbeat. Her breasts were touching his chest, even though their clothes were on. He realized she'd placed both arms around him. Her soft lips yielded to him, and their tongues met. They both moved even closer, until their hands and lips all became one.

Slowly Mark removed his mouth from hers and kissed other areas of her face. He continued a scrupulous trail of feathery kisses up the side of her face to her forehead. He paused and eased back just enough to look into her eyes.

Green!

Her eyes had changed colors again. He'd been right.

Green *must* mean she was aroused.

In that split second, he thought of the *Pernese Dragon* stories and wondered if they could come back as humans when they died.

Had he found his very own dragon?

Her now green eyes reflected passion, want, and need. He felt so electrified to see her raw emotions, it was as if he'd been struck by lightning.

"Rane?"

He held his breath and waited for her approval to go even further. If, she said no at this moment, he didn't know what he was going to do. She had him on pins and needles.

"Yes."

She said it against his lips. The exoticness of it went to his head. Then she pressed herself against his length, with her legs parted as far as her skirt would allow. When her lips touched his, he was lost. About to push her hips into his, the *Pink Panther* ring tone interrupted them.

Ending the kiss, he signed and rested his forehead on hers. The song kept playing and he relaxed his hold, giving her room to answer the annoying phone call.

He should have had her turn her damn phone off.

———

Rane froze against him.

Damn her phone. Talk about embarrassing.

Shyly she raised her eyes to him. "Sorry. That is Val. She will keep calling if I don't answer."

"Then by all means do so. I don't want her interrupting us when we're at a more critical moment."

Her heartbeat stuttered as the implication penetrated her foggy thoughts. Mark dropped his arm from her, giving her access to her phone which was in her skirt pocket. Taking it out, she tapped 'accepted' and turned away him.

"Val, this is not a good time. I'm with Mark."

"What are you doing? Are you safe."

"Yes, I'm safe and it's none of your business what I'm doing. Don't you have court in the morning? I don't want to talk about it. Bye," Rane said.

She pressed 'end' and pocketed her phone.

"Don't forget to turn it off this time. I think that's Rule Number Two Hundred and Sixty-Nine in the employee hand-book. While making out with the boss, turn off your cell phone."

Rane laughed, took her phone back out and turned it too silent. "Should we start the movie?"

He took the phone from her hand and tossed it aside. She

watched it land safely on the couch and then he gathered her hands into his, so she was facing him.

"I think there is something else we could do."

"You do, do you? And what would that be?" She felt breathless. Even with Val's untimely interruption her body was on fire. Her sexual desire for him hadn't dissipated and it was clear from his suggestion his hadn't either.

"As if you need to ask."

"Since you brought up the employee handbook, my agenda said only a movie and popcorn. Did you get a different one?" Her teasing tone had him smiling and she freed her hands from his to embrace him. Holding him close had a familiarity to it. Being so forward, had her imploring him with her eyes as she waited for his reply.

"No, but I think we're both on the same page now."

She knew he understood the playfulness of her words when he wrapped his arms around her. Then he kissed her again and one of his hands caressed her full breasts. The thin fabric of her shirt wasn't any protection against his searching fingers.

Her nipples had tightened, and they ached. She needed, no wanted him to kiss them.

Mark moved away from her, and she turned a little to give him more access to her breasts. Instead, he ended the kiss. "Will you come upstairs with me?"

She didn't have any breath to answer him and simply nodded. With one hand still holding hers, Mark reached over to the wall and pushed the button, causing the doors to close.

There was no turning back now, Rane thought.

She was about to have sex with the boss. And she wanted it to happen.

He led her to the stairs. Up they walked, hand in hand.

This is what she wanted and dreaded at the same time. When they reached the top step, she was about to pull her hand free and stop this insane train of events, when to her surprise they stopped outside his open bedroom door.

The first thing that caught her attention was the oversized bed, the focal point of a masculine-decorated room in shades of brown and blacks with a touch of gold.

She pushed away the lingering doubt. She wanted this. Her body was craving his and the web of desire he'd spun. Tightening her hold on his hand, giving him another signal, she was ready to give in to whatever the night was going to bring.

"This is my bedroom."

"I see. It's very, it's very manly."

"I guess you could say that. Are you sure you're okay with this? I'd understand if you said no. This part isn't in the employee handbook. We're on our own from here out," he said.

"If this isn't in the handbook, there's no reason for us to hold anything back. Is there?" Rane stood on her tiptoes and kissed his partly opened mouth.

The handbook be damned.

She was a woman, and he was a man. No one or thing was going to tell them what to do.

Her body and mind were crying out yes, yes, yes.

Mark took control of the kiss as his response and explored the recesses of her mouth tenderly. Again, she wrapped her arms around his body, feeling the solid strength beneath the muscles.

This was what she'd been hoping for since the day of her interview.

He deepened the kiss with an urgency, and she devoured his mouth too, as if it was going to be their last kiss.

She felt lost in an abyss of heaven. The kisses in the hallway had made her feel dizzy, but these were short-circuiting her senses. No one had ever made her feel like this. She was being kissed beyond reason and his lips felt as if they were touching her soul.

She knew if he hadn't been supporting her, she would've

fallen to the floor. Her knees were ready to give way at any moment.

Don't think. Let yourself drift away into his web.

To her surprise, just like in storybooks, Mark lifted her up into his arms and carried her to the comfort of his bed. He gently laid her down, never losing contact with her lips while he positioned himself next to her.

He released her lips for a moment, but then they were kissing again. His hands framed her face. She felt his hand move slowly down her throat, softly caressing every inch of her skin, leaving a burning path in its wake.

She murmured his name as his hands passionately explored her still fully clothed body, caressing her shoulders then moved on to claim her breasts.

She moaned, thinking, *Don't stop, Mark. Make them yours.*

His touch sent shivers of delight all the way down to her bright pink painted toes. Even through her shirt and bra, his fingers felt like fire against her skin. The fabrics and his fingers were like two separate beings working together. Somehow, he had managed to unbutton her blouse and was pushing her bra, freeing one of her nipples. Once it was free, his fingers attacked it without constraints. He rolled her hardening nipple between his fingers, pulling and tugging until the bud stood at attention.

Then his mouth broke free from her lips and began kissing the burning trail his hands had left down the side of her neck to her unattended breast. The combination of his hand on one of her breasts, his mouth on the other, along with the sensation of the soft fabric, proved too much.

Oh my god, she'd died and gone to heaven.

She was losing control.

"Rane, you're so beautiful. I'm going to ask before we go any further, are you sure? Not just for tonight, but for what else the future might bring?"

"Yes. Now kiss me again."

Mark forced himself to take things slowly. Her demand to kiss her had him smiling as he reclaimed her lips. If she had told him to stop, he didn't know how he would have been able too. He wanted her so bad; he was inching toward being out of control.

Leaning over her, he covered her now partly free breasts with his mouth, caressing them with kisses. He could tell they were now a little swollen. Giving them a break, he opened his eyes and gazed at her in astonishment. She laid there in the thongs of passion that he had created.

But before he allowed himself to totally lose himself to her, he had to make sure, one hundred percent, she was okay with what they were about to do.

"Rane, are you absolutely positive? We are about to cross the point of no return."

He waited for her reply, unable to explain these intense feelings and his body's reactions. The hard truth, through all his life, none of the other women had ever made him feel like this. This deep craving need.

Where have you been all my life, Rane?

She wasn't like any woman he'd ever known. She was different. All he had to do was touch her, and he knew what she wanted and what she was feeling. This had to be more than just something sexual.

Only once, long ago, had he felt such a strong connection with someone. He'd been young and she'd been even younger.

The damn fuckin' picture again.

Squashing the memory, he focused on Rane's face. Fear, uncertainty, and then calmness settled over her delicate features. Unbelievably, her eyes had gone from blue to green and now sparkled like emeralds.

Realizing she hadn't responded yet, Mark moved away at a

loss. Her eyes said *yes* but she hadn't spoken the word aloud. Adding to his confusion, he felt her hands pushing at him.

Damn, he'd gone too fast.

He sat up, ready to get off the bed. "Rane—"

"Mark, you talk too much."

Her voice was husky and thick. And then he watched as she began to unfasten the rest of the buttons on her shirt. Before she could finish, he moved her hands aside and completed the task.

Rane's answer was very clear. She wanted to stay with him.

Without another word, he unhooked her white lacy bra. It gave way and he took one of her perfectly sized mounds into his mouth. As her head fell back, Mark gently removed the straps from her arms. Taking advantage of her fully freed breasts, he caressed one while his lips tugged and gently nipped the other.

———

Lost again, all Rane could do was muster up enough strength to lazily move her hands to Mark's shoulders. She braced herself for the assault she knew was coming as his hot lips moved to toy with her other breast. His hands and mouth were moving from one neglected breast to the other.

To her surprise, his mouth took in both of her rosy peaks at one time. The feel of his tongue and lips on her oh-so-sensitive breasts sent tremors throughout her body. She moaned as they laid down together, glad for the reprieve from the sweet assault.

Pushing up his shirt, she found beneath it what she'd always fantasized a man should feel like. She skimmed her hands intimately over his shoulders and chest not missing an inch of his warm skin. His muscles moved in ways that enticed her to keep exploring.

And that is what she did by sliding her hands lustfully up and over his broad chest. She found the spray of his chest hairs, soft yet springy to her touch. Finding them sexually pleasing, she played with the hairs which led her to his nipples.

Continuing her journey upward, she ran her fingers over and over his nipples, deliberately making them firm, giving him a taste of his own actions.

"Rane, behave yourself."

His playful murmur had him moving just beyond her reach, as he began a slow trail of kisses from her breasts to her stomach. Unable to torture him, as he was her, she grabbed his shoulders in anticipation of what was to come with his exploration.

Chapter Sixteen

Having not had sex in a while, Mark was ready to explode. Not wanting to lose control or have his own need take over, he unbuttoned Rane's skirt, yanked down the zipper, and slowly slid the fabric over her hips and legs.

He heard her inhale sharply as his hands caressed her thighs and he rolled down one of her thigh-high nylons. "No garter belt? I like this better."

As he rolled the sheer nylons down, he placed kisses on her thigh when it revealed more skin. Rane let out little gasps when he had successfully removed one. She lay with her eyes closed, not letting him see their colors, but from her rapid breathing he knew she was enjoying the sweet torment. He reached up and began the same course for the other nylon. Rolling it downward and kissing the exposed skin, until it slipped off her foot. Then he kissed and suckled each of her toes.

One by one, and then two by two.

Her moans had his own sexual urgency rising. She was now withering in erotic pleasure. He finished and slid his hands up her calves, thighs, and over her taut stomach. Leaning in, before kissing her lips, he murmured, "Your feet are very sexy."

She opened her eyes showing him they were green. He kissed her half-parted lips and stroked her cheek and neck. Seeing she needed a minute to recover he rolled off of her and stood up.

"I'll be right back."

———

Before Rane could protest, Mark had eased himself off the bed. She immediately felt the loss of his body heat. Sitting up a little, she rested her head on her hand and placed her other arm in front of her. She watched as he discarded his shirt and went to the bedroom doors and closed them. He walked over to the wall to the left of the doors and flicked a switch. The room was instantly engulfed in soft light and, seemingly from nowhere, low music played.

Smiling, she observed Mark without his shirt.

Man, oh man alive, what a body. He was going to ruin her for life. No other man would ever be able to out do what he had to offer.

When he had turned, she'd seen an impressive gorgeous, winged dragon tattoo that spanned his muscular shoulders and back.

"Is that tattoo company approved?"

"Yes, it is. If you have a problem, send an email to the president."

He laughed and she joined him. As he stepped closer, she could tell Mark worked out more than once a week. She followed the chest hair that she'd enjoyed touching earlier as it tapered off over his tight flat stomach before stopping at his pants. Admiring the manner in which his dress slacks were tailored, she concluded he must have a female tailor. Only a woman would know when a butt and a front package were worth showing off.

And those were all hers tonight.

Mmm, mmm.

Feeling her stare, Mark turned and swallowed hard at the picture Rane unknowingly presented to him. She lay half-naked, her head resting on one of her hands, while the other hand tried to hide her tantalizing full breasts. She wore a look that said, 'come get me', like one of those eighteenth-century pictures.

Knowing he had her full attention; he slowly unbuckled his belt. As the buckle came undone, something in her intense gaze caused him to stop halfway. He couldn't help but smile as he saw Rane's mouth drop open.

He couldn't be nervous. Could he?

With his pants partly zippered, he strutted toward her. By the time he reached the side of the bed, Rane was sitting up on her knees with her arms outstretched to him. He stopped in front of her and took her breasts in his hands, then leaned down and kissed her waiting lips. She pushed his pants along with his boxers off his hips, down to his knees, and released his full arousal.

Where he found the strength, he didn't know, but he slowly caressed both of her breasts and nipples and stepped out of the confining clothes around his ankles. He ended the kiss quickly and held his breath in anticipation when he felt the warmth of her hands on his bare hips.

Her soft touch was so intoxicating that for a moment he forgot where he was. He could only think of her hands, the way the tips of her fingernails dragged over his skin, slowly exploring his hips before sliding around to his butt. Then, in one graceful motion, her slim hand took hold of him and moved slowly up his erection to the tip.

Mark stood proud but felt ready to crumble. He had to remove his hands from her breasts and place them on her shoulders to steady himself.

"Oh my god, Rane."

He closed his eyes and let his head fall back. He hadn't

expected this on their first time together. If her fingers applied just enough pressure, he would explode. With as much constraint that he could muster through the pleasure, he almost lost it when her mouth took him. As she continued to pay homage to him, he tangled his hands in her long silky strands. It was hell, but endearing as they touched his skin, almost burning it as they caressed him.

Enough. Enough, his mind screamed. She was sending him too close to the edge.

"Rane," he muttered.

If she had heard him, it hadn't affected her actions. Her mouth and tongue continued their assault. Through the thickness of his pleasure, he knew if she didn't stop, he'd come inside her mouth. This wasn't what he wanted.

He placed his hands on her chin. She released her hold, and he tilted her face upward. He felt the cool air and his heated passion slowly declined. Meeting her gaze, he saw her green eyes gazing at him with a satisfied look.

Little she-devil! Two can play this game.

Back in control, Mark eased her over so he could join her on the bed. As they settled next to each other, he captured her sweet mouth. Her own distinct taste mingling with his was proving too much for him to handle. He deepened the kiss, hoping to ease the urge to drive into her while her hands continued to stroke him slowly.

Mark let up on the kiss, moved his hands to her hips, and began a payback trail of kisses down to meet his hands. He found the barrier of her panties and, using her underwear as a tool, he placed his fingers on her mound and slowly stroked. Moving his fingers to the straps of her thong panties, he slowly slid them away, revealing their treasure.

And what a sight.

Pushing two of his fingers deep into her core, he began sliding them in and out leisurely, watching her face. Then he withdrew to replace his fingers with his tongue. He proceeded to kiss the hardened nub, flicking his tongue over the slick surface.

Rane's moans came faster and faster and her hips moved in a way that told him he'd succeeded. Smiling, he enjoyed the triumph knowing she was about to explode. He removed her panties completely.

"Had enough of my teasing?"

She was unable to reply, it was her body's actions that gave him the answer, by lifting her hips upward. He plunged two fingers inside her and kissed her nub until he felt her release and watched as the last spasms engulfed her, causing her body to go limp.

———

An amazing sense of completeness filled Rane, and for the first time ever she felt sexually satisfied. She lay there wanting to kiss Mark but didn't have the strength. She couldn't believe what she'd just experienced. The feelings had been so intense.

In her fogged and muddied mind, she realized he hadn't even entered her yet. He'd given her this pleasure with his mouth.

This must be what Val kept talking about, an intense, overwhelming, and totally mind-boggling orgasm. This man had succeeded where all the others had failed. She'd been married, had had a handful of boyfriends, and yet here she was a thirty-three-year-old woman having just had her first fulfilling orgasm.

She peeked out from beneath her eyelids only to find a pair of blue eyes staring at her.

"Are you all right?"

His question made her feel a little ashamed. "Yes, I feel so naïve. No one has ever done that to me before."

"I don't understand. You've been married."

"Yes, but-but it was just sex. There wasn't a lot of kissing, caressing, or...anything else."

"I'm confused," Mark said.

"This is so embarrassing. I've never experienced *that*-the life ending feeling before." She felt the tears ready to spill and closed her eyes to stop them.

———

Mark didn't know what to say by her admission. What decent man would be so selfish to leave their wife or girlfriend sexually unfulfilled?

"Are you trying to tell me that you have never had an orgasm before?"

She nodded but kept her eyes closed, refusing to look at him.

"Tonight was your first one. Just now?" He watched tears trail down her cheeks as her head moved up and down. He enfolded her into his arms and held her tight. "Rane, it's going to be okay."

Damn her ex-husband. Damn her ex-boyfriends.

Damn men in general that were so arrogant to do this to women. To be a good lover, you needed to know what women wanted and desired. That was the power, knowing you could satisfy them before yourself.

He felt the wetness of her tears on his chest and gently stroked her hair.

"I just never knew it could be so amazing. I'm sorry to have ruined our night. Maybe I should go," she said.

"No, I want you to stay. We should celebrate and besides we still have to watch our movie and eat popcorn."

He saw her begin to smile, then start to laugh as she wiped her eyes. Satisfied, she wasn't ready to bolt, he loosened his hold on her. "Wait here."

Getting off the bed, buck naked, he went into his closet. Grabbing his dark blue robe, he brought it out. "Here, put this on and we'll go back downstairs to watch the movie and eat popcorn."

She sat up and he helped her slip it on, all the while trying to hide her gaze from his. He tugged on his dress pants.

"Ready?"

He held out his hand and when she put hers into his, he felt her trembling. She looked helpless as she moved guardedly off the bed. He couldn't believe he was being so patient. His body ached for its own release. Having just begun his seduction, he'd had to put on the brakes. But looking at her in his robe was enough to make him forget about the movie.

Ignoring his protesting body, they descended the stairs hand-in-hand, and he guided her over to the movie theater chairs.

"Have a seat. Would you like that Coke now?"

She nodded, and he went to the bar to get them refreshments.

———

Sitting in the chair waiting for him to return, Rane wondered at the turn of events. A few minutes ago, they were making love and now they were about to watch a movie.

Insane.

What type of man was Mark?

He was so caring, so insightful it was scary.

What man in the heat of passion would stop and ask to watch a movie because the woman he was making love to had acted like a virgin?

Did he, could he care about her? Or was this just his bachelor ways? Is this how he won the women over so easily? The blog posts had implied he was an exceptional lover but hadn't gone into details. Should she post something too?

"I think we're ready. I'll flip through the on-demand titles. Tell me to stop when you see one, you'd like to watch."

"Okay, let's start in the comedy section."

"Sounds like a good plan," he said and worked the remote.

"That one, *Crazy, stupid, love*, it's pretty funny."

"Got it. I've never seen it."

"No, really? It's an older movie."

"Remember I don't do much besides work." He held out the bowl of popcorn that had been set out earlier for them and a Coke. He then plopped down into the double chair next to her. His robe that she was wearing was bulky, but she managed to slide her legs up to curl them underneath her and inch herself closer to him.

Several times during the movie, she felt Mark's hands in her hair, stroking her neck, or touching her shoulders. It was a comforting feeling. More immersed in his actions than the movie, she lost track of what was going on. His little soft touches were making her think about finishing what they had started.

She wanted him to know she was ready for the next round and placed her hand on his inner thigh. Gently, she caressed his leg and achieved the desired effect. Mark squirmed and spread apart his legs. His pants were becoming an unwanted barrier. She faced him.

All interest in the movie gone, she gave him a meaningful look and slid her hand over the telltale bulge and squeezed.

————

Mark gulped for air and saw Rane's eyes were green again. He drew her close and captured her lips. This kiss was different than the earlier ones. Somehow it now had more meaning.

Like two souls reuniting.

There was no hesitation from either of them. Both wanting and needing what the other could give. He was ready to take her right now, here on the chair. But he couldn't and wouldn't cheapen their first time together.

"Shall we continue this upstairs?"

Even to his own ears, his voice had a huskiness and a thickness to it. She nodded. That was all he needed. He stood and lifted her into his arms.

"Mark, put me down. I can walk."

"No, I need to have you close." He carried her up the stairs.

With each step he took, the robe opened, giving him a full view of her legs, and the place where they came together. By the time they reached his bed, all he needed to do was give the belt an impish tug. The robe opened like a curtain, revealing what it had been hiding.

All he could do was close his mouth and swallow. Everything about her was perfect.

Somehow, he managed to unbutton and unzip his pants in record time. Once free, he leaned over to devour her breasts with demanding kisses and joined her on the bed. With his tongue, he traced the outline of her lips, and he felt her tremble. Lower and lower he moved, placing kisses over every inch of her body. Slowly his explorations led him to her belly button. He nibbled and sucked until he heard her call out his name.

"Mark."

He stopped and moved lower until his mouth found the spot where his fingers had just been moving, in and out of. Her body quivered with what he guessed was nervousness.

"Relax. Let it take over," he murmured. He could tell she did, just as his tongue found and played with her nub.

He held her hips, as wave after wave of multi-orgasms exploded. He slowed his tongue, letting her come back to him then started a slow exploration back up to her lips, kissing them unrelentingly. Covering her naked body with his, he gently nudged her legs apart with his knees.

"Ohhh, yeahhh, Mark—"

Hearing her moans and cries of pleasure, he found the refuge he sought. He held back and slid in part way. In one slow push he filled her. A thundering tremor shredded what little control he'd been maintaining. Concentrating, not willing to give in yet, he moved slowly in and out to tease her.

Her eyes opened and she met his gaze.

"Rane, you are so beautiful. Where have you been all my life?"

———

She felt him push inside her completely at the same time as his tongue plunged into her mouth. When he withdrew, so did his tongue, and when he pushed inside her again, his tongue met hers with full force. Rane wrapped her legs around him to help enforce the thrusting motion of his hips.

Sensing he was about to give in, she relished in the power when he did. He threw back his head as he made a final thrust. Rane felt his abrupt release and wrapped her arms around him. He stopped moving and simply laid on top of her. While she waited for his breathing to slow, she caressed the strong tendons on the back of his neck.

"Now it's my turn to ask. Are you, okay?"

Mark turned to look at her as he shifted his body away from her but never removing himself from inside of her. "Ask me in a little while."

He moved his hips again, back, and forth.

"Ohhhh." Rane beamed at him in surprise when she felt him growing harder inside her. "Oh, my!"

Kissing her, he rolled to one side, so he was on his back, and she was on top of him. Rane stroked his chest and moved her hips up and down over his fully hardened shaft. He clutched each of her breasts and squeezed them, matching her movements.

She leaned forward and placed a hand on each side of his head to support herself. Her hair cascaded down around his face like a million feathers, moving with her as she rode him. His hand released her breasts and moved to help guide her rocking hips. Keeping her eyes open and focused on his face, she brought them to a full satisfying rapture. She cried out as his fingers found her nub again. The release sent her into an unexpected downpour of fiery passion.

Mark studied Rane, who lay motionless and wrapped his arms around her. The tail end of the passion they'd shared pounded through his body in a beat of its own. He could feel her heartbeat as it mixed with his. She hadn't moved or said anything for a while, and he wondered if she'd fallen asleep.

No other woman had been able to give him the total satisfaction he was feeling right now. Not once, but twice in an hour.

Just thinking about the passion they'd shared, along with Rane's naked body covering his, the seeds of desire were starting again, surprising him.

Man, oh man, alive. He couldn't get enough of her.

He hadn't made love all night long in years. Repositioning his body so, she fit into his arms, he reached for the forgotten quilt.

"I should really get going," she said. "I do have to work in the morning."

"What?"

"Leave. Work. I'm not sure if my boss will approve of me being late to work."

She wiggled out of his arms and sat up.

"Don't you think your boss would understand if you called in sick for a day?" Mark reached out to her in an effort to hold her again.

"I'm not sure if I should."

Not liking the turn of events, he sat up too. "Rane, stay the night."

"You can turn on as much charm as you want, but I can't stay. I don't have a change of clothes. And I do have to go to work."

Taking him by surprise, she rolled past his reach to the other side of the bed, but he was quicker. He caught her before she successfully escaped. He hugged her closely and felt his body's reaction. Wanting her again, was very apparent. "Stay with me for a while longer. Don't go yet."

He captured her lips to silence any rebuke she might have uttered. When they came up for air her response had him smiling.

"Three times in a night. Val is not going to believe this."

She placed her leg over his hip, allowing him to push his way into her. He felt himself shudder at her wetness as he did. She wanted this too. There was no need to hold her so close, she wasn't going anywhere.

Laying face to face, he moved his hands downward to her hips and butt. Pulling out, he pushed in hard. She matched his thrusts. Their tongues battled each other at the same time.

There was no foreplay.

Neither needed it.

In and out, he plunged into her. Hard and fast.

He waited until she reached her own release, before allowing himself to climax.

———

A five-person band played loud enough to be heard over the crowd in Mark's ballroom. Rane stood in the center and watched.

The room seemed overly packed with people, but she didn't find anyone she knew. The mass of people grew, and the heat was stifling. She couldn't breathe.

She glanced longingly toward the sliding glass doors that stood open. There was no breeze or airflow coming through them. She felt as if she was suffocating.

Moving through the crowd, she couldn't reach the open doors to the night air. She tugged on the thick cloak she wore but it wouldn't move.

Panic seized her.

She had to get out.

Spinning around and around. No one helped her. No one noticed her.

Suddenly the doors appeared in front of her and as she was

about to step outside a hand grabbed her breast. She stopped and jumped, swinging at the offensive hand.

Rane opened her eyes.

She'd been dreaming and instead of hitting the hand she had sought; she'd hit something hard.

The headboard?

Reaching out to pet Thor, who was usually right next to her, but he wasn't there. She tried to turn to find him but couldn't.

A man's hand was indeed imprisoning her breast. That part was real and not only part of her dream. Trying to see in the darkness, she covered her mouth with her hand to quiet her moans.

Oh, holy shit.

She was in Mark's bed. She'd stayed the night when she'd said she couldn't. She'd fallen asleep when she'd told herself not to. The images of the night flashed before her in a whirlwind of scenes.

The kisses in the elevator, the tour of Mark's house, her first earth-shattering orgasm, then watching the movie and the two of them making love not once but three times. That was a record for her. She lay there unmoving, ashamed, and bewildered at the same time. A rush of emotions hit her full force, settling in the pit of her stomach.

She'd clearly just had the best night of sex ever.

No, it hadn't been simply sex.

What she and David had shared had clearly been sex. Just that, sex. What she'd shared with Mark had definitely been making love.

She stole a glance over at the man who'd given her such pleasure in ways she'd never dreamt possible, and her heart skipped a beat. Was this what it felt like waking up next to the man you loved?

Loved?

The realization came fast as she continued to stare at him.

Yes, oh God. Yes, she most certainly did love him.

Val's words of advice drifted in, bringing some sense of realism to her emotions.

Never tell the man you love him. Let him say it first. That way the fall is easier to recover from if it turns out he doesn't.

She couldn't face him. She needed to get out of his house. Fast.

Escape!

Time.

That's what she needed, time alone to sort out her feelings before staring into his memorizing blue eyes. She inched herself slowly to the edge of the bed. His hand slid off her breast and unexpected waves of desire coursed through her body as it did.

Impossible. What was wrong with her? She'd been sexually satisfied not once but four times in one night and she wanted him again.

She was turning into a nymphomaniac.

Forcing herself to keep moving, she glanced over her shoulder to make sure Mark had stayed asleep. As she stood naked next to the bed, she saw the mess they'd made of his bed and room. Clothes were everywhere, pillows had been thrown on the floor, and the bedding was half off the bed. She blushed, knowing exactly how everything had gotten so messy.

One piece at a time, she gathered her clothes and stepped out to the landing. It took longer than she'd expected to dress because she kept glancing back into the bedroom, afraid Mark would wake up at any time.

Seeing that he hadn't moved since she'd left the comfort of his side, she blew him a kiss and carefully descended the stairs. With one last look around the room, she pressed the keypad to open the doors. Making her way through the house, she grabbed her purse from the table before walking through the front doors.

The morning sunlight momentarily blinded her as she anxiously scanned the driveway for her car. Someone had moved it to a side parking lot. She dashed toward her car and searched her purse for the keys. Tears of frustration came to her eyes when she couldn't find them. She didn't want to have to go back inside to look for them. Then she remembered Mark had told her to leave them in the ignition.

Swiftly, she walked the rest of the way to her car and said a silent prayer, please, God, have mercy on me and let my keys be in the car.

Hand on the handle, she nudged open the door and saw that they were there, hanging from the ignition. *Thank you, Lord.*

She didn't waste any time. She got in and started the engine. As she backed out, she took one last look toward the front doors of the house. No one had followed her.

Would the guard stop her? Or would he simply let her leave?

Hesitantly, she approached the gates. The guard came out and the gate opened. He waved to her as she drove by. In disbelief, she turned onto the road still expecting someone to come after her. Her heart was pounding so fast she was breathing hard.

Calm down.

She'd have to call Val. She'd forgotten to text her, SON. Trying not to focus on what she'd done, Rane reached for her cell phone inside her purse.

Not finding it, she hit the steering wheel with her fist.

Damn.

Mark had thrown her phone onto the couch after Val's untimely interruption.

Great, now what?

How was she going to get it back? Val was going to be furious. Would Mark find it?

There was nothing she could do to remedy the situation. She could worry all she wanted to, but it wouldn't fix it.

The clock was flashing six minutes before six. This would give her time to soak in a bath before going into work. The hot water would help her relax. She felt so wired, as if she'd drank four Cokes in less than a half hour.

During her drive home, the images of the night kept playing out one right after the other, while the radio played songs about not being able to get enough love.

———

Mark flung his arm out toward the nightstand, slapping at a buzzing sound.

How in hell had a damn fly gotten into his room?

He swatted again and the annoying hum stopped. The quietness was short lived as the buzzing started right back up. He slowly came awake and realized the buzzing sound was the phone and not some unseen fly. He felt around for the handset and hit the 'talk' button with his finger.

"This had better be important."

"Mark, Rane is in her car heading toward the front gate."

He recognized Philip's voice and sat up to find the other side of the bed empty.

She was gone. Rane had left.

"What time is it?"

"Just before six," Philip stated.

"Let her go but have someone follow her to make sure she arrives safely at her townhome."

"Yes, sir. I'll call you with an update. Ah, excuse me sir, but will you be going into the office today?"

If Philip had been within reach, he'd have punched him.

"Yes." If his one-word answer wasn't enough to indicate to Philip just how angry he was, Mark disconnected the call.

Now fully awake, he sat up on the edge of his bed with his feet hanging over the side and held his head in his hands.

Why had she left?

Images of the two of them in various positions made him wish she hadn't. He'd wanted to wake her up slowly so they could enjoy a leisurely morning of making love.

The smell of freshly ground coffee took over his senses helping to clear his sleep-muddled brain. The aroma became stronger which forced him to stand.

Man, oh man, he loved the smell of brewing coffee.

It was an aphrodisiac.

Today he sure needed a cup to give him a jolt. His body and mind were drained. He'd been dreaming when the phone call had interrupted the images. Everything had seemed so real. Lately almost every one of his dreams had some sort of dragon in them.

He could recall this particular dream vividly. He'd been wearing some sort of armor and was trying to rescue Rane, but she kept changing shapes. First, she'd been a winged dragon with green eyes, and then she'd changed into her beautiful self.

It had been dark, with only the moonlight as the source of light. He'd tried to call to her, but no words came from his mouth. All of a sudden, she changed back into the winged dragon. It had been glorious. She'd spread her wings wide and took off. She turned, scrutinized him, and he was honored with a spectacular view of seeing her eyes change colors as she flew away.

With a sigh, Mark pushed the dream away and surveyed the room. Mark grinned from ear to ear seeing the havoc they'd done. He hadn't felt this alive in a long time.

He slipped on the robe Rane had worn, and her lingering scent engulfed him. He tipped his head down and took a huge whiff of the collar. Instantly a rush of desire overcame him.

Damn! What had this woman done to him?

He was literally weak at the knees and felt lightheaded. Rane was definitely going to spend the night again tonight.

Mark headed down the stairs to get his coffee when the morning light reflected off something on the couch.

Rane's cell phone.

She'd forgotten it in her haste to leave him this morning. He retrieved it and saw fifteen missed calls and twenty-five text messages from her friend Val. He'd loved to be in the room when they finally were able to talk.

He smiled.

So even though his real-life, eye color-changing dragon had taken flight, she wasn't getting far.

Chapter Seventeen

From the garage, Rane heard the landline phone ring, but by the time she'd opened the door, it'd stopped, and the unanswered call went into messages.

"Good morning, baby. Did you like your visitor last night? Don't stay mad at me."

Thor meowed and held his tail up in the air with his back arched. She'd have to do better than that to get him out of his bad mood. Reaching down she picked him up and snuggled him to her.

"I love you, Thor. You'll get to meet the man who stole me away from you soon." This time his meow was more like normal. She set him down and got his breakfast of wet cat food out of the refrigerator. Pulling the lid off of it had Thor rubbing up against her legs. Filling his bowl, she set it on his mat. "Okay, now I'm off to put out a fire."

She realized having a landline phone was coming in handy. The reason she still had one was because of her grandma and mother. For some unknown reason, if they couldn't get her on her cell phone, they always called the landline. Pressing the play button, the most recent message played.

"Rane! Are you there? If you don't call me back in ten minutes, I'm calling the police. Do you hear me? Ten minutes. Call me!"

Val.

Smiling, she saw she had fifty missed calls and twelve messages. Time to own up to her actions. She picked up the receiver and hit redial for the last call received.

"It's about goddamn time, Rane. You had three minutes to spare."

"What, no hello?"

"You don't deserve one. Who gave you permission to stay out all night? My phone is still showing you at some location by Lake Calhoun. You had me worried sick. I was ready to call in some favors from the guy I dated who's on the Minneapolis Police force."

"I'm okay. I left my phone at his house."

"Remember the rule, at least one text message saying *SON*," Val said.

S for staying, O for over, and N for night. She'd never had to use it before; however, Val usually did.

When had she had time to text? What was she supposed to have done? Stop in the middle of one of their heated moments and say, "I have to text my friend."

Like that was about to happen. And she hadn't planned on staying. Things just ended up happening.

"Sorry, *Mom*, I didn't have access to my cell phone." Which was true. She still didn't have it. "I'll remember next time."

A wave of desire swept over her at the thought of spending the night with Mark again. She heard Val sigh.

"You're forgiven, but don't let it happen again. We, single women have to look out for each other in this crazy world. I'm going to stop by your office for lunch today so I can get all the dirty details."

"Okay, just text the time. Gotta go."

They hung up and, as Rane had predicted, Thor was nowhere to be seen now that his tummy was full. She checked the time and saw she'd have to settle for a quick shower instead of her bath if she wanted to make it to work on time. Not allowing herself to think about Mark, she raced through her morning routine.

Once back in her car, the radio DJ announced it was almost seven-thirty. Thank God. She hadn't wanted to call attention to herself by arriving late. No one could know she'd spent the night with the president of the company. It would ruin her reputation not to mention all the respect she'd earned from the employees so far.

How would the morning play out?

Would Mark come to her office? Or, on the other hand, would he call and demand she come to his? Would he be casual about the whole date thing and simply hand over her cell phone?

What if he didn't have her phone? She hadn't thought about that until now. How would she get it, or for that matter live without it for the entire day?

So many 'what ifs' were getting her nowhere. She was coming up with more questions than answers. The whole thing felt more than a little awkward. That is why she'd always vowed never, ever, to date nor have casual sex with anyone she worked with. Ever.

So why hadn't she stuck to her plan?

"Damn it! Damn you, Val," Rane said to no one and hit the steering wheel with her fist. She'd never have slept with Mark if Val hadn't made her promise to go on a date with him.

Liar, her inner voice yelled.

Pushing away the lingering doubts, she pictured the morning ahead. She could envision it now. She'd run into Mark in the hallway and say, "Hi, good to see you this morning. Do you have my phone? Oh, and by the way, thanks for the great sex."

Yea, right. Wrong.

That's something Val would do. Now on the other hand, if she did that, it could or would most definitely leave the wrong impression.

What in God's name had she been thinking?

That had been her problem, she hadn't done one ounce of thinking last night. Having sex on the first date was the stupidest thing she'd done in a long time. Not to mention, it had been unprotected sex. That was a first for her too. She'd always made sure she was on the pill but had stopped because it had given her migraines. After that, she'd insisted her dates or boyfriends use a condom. Val would say better to be safe than sorry.

How could I have been so careless?

What if Mark assumed she was on the pill and that was why he hadn't offered to use a condom?

Oh shit.

The possibility she could be pregnant was too much to even consider right now. She groaned and rubbed her forehead, feeling a headache coming on.

What if her worst nightmare was about to come true, and Mark ignored her?

By the time she arrived at work, she concluded that the only option she had was to go to her office and handle one hour at a time.

No, one minute at a time with hot chocolate and kisses. No, it was a Coke kind of morning. Caffeine and extra caffeine.

Her mind and body needed the jolt the way she was feeling. The idea of having one of those Café Mochas Mark kept pushing her to try was seriously tempting.

Arriving on the sixth floor, she masked her inner turmoil and sent a fleeting look toward the left to his office. She was about to go over to Mrs. Weber and inquire if he'd arrived yet, when she heard his deep voice call out.

Her pulse pounded and she experienced a slow burning that

reached just below her belly. She found herself heading toward Mark's office.

"Good morning, Ms. Schoen, I have a message for you."

The receptionist's words stopped her from her crazy action.

"Thank you," Rane mumbled. Taking the note from Linda's outstretched hand, common sense took over. Had Mark left her a personal message? She chanced a look in his direction again, but he hadn't come out of his office.

Opening it she read the note and gasped.

"Are you all right, Ms. Schoen?" Linda asked.

"Yes, just a paper cut."

Hoping her lie went undetected, she shook her head and read it for a second time. Her heart began to pound fast, and her stomach became queasy. She walked slowly to her office, as her mind tried to work through what the note had said.

The message was from David, not Mark. It said to call him.

How in the hell had he found out where she worked? Why now? Why did he always have to complicate things?

So engrossed in her shock and dismay she failed to notice that her door stood open instead of closed as it always was in the morning. Flicking the light switch, she stood speechless for a second time in a matter of minutes as the unwanted note fell to the floor.

A single red rose lay on her desk.

What did it mean? Who'd left it?

Rane glanced out into the hallway. Not seeing anyone, she closed the door partway and hesitantly stepped closer to the rose.

Didn't red symbolize love?

Moving to the back of her desk, she slid out her chair to sit and to her surprise, an envelope along with a gold-wrapped little box greeted her. She quickly picked up the items and sat down slowly. She held the two pieces for a while, not sure which to open first. The card won.

Her smile deepened at the sight of it. More roses greeted her. They covered the entire front of the card. She imagined their sweet aroma. The inside revealed a thick heavy handwritten message:

I wonder what it would feel like to wake up with you in my arms. Maybe next time? Dinner at 8:00. Mark

Reading the note a second time ignited a soul-stirring need.

Mark still wanted to see her. She hadn't been a one-night stand. All wasn't lost.

She knew it would be heaven to wake up naked next to him. The thought of his strong yet gentle hands on her breasts had her wishing she hadn't left his side and had called in sick.

Had it only been hours since his lips had covered hers in never-ending kisses? Since his arms had enfolded her naked body, pulling her into his web of magical delights? Sighing, she opened the wrapped present, not sure what to expect.

She gasped and sat back in her chair. Lying on black velvet sat a gold necklace with a golden-winged dragon pendant. It was the most beautiful thing she'd ever seen. It sparkled like an array of colorful lights. The dragon's eyes were two rather large emeralds, and its wings were adorned in diamonds.

"Are you going to accept my dinner invitation?"

Glancing up, she found Mark had come into her office smiling and was closing the door behind him.

"I'm-I'm not very nice in the mornings." Her words had come out sounding breathless. She'd been so engrossed in her gift she had failed to see or smell Mark as he came into her office. Rane tried to mask her feelings as he walked toward her.

"I'm a very likable person in the morning."

He now stood on the other side of her desk. As if she was under some sort of spell, she watched as he leaned in toward her. She was sure he was going to kiss her right now in her office. His lips were so close.

Just one little kiss wouldn't matter. Would it?

Blinking, she came to her senses with only a millimeter to

spare. She sat straighter and pushed her chair back a little to put some extra space between them to stop him.

"Mark, I can't possibly accept this gift."

She closed the lid of the box and held it out to him. She couldn't meet his stare, knowing if she did, she'd be lost.

"No, I want you to have it. You are my dragon. I want—"

Their glances met for an instant, as they both eyed the opening office door. Bad timing, and karma, Val would have said.

"Rane, I think we need—"

Richard stopped in mid-sentence. Mark turned toward him. Even from her sitting position, she saw that the look Mark gave him was one that said, *what are you doing here?*

"Oh, I didn't—Sorry, Mr. Christmenn, I didn't know you were in here. I was actually looking for you, too." Mr. Adams paused for a moment, regaining some confidence. "I guess I should've knocked."

If the situation hadn't been so bizarre, Rane would've laughed aloud. Seeing a grown man turn into a mumbling fool by a simple look was something to see. Rane discreetly used Mark as a shield to remove the rose from her desk. Placing it, and the other items, onto her lap, she slid her chair closer to the desk to further conceal the gifts and hoped Mr. Adams couldn't read her face.

"Richard, the traffic was bad this morning. I just got in. I need to change our meeting time to nine-thirty. Does that work?"

"We can skip our meeting. I'll see you at ten-thirty for the department meeting," Richard stated.

"Thanks. I finished most of everything last night. I'm sorry for not being ready," Rane said.

"It's understandable. See you at ten-thirty."

She watched Richard leave knowing he had been nervous. The instant the door clicked shut Mark turned around, placed both of his hands on her desk, and leaned in toward her again.

"Dinner?"

Mark was closer now than before when she had thought he

was going to kiss her. What if she moved her head, just a little? She'd be able to capture his incredible lips with hers.

One little touch of their lips against the others, wouldn't hurt. How could it?

"Rane?"

She didn't want to talk. In fact, she wanted the man in front of her so bad she was aching in spots only he would be able to satisfy. Rane placed her right hand on top of his and slowly stroked his fingers. She took special care to go the full length of each of them and then back to his palm.

———

"Rane, you'd better stop this teasing before I take advantage of the situation."

Mark tried to put authority into his request but failed. It had come out as an enduring sexual whisper.

He wanted her right now too. What had he been thinking of by coming to her office? He should have requested she come to his and given her the gifts there. They might have been in his private apartment right now making love.

Her hand was soft and teasing, stroking his fingers as if they were another part of his body; one that was so hard and ready to spring into action it hurt. He was in pain and almost groaned aloud as a surprising rush of passion came over him. He hadn't moved and wasn't going to. He was afraid that if he did, he'd embarrass both of them. Her office just wasn't private enough for what he wanted to do at this moment.

She didn't remove her hand, just stopped her fingers. He found her gazing up at him.

"Are you the planned dinner?"

Her reply was said in a seductive tone, it took him by surprise. He moved his right hand to her cheek and gently stroked her jawline.

"No, but I could be the dessert if you agree to have the main course with me. I'd also like to take you away for a weekend."

"I think I'd like to have dessert before dinner," she stated, "but I'm not sure about a weekend thing. I have Thor to think about."

He took advantage of the inches separating them and kissed her lips as if to seal their agreement. He eased back and straightened, placing his hands in his pants pockets to conceal the effect she was having on him.

"I see our kiss has had the same effect on you as it did on me. But no matter how hard you press me, I have a job to do. Mr. Adams and a room of other people will be waiting for me."

"All I would like to do right now is make love. Do you know how tempted I am to have you come to my office at lunch time for a little afternoon delight?" He was trying to stall so he could get his body under control before having to leave her office. "You're right. You had better gather your reports for your meeting. You have about an hour."

He withdrew his hands from his pockets and hitched up his slacks. Shrugging and rolling his shoulders, he smoothed out his suit coat, knowing she watched his every move. "Stop by *my* office when you are ready to leave for the day."

"It won't be till about four o'clock. My last meeting runs until three."

"That's acceptable."

Mark had seen her eyes turn to green and were now just beginning to go back to blue. He couldn't help but smile. Turning, he walked to the door and opened it. Leisurely, he headed to his office to make plans for their night together.

———

Rane watched his retreating figure, enjoying the view, but wished his suit coat hadn't hidden his tight ass.

Crap.

She'd forgotten to ask for her phone. Knowing, she couldn't chance going to his office, because she might not leave, she'd have to wait until after her meeting. It would be around lunch time. Maybe some afternoon delight was in her future. She clutched the rose and the necklace on her lap.

They would have to discuss this gift tonight.

She placed the box in her briefcase and laid the rose in front of her computer. Standing, she went over to the table and finished sorting through the stack of papers she'd left last night in her rush to go to Mark's house.

———

Mark couldn't help but grin. He felt so alive. He hadn't felt like this in years. As he passed Mrs. Weber's desk, she raised her eyebrow at him in a manner that reminded him of Mr. Spock from *Star Trek*.

He didn't acknowledge her and didn't stop. He simply strolled straight into his office, and then to his private bathroom, letting the door close loudly. He needed some time to think without interruptions. After pacing back and forth for a few minutes, he stopped in front of the mirror.

Fool. A lovesick fool. That's what he saw.

Fucking A, what had he just done?

Why had he gone and kissed her?

Anyone in the company could've seen them if they entered like Richard had. He had no business taking advantage of Rane like that and potentially damaging her hard-earned reputation.

Shit!

He'd never kissed a woman in the workplace. Even if one of the women he had been dating showed up at the office, he *never* kissed them in front of the employees.

If his father had been alive, he'd have lambasted him and thrown him out with the trash, if he had gotten word of him kissing someone in the building. It had been out of fear of his father's wrath, mixed with not wanting to disappoint him, that he had kept his sexual attractions for women employees at bay over the years. There had been plenty of women whom he would have liked to have had a sexual fling with but couldn't bring himself around to doing it. Plus, that picture had saved him on many occasions too.

Mark shifted his stance, placed his hands on the sink, and dropped his head. His body was still heated over Rane's little stunt. He hadn't been able to hide his erection from her.

Man, I'm losing it!

This was a working office. He needed to keep his and Rane's private dealings private. But then again, her lips had been so tempting, so ready to yield to his.

Shit, this was insane. Who would've guessed, the guy who kept all his relationships cool and low keyed, had allowed a woman to get to him?

The question was *why* was she affecting him in this manner? He couldn't allow Rane to get too close to him not with his date with the artist of the picture fast approaching. He'd made sure over the years not to let any woman truly capture his heart.

Mark pounded his hands on the rim of the sink.

The damn picture again.

Rane was real. Philip was right. He needed to throw the thing away.

As the last signs of his heated desire faded, he was able to focus on what he needed to do. First thing, he'd have Mrs. Weber put out a memo about walking into an office when the door was closed. Thankfully he hadn't been kissing Rane when Richard had barged in. It would've been very embarrassing for all of them.

Splashing cold water on his face had its desired effect. All of his lingering sexual emotions were gone. He exited the bathroom and headed to his desk in a better state of mind than before.

Without thinking, he took the twenty-year-old picture and

shoved it into a desk drawer. He wasn't quite ready to trash it, but out of sight was better now that Rane was a part of his life.

"Mrs. Weber, will you please come in here?"

"Yes, Mr. Christmenn?"

She came in and sat down with her pad of paper and pen in hand.

"Please take down this memo and have it distributed immediately." He paused for a moment: "To all employees, this is a reminder that proper office etiquette is needed to be practiced at all times. It has come to my attention that boardroom doors, conference room doors, and office doors are being opened without a proper announcement. When a door is closed, it is proper etiquette to knock before entering. Please practice this in the future." Mark cleared his throat and added. "Do you have any questions?"

"No, Mr. Christmenn. I'll have this ready within the hour. Do you want this e-mailed or a paper memo?"

"Both."

"Is there anything else?"

He had called her early this morning and had instructed her to pick up the necklace from the jeweler and a single red rose. She hadn't asked or questioned him as usual, she just did what he requested. Sooner or later, he would confide in her.

"Yes, I'll need you to come back in an hour to handle some reservations for this weekend." Not looking at her, he got up to pour himself another cup of coffee. "That will be all."

Mark half expected her to lecture him, but she didn't, she simply left. Puzzled a little since it wasn't like her not to voice her opinion, he wondered why she hadn't taken advantage of the opportunity.

He concentrated on making plans for the weekend. Dinner and a play?

No, he didn't want to go to a play. Too public and it would be torture sitting next to her for so long without being able to touch her. Then he recalled Rane saying she'd wanted dessert first which was something that was sounding better and better by the minute.

Maybe a cozy dinner for two at his house. They could spend as much time as they wanted in bed and then have dinner brought up to them. He'd have to call Chef Motzer to prepare dinner for two.

He could picture it now. They'd start with oysters, as the ultimate mood setter, and then some blackened tuna steaks with fresh greens. It would be light not heavy. Perfect for the special dessert.

The phone was in his hand when a compelling plan hit him like a slap in the face. He'd spirit her away for the weekend down to his villa on Marco Island in Florida.

Why hadn't he thought of it before? And he could make sure she got her dessert before dinner as a member of the mile-high club.

Instead of dialing Chef Motzer, he quickly punched in Philip's number.

"Hello?"

"Philip, we need the plane for tonight. We're going to head down to Florida and come back Sunday evening. I'll be bringing a guest."

"It's Ms. Schoen, isn't it? I know you can't talk freely at the office."

"Yes, it is. We can discuss this at lunch." Not wanting to say much more over the phone, he waited for Philip to say something. His door was open and Danny, who was in charge of shipping, was due any minute to discuss next week's coffee bean shipments. They would be the first drug-free ones since the whole Massaro mess.

"Okay, I'll call Hal and have him ready the flight plans. I'll come get you for lunch," Philip said and hung up.

Mark now had to figure out a way to get Rane to agree. He'd seen it done in the movies. It wasn't his problem if she assumed they were staying in Minnesota. She had, after all, agreed to dinner and he'd never said which state they'd dine in. How could she object when she found out their dinner was going to be in Florida? Laughing to himself with his new set of plans set into motion, he finished a to-do list for Mrs. Weber, minutes before she announced Danny.

"Come on in. I hope you have good news for me." Mark got up and took a seat at the conference table and Danny joined him.

An hour later, per his earlier instructions, Mrs. Weber interrupted the meeting. "Excuse me, Mr. Christmenn, you wanted to go over some important matters concerning this weekend. Do you want me to come back?"

"No, we've just finished. Thanks for the updates, Danny. It'll be nice to have our shipments coming in on a regular basis again. Let me know when you have the estimated time of arrival."

"Yes, Mr. Christmenn, I should have their expected arrival date by Tuesday. The numbers are improving which should be reflecting in our sales."

He waited for Danny to take his leave and to get out of earshot before addressing Mrs. Weber, who still stood just inside his office. "Please shut the door and sit down."

When she did, he handed her his list of things that he needed done for his weekend getaway. "I'm going to be leaving for Florida in a few hours."

He watched Mrs. Weber raise her eyebrow in that arched way again. "Don't act like you know nothing. Yes, I am and as you've probably guessed, Ms. Schoen will be accompanying me."

Immediately, he knew his tone of voice had been too stern and wished he could take it back.

"Mark, is this a good idea? I don't want to see her get hurt. She is a very sweet person."

"I know what I'm doing," he paused, for a second. She had used his first name. It was something she rarely did. Did he really know what he was doing? "I kissed her. Here, at the office."

244

He went to the window that overlooked parts of downtown Minneapolis and looked out. Instead of hearing a scolding from Mrs. Weber, he heard her laugh. He turned and glared angrily at her. He was about to go into his private apartment when her words stopped him.

"You're so much like your father." The laughter in her voice disappeared as she added, "I think it's time you know something that I've been hiding for a very long time."

His chest suddenly tightened. Mark met Mrs. Weber's watery gaze. He really looked at her. She had aged gracefully over the years and had kept a slim figure. She had stopped coloring her hair, which was a white-grey blend and short. He swallowed and inclined his head. "Yes?"

"Your father-Sam and I were lovers, up until the day he got sick and passed away."

Mark shook his head. "No surprise. I've known that for years."

"I'm sure you did. Now let me finish. You see, Sam-your father, was very taken aback the first time he kissed me in this very office, which was over forty-five years ago." Mrs. Weber paused and took a breath. "That's the reason he was so hard on you about not getting involved with any of the employees."

"Are you my mother?"

The question he'd been holding back came out. What would she say? Would she deny she was? Or would she confirm his suspicions. He saw that her eyes were now brimming with tears. She stood, set her pad of paper and his list on the chair, and walked over to him.

"Yes. He wouldn't allow me to recognize you as my son. Even after he died, it was stated in Sam's will that no one could know the truth. I hated him for that." She raised her hand and gently smoothed back his hair in a motherly gesture. "I knew you struggled with the idea, but I-I couldn't tell you. Damn it, but it's time you knew. I love you so much. I'm so proud of you, too. You're all a mother could wish for in a son."

Mark stood frozen, unable to think of a thing to say. Out of the blue, his suspicions had been confirmed.

"Mark?"

"I'm so glad you're my mother." He engulfed her in a hug that was long overdue. "Why did you wait so long to tell me? Why didn't Father just divorce Helen?"

"He couldn't. It was very complicated. You see, your grand-daddy promised her parents he'd take care of their daughter. He made your dad marry Helen."

Mark led her over to the couch and handed her a Kleenex. "I never heard that story. Why would Father ever agree to anything like that? He was so strong. I can't see him taking orders from anyone."

"Your father should've told you before he died. He made me promise not to ever tell you when he became ill. You see, your granddaddy and Helen's father were in the Korean War together. They'd made a pact, if anything happened to either of them the other would watch over their families."

The pieces started to slide together, and he waited for Mrs. Weber, no, his true mother, to continue.

"Well, Helen's father was killed in the war. Your father and I had been dating for a period of time, but your granddaddy stepped in. He couldn't have his son dating a lowly secretary. He ordered Sam to marry Helen."

Handing her the entire box of Kleenex's, Mark put his arm around her shoulder. She continued to wipe the tears from her eyes. "If it's too painful to tell me you should stop."

"Thank you, sweetie, but I've been holding this in for a very long time. I need to tell you. You need to know."

"Okay, I have all the time in the world."

"I know you don't. Your schedule is full. But I'll tell you. Sam —your father put up a huge fight. We loved each other. After days of fighting, he gave in when your granddaddy threatened to disown him, take him out of the will, and fire him from the company. We attempted to stay away from each other and did for a while. But we were in love, and you were created during that time."

Mark took her hands into his.

"Your granddaddy never knew you were my son. Helen wanted your family's wealth and power, so she agreed to pretend to be pregnant and would raise you as her own. But I could never be a part of your life."

"But you stayed his mistress?"

"Yes, that was also part of the deal your father made with Helen. When he brought you to the office, it gave me some time with you. And no one was the wiser. I'm sorry for the deceit. You were never very far from me, yet you were out of my reach. Do you forgive me?"

"What is there to forgive? I'm happy the truth is finally out in the open. Does this mean I get to call you mother? Or at least by your first name, Joan," Mark said and once again hugged her.

———

Reports.

Spreadsheets.

Who needed them?

Mark paced the office. Damn, he couldn't concentrate. The board would have to be happy with what he'd gotten done so far. As long as the annual reports showed they were making money, lots of it, and the drug problem was taken care of, they'd be happy.

The fact remained that Mrs. Weber, no Joan, he corrected himself, was indeed his mother and the story she'd revealed had been astounding. All these past years, wasted why?

What if he had been able to see his father before he'd died? Would he have told him who his real mother was? His life was a mess. None of this changed the fact he both hated and respected his father for sticking to his guns. He'd never left the woman he'd loved.

What difference would it make now if the world knew their secret? Would his mother, no, his . . . He didn't even know what to call the woman he'd thought was his mother all these years.

Should he tell Helen he knew everything? The secret.

Would she even care?

Torn, Mark ran his hand through his hair. She had been a mother to him, and the only one he'd known. He'd have to ask Mrs. Weber—Joan if he should tell Helen.

It was all so complicated it hurt his head to think of all the possibilities, but he did know things were going to be different from now on. Pushing his chair back, he gave up on the papers and reached for his suitcoat. As he did, he felt something in his breast pocket vibrate.

Rane's cell phone.

He'd forgotten to give it to her earlier. Slipping it out, he saw a new message alert from her friend Val. How was he going to give it to her?

"Mrs. Weber, I need you."

She came in, looking anxious.

"Sorry, I didn't mean to scare you. But I have another problem. I need to give Ms. Schoen her cell phone. I wasn't able to earlier."

"I see. Give it to me. I'll leave it in her office."

Mark shook his head. "I don't think that will work. I noticed several messages from one person."

"Right. Don't worry, I'll get it to her immediately."

"Thank you. Can you move up my lunch reservation to eleven-fifteen and let Philip know too?"

"Consider it done."

She held out her hand and he gave her Rane's cell phone. Putting on his suitcoat he waited for Philip.

"What is so important that you had to move up our lunch

time? What if I'm not hungry yet?" Philip asked from the doorway.

"If you want the low down on our bird in flight, we'd better get going now." Mark cruised past a stunned Philip, who was staring at him with his mouth opened. Philip caught up to him and together they proceeded to the Café Loon, which was around the corner from the MAC building. Neither tried to keep up a conversation while they walked, but that changed once they entered the restaurant, and the hostess sat them immediately.

"Spill your guts, man. What is going on? First, you have me follow the woman to her car. Next, you order an investigation into her background. Then you invite her over to your house and she spends the night. And now you are talking about taking her to Florida."

Mark took a sip of water and unfolded his napkin. "I think I'm in love with her."

"For Christ's sake."

"That's right. I think I've fallen head over heels for her. You can make fun of me but all I know is that she isn't like anyone I've ever met. She makes me laugh. She fascinates me as no other woman has been able to do. It's odd. Sometimes it seems she can read my thoughts." He paused, took another sip of water, and waited for Philip to say something. When he didn't, Mark continued. "You know I don't rush into anything. I'll bet you didn't know I've been going to lunch with her for the last couple of days."

Philip's mouth opened but he quickly closed it into a tight smile. So, he hadn't known. Seeing he had the upper hand, Mark decided to further divulge even more of his feelings. "The more she and I talked, the more I want to get to know her better. I almost feel as if I've met her before. As if I've always known her."

"How could that be?" Philip asked.

"It can't be. I've gone over and over your report and I can't find anywhere that our paths might have crossed. I'm sure you've read the report yourself and know she doesn't need money. Therefore, she can't be a fortune hunter. I'm not sure why she's working but she's good at what she does. What do you think? Am I losing it?"

"Yes. I know what the report says. Did you want me to dig deeper? I can if you want."

Mark shook his head. It somehow felt like he'd be overstepping the line, if he did have Philip go searching for more.

"Awesome. After all these years, you're finally showing interest in someone. Does this mean we don't have to go to Florida to Walt Disney World, the place that makes dreams come true?"

"That dig wasn't necessary. I look at the picture every day. Every now and then, I wonder why I've kept it all these years. Why would a woman remember she asked me to meet her when she was like thirteen? Who would wait twenty years to see someone again? Why have I waited all these years?"

"Sometimes people see things in other people that others don't. Mark, you're one of those people. That's why you've been so successful. You can smell a rat a mile away. You know when someone is lying. That young girl was a glimmer of something that would be simple." Philip put up his hand to stop him from saying anything, then continued. "When you met her, your life was just beginning to become complicated. You were trying to finish college. Your father was dying, and then the Board of Directors didn't want to hand over the companies to you. She and the picture have gotten you through the tough times."

"You're right. Since Massaro entered the scene, the drugs, and the attempts on my life I've become aware that there is something missing from my life. There has to be more than my work, the companies, and my wealth. What good is it all if I have no one to share it with? But there is still something about the promise on the picture . . ."

"I'm telling you one last time, let her go. She isn't real. You've created an image of what you want her to be, and it is not real. Since Agent Nelson put Massaro in jail and you've been taken off the drug cartel hit list, you're free to begin to live again. The trial isn't for another six months. It's time you searched for someone who IS real. Rane is as real as you can get," Philip said.

"I guess you're right. I have something else to tell you."

Their food arrived and Mark waited until the waiter was out of earshot. "Mrs. Weber just came clean and told me she is my biological mother."

"No way. You always thought she might be. Do you want a DNA test done, just to be absolutely sure?"

"Not now, but maybe in the future for when I change my will. I'm still a little shocked and relieved. I guess there is a whole other side of my father that I need to discover."

"I only knew him a few months before he became ill and died. None of the other security guards included me in on things. I had been hired to train them. They were all tight-lipped. Then when he passed and you took over, I became your personal bodyguard, and the rest is our history. Is there anything you want me to do? Anything you want me to confirm?"

"No. Life was so different back then. College. Parties. Drinking. After he died, I couldn't be that person. The board made sure of that. I had to take ownership of my actions and I thank God you were there for me. Let's finish our lunch. We have a lot to do this afternoon before flying out."

"I'm glad you're going away with Rane. You need and deserve this happiness. The contracts on your life are no longer a threat, and the coffee bean shipments are now drug free, it's time for you to relax. And to start enjoying life," Philip said.

"Are we sure all the hit men have been found and they've stopped any future ones from showing up?"

"Agent Nelson can't say one hundred percent, but he feels they've plugged the holes. The last one they found was trying to enter into the United States. He was deported to Colombia and the government there has to deal with him."

"Thanks for being there for me all these years. You are the best friend anyone could have," Mark said.

"Yeah, that's because I'm your only friend."

Staring into his glass of water, Mark prayed his life would be normal again. But could it ever be? Was he destined to live his life without true love like his father?

No, goddamn it.

He was going to make Rane part of his forever.

Chapter Eighteen

Taking the jump-drive from her computer, Rane stepped around her desk and spotted the note from David lying on the floor.

Damn him.

Picking up the disgusting note, she crumpled it and shoved the wad into her pocket not wanting to deal with it or the emotional roller coaster of curiosity.

"Ms. Schoen?"

Rane looked toward the door and saw Mrs. Weber there. "Good morning, can I help you? I'm on my way to a meeting."

"This won't take long. I have something, Mr. Christmenn says belongs to you."

From under a note pad she was holding; she withdrew a cell phone. Not sure how she should act or what to say, Rane hesitated.

"He said you might need it." Mrs. Weber held out the phone.

All the precautions she'd taken went out the window. She took it and laid it on top of the papers she was holding. "Tell him thank you."

"For what it's worth, Ms. Schoen, tread lightly where he is concerned. Your time after hours is yours alone."

Totally confused, Rane watched Mrs. Weber leave her office. Why she thought no one in the company would know about her and Mark's time together was so naïve. Of course, Mrs. Weber would know about their lunches.

Sighing, she headed down the hall, forcing herself to focus on the agenda. Luckily, she managed to arrive on time. Richard and all the other employees were seated at the conference table. Taking charge, she had the group effectively working on projects that were long overdue.

During a fifteen-minute break, she took a moment to text Val since she had her phone.

David called.

You told me. Val's response came back quickly.

No, today at work.

Scumbag. Val's way with words made her smile and she sent a reply. *What should I do?*

Remember we have lunch at twelve-thirty.

Where? Her buzzer went off signaling the end of the break before Val's reply came through.

Rane switched her phone to 'silent' and slipped it into her pocket. Richard had excused himself almost as soon as she arrived, leaving her in charge of the meeting. At first, she'd been a little surprised, but she realized he must've felt comfortable with what she was doing. Talk about a confidence builder. Before she and the group realized it, her buzzer went off again. "I want to thank everyone for all the hard work you've done this morning. I know it's lunchtime and it is Friday."

Hearing some remarks about not coming back, she added quickly, "I would like all of you to remember how hard we've worked. After lunch, we'll meet back here just long enough to table any items we haven't gotten to until next week. Just like you, I'm ready for the weekend."

The group laughed and applauded on their way out.

It wasn't a lie.

She had an unquenchable appetite for Mark and wanted to get him back into bed. She was craving the feel of his lips and the unforgettable orgasms he'd given her. She'd been tempted all morning to excuse herself and wander into his office, secretly hoping they'd end up in his private apartment.

The group thinned out and she took out her cell phone. Val's reply was waiting.

Your place.

It figured. Val loved the company's cafeteria. It had everything she could want, and she loved the coffee bar.

Rane checked the time, almost twelve-thirty, then headed straight to her office and told Linda that she was expecting a guest.

Val hated to wait. It was a lawyer thing since sometimes verdicts weren't reached immediately. In addition, some judges took matters under advisement before ruling on them. So, when it came to everyday things, she couldn't handle delays.

Rane putzed around her office. Her stomach growled reminding her she hadn't had breakfast. Between sneaking out of Mark's house, rushing to get to work on time, her morning encounter with Mark and then her meeting, she hadn't had a spare minute all morning. When the phone did ring, she jumped a little and told Karen to send her lunch date up. The elevator bell went off quicker than she expected, and she bent down to grab her purse from the bottom drawer.

"Ro?"

She popped up so fast she hit her head on the desk's edge. "Ouch!"

She hesitated a second before opening her eyes. When she did, she blinked fast, thinking she was seeing things, or she'd hit her head harder than she originally thought. It wasn't Val standing in front of her desk as she'd expected. To her shock and disbelief, David stood smiling at her.

"David, what are you doing here?"

"I sent you e-mails and text messages. When you didn't respond, I thought it best to come see you in person."

Unable to say anything more, she struggled to take in what was going on. She hadn't seen or verbally talked to him, except for the recent emails, in over three years. Now, when she'd fallen in love for a second time in her life, he showed up to complicate things. She sat down in the chair and stared at her ex-husband.

"You're a sight for sore eyes, baby-doll. You're looking fantastic."

She continued to sit and stare at him, not affected by his words. He hadn't changed much. Some gray hairs mixed into the blond ones, and he had the beginning signs of wrinkles around his eyes. It gave him a certain look of distinction and made him more handsome than she remembered. Her pulse quickened but instead of feeling a whirlwind of love and desire, she felt a mixture of hatred and disgust.

"My little Ro, I want you back."

His soft tone was laden with desire, the one she well remembered. It meant he wanted to have sex. In the past, she would've jumped at the opportunity, as was expected of a good wife.

Anger swept over Rane, giving her the power, she needed. "Don't you ever call me by the nickname my grandmother uses. No, no, no. Get out of here. I don't want to see you."

"But, baby, don't get upset. Let me explain."

David moved and came around the desk to stand next to her, blocking any path of her escape.

"No!"

She shouted the word and raised her hand to stop him from coming any closer to her. Her earlier assessment of him hadn't been accurate. Her mind had played a trick on her. Up close, he wasn't as handsome as she once thought. His eyes showed a loneliness and a sadness that had never been there before. His cheeks looked sunken. Life in the fast lane had taken its toll on him. He was so different from Mark.

"I don't want to hear anything you have to say. We are divorced. I'm so over you."

"But Ro—"

"No, stop! Oh yeah, you lost me years ago. There's no turning back the hands of time here. You might be able to do it on your patients' faces but you can't on peoples' emotions. Now get out of here!"

"Do we have a problem?"

Hearing Mark's commanding voice, her blinding anger faded. Their eyes met. Her knight in shining armor was blocking the door and ready to take charge.

"This is a private matter." David took a step closer to Rane. "Close the door on your way out."

Mark raised his hand toward Mrs. Weber, who stood a few feet from him waving her in and then pointed his finger at David.

"You, sir, are someplace you shouldn't be. Ms. Schoen has asked you to leave. I think you'd better do as she says," Mark said.

She saw Philip and other security guards pushing past Mark and Mrs. Weber.

"Tell this man and the others to leave, Ro."

Rane cringed at David's sickly sweet tone. She knew what it meant and almost opened her mouth to do as he'd instructed when another voice entered the conversation.

"David Moore, get your sick, abusive, two-timing ass away from Rane. If you know what's good for you, you'd better leave, or I'll stick you with a court order at your expense."

She had two knights in shining armor. Val barged past Mark, the security guards, and stood nose-to-nose with David, who had turned to face her.

It was a classic *OK Corral* standoff.

No one said or did anything.

No one was going to back down.

"Mark, give me a moment. Val, please wait outside too," Rane said, taking control of the awkward situation. David wasn't going to know what hit him when she was done with him.

"I don't—" Mark began but Val cut him off by taking him by the arm, then leading him out of the office. The others followed and it was Philip who shut the door.

Gathering her courage, Rane stood. "David, I don't know you anymore and you don't know me. I'm not the little obedient wife anymore. I used to dream of hearing you say you wanted me again. I waited and waited for you to come back to me, but you never did. As much as I would have liked to hear those words years ago, they don't mean anything to me now. I've moved on. I have a life now that doesn't include you or your memory."

"But, baby—"

She closed her eyes, refusing to listen and said, "I don't love you anymore. Now please leave me alone."

When she opened her eyes, she saw disbelief on David's face. He opened his mouth but before he could say a word she simply said, "No. Now go, before the police have to take you away. I'm sure Val is calling in a restraining order right now."

David glared at her. Turning, he stormed out of her office, forcing the door to hit the wall. He was met by Philip and the security guards who led him to the elevators.

Val rushed in and came to her side. "Are you okay? Did you know he was fired? Plus, he has several lawsuits levied against him for misconduct and inappropriate relationships with clients. Tell me now, should I file a protection order?"

"Fired? No wonder he was tracking me down. There isn't a need for a protection order, he wouldn't hurt me. I think I've seen the last of him."

Rane saw Mark standing just outside of her office. His face was taut, and his jaw clenched. His obvious concern touched her in a way she'd didn't think possible. He nodded, turned, and walked away.

"Oh, Val, what just happened?"

"You slammed David up against the wall. Not literally, but just as good as if you had. Just say the word and I'll make sure he never comes within twenty feet of you again," Val said and hugged her.

"You know what? It was gratifying but sad at the same time. Man, I need a drink. Maybe we should have a liquid lunch."

"That's my girl."

"I can't really, you know. I have a training session to finish up. But let's go eat."

Val laughed, dragged her out of the office, and headed down to the cafeteria. Once there, she ordered Rane a Marble Mocha Macchiato.

"This is surprisingly good. I can't even taste the coffee," Rane said, thankful she could finally tell Mark she'd tried his coffee. "Do you think my chances with Mark are over now?"

"Hell no, you should've seen the anger on Mr. Wall's face. You have him wrapped around your finger. You've landed yourself a hunk."

They laughed and began to eat their lunch. The rest of their lunchtime went quickly, and they said their goodbyes. It wasn't until they separated that she realized she'd forgotten to ask Val to cat-sit Thor for her.

Suddenly as she entered the elevator a sliver of doubt sipped into Rane's happiness. Could Mark have been turned off by the confrontation with her ex-husband when he'd walked away without saying anything? Had she ruined her special weekend before it actually started?

————

Mark swiveled in his office chair as a knock sounded on the door. "Come in."

"I wanted to let you know I turned Mr. Moore over to the

police for trespassing," Philip said, closing the door behind him with a click.

"Thanks. I tell you, Philip, that man is a number one fuck! Call in some favors and make sure he doesn't get out for a day or two."

"Sure, anything else?"

Mark hesitated. "Did you hear Rane's ex call her Ro? Do you think there is any possibility Rane is the girl from the plane?"

"There wasn't anything in her reports that would lead me to believe she is or was."

"Yeah, you're right." Mark ran his hand through his hair and stood. "Just make sure the plane is ready."

"Okay, no problem."

He watched Philip leave and thought he'd seen him smile. Maybe he had enjoyed the morning's excitement too much.

Now he had some special plans to make. Four o'clock wasn't coming fast enough for him. He glanced at his watch. Philip had called several times to confirm the flight plans and limo arrangements. Mrs. Weber had completed her calls to the house staff in order to get the villa ready for their arrival. All was in place, but he was missing the main person, Rane.

Finally, Mrs. Weber called to let him know Rane was on her way to his office. He was ready for her when she appeared in the doorway.

"Hi, I'm finished for the day. I-I'm sorry about my ex-husband. I haven't heard from him in years. It was a shock to see him, and I can't believe he showed up here."

"As long as you're okay, I'm okay."

What he didn't tell her was that Philip had taken measures to ensure her ex would never threaten her or them again.

"Yeah, Val is going to file some orders of protection," she paused then added, "I want you to know I don't have any feelings for him and haven't for a long time."

"I didn't think you did. Now, no more talk of your ex. I've been planning a special weekend for us."

He took her hand, ushered her fully inside his office, and closed the door. Never letting go of her hand, he imprisoned her in his arms, giving her a kiss as if there was no tomorrow. He felt her tense at first. Then her body relaxed against his, responding to his searing lips and matched them with her own demanding ones. He kissed her with all the passion he had inside of him and reached out to unbutton her blouse to release its hidden treasures.

Ending the kiss, he led her to the couch where they landed in a heap. They broke out in laughter still wrapped in each other's arms. His heartbeat matched her racing heartbeat.

"Do you really think your memo will work?" She moved to lean back on the couch. "As tempting as your embrace is, it's so like you to think a memo will solve a problem."

"It had better! If anyone enters my office when the door is closed, they will be fired!"

"Off with their heads."

They laughed at the joke, but it was a relief knowing no one dared to interrupt their moment. She snuggled up closer to him and unbuttoned a couple of his shirt buttons. Sliding her hand inside, she stroked the hairs on his chest, and tugged at his nipples. Reluctantly, he held her hand.

"As much as I would enjoy making love to you right now in my office, we can't. Plus, we need to discuss the plans I've made for the weekend."

"Right, plans for dinner. Where are we going?"

She began to rebutton her shirt and he did the same.

"I have planned our dinner in Florida. We are going to fly there as soon as we can. And we will stay the weekend at my villa on Marco Island. We can stop at your place so you can pack some clothes."

He turned to face her and saw her eyes were green.

"Not that you will need any clothes. I plan on keeping you in bed all day and night."

———

Rane gasped at his unexpected announcement.

Florida for the weekend.

Mark sure did know how to impress someone. She'd thought they would spend the weekend at his house. Something simple. She didn't spend money on extravagant things, like hotel stays.

Then it hit her in the pit of her stomach.

That was the old Rane's way of thinking. David had created that dull person.

This was the new her. She found herself becoming excited thinking about going away for the weekend with Mark. "That sounds thrilling. What time does our flight leave?"

"Whenever we are ready to go. We'll be using my private jet."

"Ohhh. I love Marco Island. I used to have my grandma take me there when I would visit her." She headed toward the door. "Well? What are you looking at, let's get going."

Laughing, he gave her a fast kiss. "I'll be by your house in about an hour. Will that give you enough time to pack?"

"We could leave right now under two conditions. One, I have time to call Val and ask her to watch Thor. And two, that you allow me to go shopping for some clothes and other items once we land."

The old Rane was gone.

She wanted to take chances like she had when she was younger. She had enough money to do what she wanted when she wanted. Having saved all the money from David as part of the divorce agreement, it was time to enjoy life. Mark was showing her what it felt like to be free and have fun.

"Are you sure? If we leave now, I can arrange for the mall to stay open late for us. Would you want all the stores to be open or only the department stores?"

"Mark, can you move mountains, too? Only one of the department stores would be fine. I could pick up everything in one store. You are amazing."

"Great, it's settled. We'll leave from the office. Give me your car keys. Philip can arrange for your car to be driven to your house."

When she picked up her briefcase to leave, he stopped her. "Be sure to leave your briefcase in your office. We are not going to be doing any work this weekend."

She laughed. "It depends on what you consider work."

The play on words hung in the air as he followed her to her office. He stood in the door watching her. She set her briefcase on her desk chair and took out the box and the rose.

"We will need to talk about this." She placed the box with the necklace in her purse and held the rose in her hand. Together they walked to the elevators.

Downstairs in front of the main entrance, she saw Mark's limo waiting. The security guards called out goodnight to them as they exited the building. Inside the limo she sat next to Mark, in a state of shock. She couldn't believe she was on her way to the airport to fly to Florida.

Talk about a spur of the moment decision. The fact she'd actually agreed to this was craziness. She'd wanted an escape, but this was outrageous. Val was going to die when she told her.

"Are we really going to Florida? Tonight?"

"Yes."

"I just wanted to make sure. You know this is insane, right?"

As if he sensed her nervousness, Mark took her hand. "You're going to love the villa. It's on stilts and you can see the Gulf of Mexico. After Florida had those two hurricanes, it had to be fixed. I had it rebuilt with state-of-the-art features to hopefully withstand any future storms or water surges."

"Those storms caused a lot of damage."

"It was awful. Fort Myers Beach was destroyed. They are still trying to rebuild," Mark said.

The drive to the Flying Cloud airport took less time than she thought. Their hands remained entwined the whole way. When they reached the small airport, the limo stopped next to a waiting plane.

Her first glimpse of it had her smirking. She should have known Mark didn't do anything small. She'd been expecting a small four-person plane of some sort, not the plane that they entered. The jet was large enough to have belonged to a commercial airline.

The interior resembled an office and there were four rows of two seats on each side up toward the front of the plane. Behind these seats, were booths with tables. Continuing down the center was a small open area with a door that stood open part way, and she could see what appeared to be a bed. She'd only seen airplanes like this on television and she immediately felt like a movie star or a jet setter.

Mark told her to sit anywhere she'd like, and she quickly chose the last row and the seat next to the window still holding the rose. Mark didn't join her at first. He had gone up to the cockpit to talk to the pilot.

Just then, Philip entered the plane and came over to stand next to her seat.

"Hi, welcome aboard. I have the department store in Naples waiting for your arrival. I'm acting as a steward for this flight. Would you care for something to drink?"

"Thanks. Do you have a Coke?"

"Yes, I do." Philip turned and left.

Then Mark was standing next to the seat.

"I thought you might be hungry. I made a tray of snacks," he said and held out a platter of various cheeses, crackers, and fruit. "We'll have dinner once we've taken off."

"Thanks. I'm still not sure that this isn't a dream. I feel kind of like Cinderella. Will you be sitting with me, or do you have to be up front?"

"No, I'll be joining you in a few minutes. I'm not the pilot this weekend but Philip is the co-pilot. We'll be ready for takeoff in a couple of minutes."

Mark placed the tray on the table in front of her and Philip appeared with her Coke.

"I'll be back to sit down just before we take off," Mark said.

While she sat alone and munched on the crackers and cheese, she attempted to take in everything. The afternoon had gone by quickly after she'd told David off, which still shocked her. At first, she'd been embarrassed people might have overheard his parting comments but then Val had been there as always, to put her at ease.

Val. Thor.

She needed to call her. Quickly, she took out her phone and tapped favorites and then Val. The phone rang.

"Hello, girlfriend, how did the rest of your day go?"

"Just peachy. You're not going to believe where I am."

"Let me guess, *his* house?"

Rane cupped her hand and placed it over the bottom of the phone and her mouth. "No, I'm in his private jet and we are flying down to Florida."

"Shut up. Really?"

"I'm not kidding. But I need a favor. Will you take care of Thor for me? He's going to be really mad when I don't come home again."

"You know I will. He's the only stable man in my life right now. Oh, I filed the papers on David. You won't have to worry about him barging in on you at work again."

"You're the best. I'll call you when I get back," Rane said.

"Enjoy all the sex. Bye."

Val hung up and Rane saw Mark standing next to the seat.

"Is everything okay? We're about ready to take off."

"Yeah, I had to call Val about watching Thor for me."

"The other man in your life, right," Mark said and grinned.

"Do you go through the safety things? Keep your seatbelt fastened. In case of an emergency, the air thingy will come down. You know?"

"No, but I can if you need me to."

"I think I remember all those things. Unless, you have special instructions that I need to know."

He bent down and kissed her. "Those instructions will come later."

Speechless, she watched him strut away from her to the cockpit. She could think of a lot of things she'd like to instruct him to do.

———

Soon the plane lifted off and they were on their way to Florida. Mark had a strange sensation of déjà vu of sitting next to her and watching Rane gazing out the window. He had an odd feeling he'd done this before. He was almost one hundred percent sure now that she was the girl from the plane twenty years ago after hearing her ex call her Ro.

Seeing Philip's signal from the cockpit that it was safe to get up, he turned to her. "Would you like a tour of the plane?"

"That would be great. I've never been on a private jet before."

He stood and waited for her to stand before pointing to the front of the plane.

"That's the cockpit. There is one restroom in the front. You have our regular seating in this area here," he said, indicating the section they had been sitting in. He turned and pointed to the next area. "And this is what I call the conference room. I have power outlets for laptops and tables set up here. I've had to conduct many meetings in the air."

"I'm sure all your guests have found this area very convenient."

Smiling, he continued to the center. "This is the galley. I usually have two flight attendants, Dawn, and Josh, when I fly. They prepare the food here. I installed a regular-size refrigerator. There are three microwaves, and an oven. This allows them everything they need to properly entertain clients in the air. There are two restrooms back here."

"I see a couple of expresso machines too; you've thought of everything."

Next, he opened the door that he had seen her looking at. "And this is a bedroom with its own bathroom."

"This is unreal. I can't wait to tell my mom and Val about this plane. No one is going to believe me." She took a step, so she was in front of him. "Mark, what—"

She wasn't able to finish her question because the plane hit an air pocket, causing her to lose her balance. Mark caught her, pulling her hard against him.

"The gods have granted my wish. I've been thinking of numerous ways to get you in my arms." Holding Rane close, he lowered his head and kissed her parted lips. The intensity of her own eagerness consumed him. He'd thought last night's kisses were fiery, but this kiss was a fast burn all the way down to his aching loins.

Somehow through the fog he heard a noise, as if someone was clearing their throat, and Mark ended the kiss. He gently moved Rane to the side and peered over her shoulder.

"Excuse me, we should start dinner now. You can have dessert later," Philip said.

Mark saw Rane blush and kissed her lips one more time before replying. "Right. Rane, feel free to roam the plane. I have Wi-Fi and the internet. The remote should be in the cup holder by where you were sitting. I have to help get our dinner ready."

Releasing his hold on her, he moved into the galley to help

Philip gather the already prepared food. He fended off Philip's questions by not responding to them. Philip got the hint and they assembled the food in silence. Even though everything was cooked, it proved torturous as he assembled it onto a plate.

"After, we've eaten dinner I don't want to be disturbed."

"I sure hope you know what you're doing. Getting this involved with someone could lead to disappointment."

"You are overstepping boundaries, Philip. I'm a forty-two-year-old man, not a kid. Now if you'll excuse me, I'm about to serve Rane's and my dinner." Taking the plates, he pushed past Philip and went to where Rane was seated.

"I hope you enjoy our menu selection," he said and handed her a plate before settling in the seat next to her. "I had the chef from Jack's prepare us chicken cordon bleu with rice and string beans. All we needed to do was heat it up. I'm not a very good cook and neither is Philip."

"It smells wonderful."

"I think so, too," Mark said.

"Do you know that when I was little, I read all the books I could find on flying? It held my interest for several years. My mother would never let me take flying lessons. I still would like to learn how to pilot a plane. Someday I'm going to take lessons. The Wright Brothers' passion for flying has always inspired me. When I feel I'm unable to accomplish something I think about their dream and how they made it real."

Mark choked on a bite of food, not sure he'd heard Rane correctly. He stared hard at her, trying to see if the girl was there. Here it was again, the déjà vu feeling. The girl etched in his memory had also referred to the Wright Brothers. It was one of the reasons he'd gotten his pilot license. He was getting more and more anxious with every mile they got closer to Florida.

"Tell me about your spring vacations with your grandma in Florida." He needed to confirm without a doubt that she was the girl. What could they-no he-have missed in the reports?

Philip wasn't going to believe it IF Rane turned out to be the girl.

"Oh my gosh, that was so many years ago. Let's see, I used to make my grandma take me to Tiger Tail Beach on Marco Island almost every day. Now don't laugh when I tell you why. When I was thirteen, I had a crush on a boy who had sat next to me on my flight to see my grandma," she paused and set down her fork before continuing. "I haven't thought about this in years. Val poked fun at me for the longest time saying he hadn't been real. I remember him being the cutest boy I'd ever seen. I don't know if I should say boy, I think he was in college. He'd mentioned going to Marco Island, so I told my grandma that we needed to go to the beach. However, the real reason was so I could find him. That was what I call my first real crush."

"Your first crush?" Mark forced himself to stay calm as his heartbeat pounded, like with Mrs. Weber. He knew at that moment his suspicions were correct. "Was your search successful?"

Rane laughed. "No, I had fallen so hard for him during the flight I even asked him to marry me."

"For real?"

"Yeah, to be that young again. My mom said it was my hormones gone wild. The boy had been so polite to me when I popped the question. He hadn't laughed or teased me, he just told me he would when I was old enough to marry."

"That was big of him."

Mark was busting out to tell her that he'd been that boy. What should he do? Should he fess up now?

His mind lingered on the memory of that day. He shivered. Turing to look at her, he smiled.

She was the girl.

He knew without a doubt at that moment, she was the one he'd been waiting twenty years for.

But what proof did he have? Words and a story.

With caution he proceeded. "Did you get the boy's name?"

"I did. It was Mark, like yours."

"What a coincidence. You must really like the name Mark. Maybe I should have Philip do some research on him. I don't want any male coming out of the woodwork once we are together. You know, not to ruin what we have."

"No need. That was a long time ago. I've been over him for years. My grandma never said a word about going to the beach, but I think she knew it was to look at the boys. I would walk the beach looking for him. I did it every year during my spring break."

"Did you ever find this boy?"

"Oh, no. My freshman year in high school, I met another boy. You met him today, my ex-husband. I was young and thought I was in love with him, too. Now, looking back, I know it was just an illusion. Remember I told you everyone expected us to marry. So, when he asked, I agreed, not really understanding what it meant."

Rane sipped on her Coke, seemingly deep in thought over what she had just admitted.

"I had a girlfriend in school. We had talked about getting married, but then my dad sent me away to boarding school."

"Did you get married?"

"No. She changed."

"I totally get that. My ex was a good boyfriend in school, but an awful husband. He hadn't wanted high school to ever end. Then, in college, he realized that there was a whole world of women out there trying to get his attention," Rane said and placed her napkin on the plate.

"Why did you stay with him for so long? You said you'd been married to him for over ten years, wasn't it?"

"Yeah, I thought we were the perfect couple. What a joke that was."

Sensing her mood change, he knew a change of subject had to happen. Enough about her ex. He wanted to find out more about what she thought about *him*. "What made you give up on the boy in Florida? Didn't you ever see him again?"

He already knew the answer. No. But why?

His house was on Tiger Tail Beach and the property line bordered the beach preserve. Still to this day, when he would stay at his house on Marco Island, he cruised the beach to look closely at all the women.

Had they been two star-crossed souls until now?

"No, I only talked to him for, what, about three hours on the plane. I never got his full name. I only knew that he was the cutest boy I'd ever seen. He didn't talk much about himself. I even told him my silly nickname."

"You have a nickname that you haven't shared with me?"

This was it, the moment he'd been waiting for.

She chuckled before going on. "Yes, my dad used the Scandinavian pronunciation of my name. You see, the letter A should have these two little dots over it. It means that letter has the sound of the letter O. R-oo-n. But he called me Ro. that's why I got mad today when David said it. Only my true friends use it."

"I hope someday I'll fit into the category of being your true friend so I can use it. If you're done with your dinner, I'll take the trays to the galley."

"Thanks, the chicken was fantastic, and I loved the beans. They were delicious, but I'm too excited to eat much." She smiled and handed him her half-eaten dinner.

Mark quickly took the trays and went into the galley. He took a quick sharp breath. Thought after thought roared through his mind. She'd just confirmed all his assumptions.

Rane *was* the girl.

He needed a few minutes to process it. Setting the trays down, he leaned against the galley counter, closed his eyes, and covered his face with his hands.

Doubt set in.

The girl he'd pictured all these years was not anything like Rane.

What if she wasn't the girl and he was just seeing things that weren't there? Maybe everything she said was just a coincidence.

She hadn't mentioned anything about drawing the picture. A lot of kids went down to Florida during vacations. Summer crushes happened all the time.

Damn.

His excitement from moments ago was gone, leaving him more confused. Who could help him sort through all the questions?

No one, his mind shouted.

Then an idea came to him. Perhaps Rane's grandma could help solve the mystery. If he was able to get a glimpse of her, it might trigger his own memory and all the pieces would fall into place. He'd watched the girl run to an older woman and give her a hug. He knew he'd recognize the older woman if he saw her again.

With a new plan in motion, he composed himself and returned to the conference area.

"Which restroom do I use?" Rane asked.

"The one through the bedroom."

Hearing the door close, he slipped into the bedroom. The mile high club was calling him. He quickly shed his suit coat, pulled out the tails of his dress shirt, unbuttoned several buttons, and discarded his tie. Just before the door opened, he flipped the switch for music and sat on the end of the bed.

"Oh my..."

Mark stood and tenderly cupped her face in his hands. "Is it time for dessert?"

"I didn't think we'd get to this point. It's all I've been thinking about."

He kissed her. Their tongues danced in perfect unison. She wrapped her arms around his neck, and he felt her fingers play with his hair. He had to let up on the kiss because it already had him aroused beyond his comprehension. Unwrapping her arms from his neck, he took her hand to lead her to the bed.

"Making love thousands of miles in the air, has a certain expectation to it."

"I don't think you will be disappointed. Nothing can top what we shared last night," Mark said. Still standing, he slowly undressed her.

Leaving her in her bra and panties, he took her clothes and carefully laid them to the side. She slid onto the bed as he discarded all of his clothes. He joined her on the bed completely naked.

His arousal was very evident as he pulled her into his arms. She kissed him and he reached down between them and unhooked her bra from the front, freeing her breasts. He left her inflamed lips and began a trail of kisses to them. He fondled and caressed each one, and osculated her nipples, causing her to arch backward in pleasure.

"Mark, don't stop."

"There are other parts that need my attention too."

He continued downward with kisses until he reached her panties and removed them. Mark found what he knew was going to bring her to the highest point he could take her. He suckled the nub and used his tongue to give her the release, she was waiting for. It came hard and fast, and he held her hips feeling her quivering against his lips.

When the orgasm ended, he eased her legs apart and allowed himself to sink into her heated core. The rhythm was slow but soon it, too, changed. She was pushing him harder and faster than he had wanted. Her pulsing core sent him over the edge.

"Rane, I love you."

Mark wasn't sure if she had heard him or if he had really said the words aloud. However, he didn't have time to dwell on it now. The yellow light flashing above the door meant they were descending for their approach into the Southwest Florida

International Airport. They needed to get dressed. Gently he pushed her hair away from her face so he could see her eyes.

"Hey, honey. We'll be landing in about a half hour, and we need to get dressed."

Smiling at her incredulous expression, he realized it no longer mattered if Rane was the girl who he'd met all those years ago or not. He was certain that this was the woman who could fill the void in his life, the one he wanted to spend the rest of his life with. Now all he had to do was figure out a way to get Rane to feel the same way.

Chapter Nineteen

Rane found her clothes lying on the end of the bed. She grabbed them and had to reach under his legs for her panties. Then she saw Mark holding up her bra with a finger. Snatching it, she rushed into the bathroom as he laughed. She refused to look at him.

In the throngs of their passion, he had proclaimed his love to her.

Proclaimed?

Why had she used that word to describe him saying he loved her?

She hadn't expected him to say that. How could he?

They hadn't known each other for very long but hadn't she admitted to herself, she loved him. No, she thought she was falling in love with him.

Was there a difference?

Turning on the shower she stepped in and quickly washed herself. Having a shower at twenty or thirty thousand feet in the air was odd, but exciting.

Patiently waiting for Rane to finish so he could take a quick shower, it became apparent to him that Rane didn't remember anything about her promise. He'd been wrong to think the need to find the other had been one-sided. She just hadn't thought he; the boy would try to find her.

For some unknown reason they were meant not to find each other until now.

"I'm done. Thank you for letting me in first."

"No problem. I won't be long," he said and went into the bathroom. As the water cascaded over him, he remembered a story about a dragon. It had explained that sometimes it took a human years to understand the yearning and to find the creature that was the cause. The human in the story had saved a young dragon from dying. But, when the dragon woke, it had been so afraid it flew away. Later, that same dragon struggled to find the human. The story ended with them finding each other and becoming life-mates.

Would Rane and he end up being life-mates?

Yes, they would. He knew it to be true in his heart.

He quickly finished dressing and exited the bathroom. The first thing he saw was the flashing red light. Not finding Rane in the bedroom, he noticed the bed had been made. He returned to the front of the plane and found her sitting in the same seat and sat down next to her.

Taking her hand in his, he kissed the palm. Rane smiled and rested her head against his shoulder. He placed his arm around her, holding her close.

Philip came out of the cockpit and stopped next to them. "Mr. Christmenn, we have the okay to start our descent. I've secured everything in the galley. Is there anything that I need to check in the back of the plane?"

"No, we are good to go." Mark squeezed Rane's hand.

"Fine, we'll be on the ground in a few minutes," Philip said. He made some last-minute checks before going back to the cockpit.

Then the fasten seatbelt sign illuminated.

———

Rane watched Philip close the door to the cockpit. They'd almost run into each other as she was leaving the bedroom while Mark was in the shower. He'd been very polite. She was glad he hadn't mentioned the dessert she'd had minutes before. He had simply inquired if he could get her anything. Declining, she went and sat down to look out the window.

Love.

It was a hard emotion to ignore.

Yes, she could admit she loved Mark.

She loved his smile, the way he made her feel in bed and out of bed. Who couldn't fall in love with one of the world's most eligible bachelors?

But that wasn't why she had fallen for him. He made her laugh. And could make her feel sexy with a glance.

As they sat, cuddled close to each other, she made up her mind. Lifting her head off his shoulder, she placed a kiss on his neck below his ear.

"Mark, I love you, too," she whispered.

He looked down at her and kissed her forehead. "We'll have to talk about this when we get to my villa. We don't have time for me to show you how happy that makes me."

It wasn't the reaction she thought she'd get from him, but then he wasn't the typical guy.

They landed. It didn't pull into a gate as a commercial planes would have, instead, it stopped in front of a hangar. When they departed the plane, a limo was waiting, and Philip was already standing next to it with the car door open for them.

"How many limos do you own?"

"A few. Some are rented, but this one is mine. Are you ready to do some shopping?"

Inside the limo she asked, "shopping?"

"Yes, remember we have the mall staying open for you."

"Do you usually shop this way? I mean, do you have to shop when the mall is closed?"

"Sometimes, or I have a personal shopper bring the items to my home or office. You would think I would be safe in a mall. Who would know me in a mall? Right, but it never fails, someone recognizes me and then it becomes a madhouse. Philip has outlawed those types of pleasure trips."

About ten minutes later, the car stopped in front of the mall entrance.

"Are you ready to have some fun? I'm going to do some shopping, too, since we have the store to ourselves. Make sure to get a dress. I made dinner reservations for tomorrow night. And swimsuits are optional."

"Oh, what makes you think I use them. Maybe I prefer skinny dipping," she stated.

"That's why I said they are optional. I want you to pick out anything you might want but most of all have fun."

She didn't get to respond because Philip opened the door and ushered them into the store. Several employees were waiting inside when they entered. An older man with dark brown hair stepped forward and extended his hand to Mark.

"Mr. Christmenn, I'm Mr. Russell the store manager. It's a pleasure to see you again. I hear you just landed. May we get anything for you or your guest to drink or eat?" he asked while shaking Mark's hand.

"Good evening, Mr. Russell. Thank you again for opening your store for us. We shouldn't take up much of your time or your employees' tonight. Yes, we could use some water and soft drinks when you get a chance." Mark placed his hand in the small of Rane's back. "Mr. Russell, this is Ms. Schoen, and she is the main reason we're here tonight. I whisked her away from Minneapolis on short notice. We've come down here empty-handed."

Rane extended her hand. "I'm pleased to meet you, Mr. Russell. I would also like to thank you for your services tonight."

"Mrs. Little will be able to show Ms. Schoen around and help her pick out all the items she will need."

As if on cue a middle-aged woman with short, curly black hair, stepped forward.

"Have fun." Mark winked at her and gave her a little push forward.

"Okay." In a daze, Rane followed Mrs. Little to the BCBG Maxazria department. She had to be dreaming. She felt like Julia Roberts in the movie *Pretty Woman*, which happened to be her most favorite movie.

Val was going to be so jealous. She took out her cell phone and sent a text message. *Guess where I am?*

I give up. Val's reply came with a smiley face at the end.

Dillard's in Florida.

No way. This time her text had a shoe and a heart symbol.

Yes way. LOL.

Thor is fine. Stay in touch this time. TTYL. Added to this message was a real picture of Thor sleeping next to Val.

TTG.

Rane tucked her cell phone away and let Mrs. Little show her all kinds of clothes. Her pile of keep items was growing. She'd selected panties and bras that matched. Along with sunglasses and makeup. After trying on several items, she picked one black dress that she'd be able to wear to dinner, some shorts and tank tops, and even a suitcase for traveling back home.

She and Mrs. Little had so much fun Rane didn't realize how much time had gone by until Mark appeared.

"Are you ready to leave? What time is it?"

Mark leaned against the counter. "Almost midnight. The real question is, are you ready to leave?"

"Yes, we've just finished." Rane turned to Mrs. Little. "Thank you for all your help. You've been great."

"Ms. Schoen, it has been my pleasure. Enjoy your stay in Florida. If you don't need anything else, I'll be on my way."

"No, I think I have everything. Thank you for your time."

"Make sure to stop by again on your next visit," Mrs. Little said and turned away.

"Mark, I had so much fun. It was unbelievable. This is better than shopping the normal way."

"I'm glad you enjoyed yourself."

She continued to chatter all the way down to the main level and to the door. Mr. Russell stood at the door ready to let them out of the store.

"Goodnight, Ms. Schoen, goodnight, Mr. Christmenn. The other item, I'll have delivered in the morning. Call if you need anything else."

As they exited the store once again the limo was there waiting with the door open. She could see all the packages lying on the seats. They barely had enough room to sit when Mark folded her into his arms and gave her a deep and passionate kiss.

"What was that for?"

"I missed you. It's about an hour's ride to Marco Island. Rest here against me if you get tired."

"I might be able to stay awake but I'm not going to guarantee it. I am tired," she said and hid a yawn.

"If you fall asleep, I'll wake you when we arrive."

———

Mark slouched down to get a comfortable position for both of them. Like last night, he knew the moment she fell asleep, and he was able to close his eyes, too.

"Rane, wake up. Rane. Rane, we're here."

He saw her eyes flutter open, only to close again. The

humidity and the smell of saltwater overwhelmed him as soon as Philip opened the door. It was something that always made him feel at peace. He carefully detached himself from Rane's arms and slid out. He then reached back inside, lifting her out, and carried her inside the house and up the stairs to the master bedroom.

She murmured words for a couple of minutes but never fully opened her eyes. He could tell she was exhausted. He undressed her for a second time that night and was tempted to awaken her slowly to blissful feelings. But he controlled his wantful need, by telling himself they had all weekend.

He then lovingly tucked Rane into the king-size bed and only gave her a kiss. Leaving the room, he went back downstairs.

All their purchases now filled the entryway. She'd done some damage, he saw. Mark heard footsteps and turned. The housekeeper, Rita, and Philip had joined him.

"Rita, please put all the purchases in the guest bedroom. Ms. Schoen is asleep in my bedroom."

"Yes, sir. It's good to see you, Mr. Christmenn." She picked up some of the bags and headed up the staircase.

"Philip, we need to talk. I'm in love with Rane." He stood back and watched as Philip did a double-take and stopped in mid-stride. Mark saw he had his full attention now.

"Did I hear you right? Now you're saying you love her. Before, it was I think I love her."

Mark closed his eyes and shook his head. "Yes. Yes, I know I love her. And I told her that too."

"You said it to her?"

"Yes."

Philip moved into the parlor room and headed straight to the bar. "What did she say? What did she do?"

"Nothing, at first. Then when the plane was getting ready to land, she told me she loved me. I know she is the girl I met on the plane all those years ago. I just know it. I can tell. It's a feeling. I knew something was different with her. Now as I think about it, it's the same feeling I had all those years ago."

"If you're so convinced, she is the one you've been looking for all this time, what do you want me to do? I can run another check on her."

Philip poured two glasses of bourbon and handed him one.

"I want to meet Rane's grandmother, who lives in Naples. I remember what the young girl's grandmother looked like. She isn't likely to have changed that much over the years. I'll talk to Rane in the morning about going to visit her today. Even if Rane doesn't turn out to be the girl, I'm going to propose to her. I've arranged for a ring to be delivered here by breakfast time."

Mark sipped the golden-brown liquid. It hit the spot and he began to calm down. Twenty years in the making, and here he was hours away from finding the truth.

"All right, I'll make plans to leave mid-morning." Philip downed his entire glass of bourbon in one gulp.

"Philip?"

"Now it's my time to say mind your own business."

Mark watched as Philip set his glass down and walked toward the door. "I know I can be a dickhead and I don't always tell you, but I do appreciate you being here for me."

"You owe me big time for this. I can't think of what I'm going to charge you yet but whatever it is, you can be sure it's going to be *big*. I think it's time I got a Jaguar, or maybe my own house in the Bahamas, or... I know, a million dollars?"

Philip ambled out of the room still spouting ideas. Mark smiled. He finished his bourbon a few minutes later and headed up to the woman he loved.

———

Rane awoke with the feel of a hand on her breast for the second time in two days.

This time she didn't want to scream. She wanted only to snuggle closer to the warm body. She lay there going over everything in her mind from the last twenty-four hours.

It all seemed a blur.

She had flown to Florida.

She was in Mark's house, and she'd awoken next to him. His hand continued to caress her breast. Turning so she faced him, she found his blue eyes staring at her.

"I warned you before, I'm not nice in the mornings."

"And I told you I am." Mark then captured her lips with his.

The kiss had a dreamlike quality to it. His lips were coaxing her into a sweet blissfulness. She didn't want it to end. She wanted to wake up every morning to this.

———

Mark took his time awakening her desire. He wanted to fully enjoy the intimacy of waking up next to the woman he loved. It was the most powerful feeling he'd ever experienced. Only in his early college days had he allowed himself to sleep with anyone all night long.

The feel of Rane's arms wrapped around him and her response to his slightest touch heightened his passion.

They enjoyed a slow but satisfying morning of making love.

When their heartbeats returned to normal, he got off the bed and dragged Rane with him into the shower. With the water running all over their bodies, he didn't think he'd ever experienced something quite so erotic and arousing.

"Rane . . ."

With the water and the shower walls as their bed, they made love again. After they'd satisfied each other, Rane pushed him out.

"Go, so I can shower in peace."

"Fine, be that way. There's always later."

However, he stayed in the bathroom to watch her distorted

figure through the frosted glass door for a little while. Still not believing he'd found the girl he'd been looking for all these years, he took one last aching look at her and reluctantly left. He needed to get downstairs and wait for the special package to arrive.

———

Still thinking she was in some sort of parallel universe, and she was going to wake up back at home just like Dorothy in *The Wizard of Oz,* Rane finished her shower.

She loved Mark.

And he loved her.

What else could she wish for in life?

Walking into the bedroom with a large fluffy bath towel wrapped around her, she saw all the clothes she'd picked out last night lying on the bed. Looking in all directions, she couldn't find Mark. She let the towel drop and quickly dressed in one of her new outfits, a teal and yellow-flowered Ralph Lauren sundress.

She wondered what Mark had scheduled for them today. The sun streaming through the sliding glass door revealed it was going to be a glorious day. Maybe they'd be able to go to the beach. On the other hand, would he say we're flying down to Key West for dinner?

Following the smell of food and the aroma of coffee, Rane made her way to the kitchen, a spacious open area where she found Mark seated at a table in the sunroom. It had all glass windows and a sliding door that opened to a patio, filling the room with Florida morning sunlight.

"Are you hungry?"

"I thought we already had breakfast. But I can see you're clearly still hungry." She grinned when he almost choked on the food in his mouth and motioned for her to sit down. "And yes, I'm hungry, and it might not be for food alone."

"You are a devil in disguise. Not only are you not nice in the morning. You are direct and to the point. That is an extreme combination. You could've given me more warning."

She saw his lips curl into an inviting smile as he handed her the bowl of scrambled eggs and the plate of bacon. He watched her devour her breakfast in silence. When she was almost finished, she heard him clear his throat.

"I was thinking since we are so close to your grandmother's house you might like to visit her and your mother today?"

Holding her fork midway to her mouth, Rane looked at him. "That would be so nice. Grandma Gretta will be so surprised. I haven't had a chance to come down here since my mother came to live with her. Could we really go see her?"

"Yes, whenever you're ready."

"I'm ready now." She shoveled the last of the eggs on her plate into her mouth, grabbed a couple of pieces of bacon, and stood.

"Slow down," Mark said and laughed. "I'll call Philip to bring the limo around front. We'll leave in about fifteen minutes."

"Sorry, I'm forgetting my manners. You're going to love Grandma Gretta. I think we'll miss my mother. She has to work on Saturdays."

"Maybe we should invite them to dinner tonight. I know several excellent restaurants in downtown Naples."

"You would do that?"

"Yes, give me her address so I can give it to Philip."

"She lives in the Ruby Lakes Community, on Diamond Cut Lane. Do you think I should call her?"

"Let's make it a surprise. Finish your breakfast and meet me out front. I need to check on a few things." Standing, he bent down and gave her a kiss on her cheek before walking out of the room.

She sat back down and took a drink of the orange juice that was clearly freshly squeezed. Enjoying the view of the Gulf that the windows provided for a moment, it was just as beautiful as she remembered. She couldn't come up with any words to describe what she saw with the waves crashing into the white sand. From the landscape, she couldn't tell if Mark's house was north or south of the public beach.

Since she'd been asleep when they had arrived, she wasn't sure. Besides, it had been several years since she had been to Tiger Tail Beach. Rane was tempted to walk outside to get her bearings. She took a guess, assuming they might be in the restricted part of the beach.

As a teenager, she'd never been able to cross the line. There had been guards posted by the invisible line and they knew everyone who lived in the area. If they didn't recognize you, they asked for your card showing you were a visitor or an owner in order to cross back into the area.

Sometimes when she would come to the beach, she made sure she could see everyone who left this protected area to see if the boy from the plane would walk out to the public beach.

The sound of a door closing brought Rane back to the present. Clearing her thoughts, she grabbed her can of Coke, which Mark had so thoughtfully set out on the table and walked out to the foyer.

"Are you ready?"

"I need to run upstairs for a moment. Then I'll be ready to go." Rane took the stairs two at a time.

———

Mark waited patiently by the front door and patted his front pocket and smiled. Today was going to be a win-win situation for him, with an answer to his twenty-year-old quest close at hand.

He was rejuvenated.

Even if his suspicions turned out to be wrong, it wasn't going to stop him from asking Rane to marry him.

She reappeared wearing a hat and carrying her purse. Together they got into the limo.

"Thank you for making this happen for me."

"It really isn't a problem. I knew if I didn't get you out of the house, I'd be carrying you up the stairs to the bedroom."

"Oh Mark, stop it. You're making me blush." But to his surprise, she reached over and cupped his groin area. "I've never made love in a limo before."

Clearing his throat, he removed her hand. "You are most certainly not nice in the morning. Not that I'm complaining. But I would like to table the making love in a limo, for when we have more time. I will make it very special for you."

"I did warn you." She laughed and kissed his cheek.

What had he gotten himself into? He had never turned down the opportunity to have sex. She was an amazing woman.

Thankfully, they arrived at the Ruby Lakes community in Naples. The limo had barely come to a complete stop when Rane opened the door. She got out and ran to the front door and pressed the doorbell. She turned and waved to him to hurry. He made it just in time as the door opened.

Rane let out a squeal of joy at the sight of her gramma. "Gramma Gretta!"

"Ro, is that you sweetie?"

"Yes, it's me Grams, and I've brought someone with me today."

"Why didn't you call to let me know you were coming? Come on in and get out of the sweltering heat. A friend? Is it Val? I haven't seen her in a long time," Gramma Gretta said as she held open the door wider.

"No, Grams, Val didn't come this time. She's cat-sitting Thor for me. You haven't met this friend." Rane hugged her grandmother. "His name is Mark." She moved a little, so the two of them could see each other. "Gramma Gretta, this is Mark. Mark, this is my Gramma Gretta."

"Gramma Gretta, I'm very pleased to meet you," Mark said.

He couldn't stop himself from staring at the woman. Then he smiled.

Damn. He'd been right.

The woman who'd greeted the girl so long ago stood before him now. Gramma Gretta hadn't changed very little with age. She now had more gray hairs, her face had more wrinkles, but she was definitely the woman the girl from the plane had hugged on that day, so long ago.

"You tell Val, I expect her to call me more often. It's a pleasure to meet you, Mark," Gramma Greta said as she held out her hand and shook Mark's.

"No, it's my pleasure."

"My, my, aren't you the flirtatious type."

"Gramma!" Rane exclaimed.

Gramma Greta waved her hand and smiled. "Come on in and sit down. I'll bring some cold lemonade to drink and some cookies. If I'd known you were coming, I could've baked your favorite ones, Ro."

Rane rolled her eyes as her Gramma went to the kitchen. She turned to Mark. "Well, what do you think of my Grams?"

"She's like the grandma I never had," he said meaningfully.

———

Once settled in the living room area, Mark sat down next to Rane on the couch next to each other and waited for her grandmother to rejoin them. This was all new to him because he'd never had a chance to know his grandparents or members of his extended family.

As he took in everything in the room, his gaze locked in on a single picture on the entertainment stand in front of him. He felt his palms perspire and nervously brushed his hand through his hair as his breathing quickened. He couldn't believe what he saw.

There, on the stand, right in front of him, next to a current picture of Rane, was the other half of the picture that he kept on his office desk.

Hot Damn. Sweet mother of Jesus! His instincts had been correct. Philip had been wrong.

He studied the other items on the stand and found a picture of a younger Rane, which is how he remembered her. He glanced over at her and saw the similarities in the teenage girl to the woman she had become. Her eyes still sparkled with mischief. She now had pouty cheeks that made him look twice at her.

Why hadn't he been able to see the similarities? The adult Rane had the same self-confidence as the teenage Rane. Her *never disagree with me* attitude was still there in the grown-up Rane. And her unique eyes caught his attention today as they had on the plane.

Everything started to grow clearer and made more sense. The feelings he'd been having since he had knocked her down, the attraction he kept dismissing, and the comfort level he'd felt whenever he was around her. It was as if fate hadn't been on their side until today.

Rane obviously hadn't made the connection yet. How was he going to bring up her promise to meet him in two months, twenty years after their original introduction?

———

Rane couldn't stop smiling when Gramma entered the room. It'd been too long since she'd been able to visit.

"Here we are. I've got some goodies to eat and nice cold lemonade to drink," Gramma Gretta said. She placed the tray down on the table in front of them.

"Thanks, Grams."

"Ro, honey, tell me what brings you here. I didn't know you were coming down to visit. Your mother didn't say anything, and she just left for work. She won't be back until suppertime."

"It's okay. I'm sorry for not calling. Mark and I flew in last night. We're only staying for the weekend."

Rane felt her cheeks heat. She couldn't tell her grandmother that the real reason was it had been a spur-of-the-moment trip to be alone with her new boyfriend. It was going to be tough enough when she introduced Mark to her mother. What would she think of him?

"Oh, that's too bad. Will you be able to see your mother?"

"Yeah, Mark suggested perhaps we could all go out for dinner tonight," Rane said, playing with her hair. "Do you have some-place you'd like to go?"

"Gramma Gretta, you have some interesting pictures on your shelves," Mark stated.

"Yes, I do! I'm so glad you noticed them. They are my memories of the times Ro spent with me during her spring vacations. Each item has a special memory of our time together, doesn't it, sweetie? Do you remember these?" She went over to the shelves, picked up a cup of seashells and continued, "Take this cup of shells. We would have to—"

Before Gramma Gretta could say another word, Rane said, "Oh, Gramma, stop showing off items from my youth. Mark doesn't need to hear about this stuff."

Embarrassed, Rane studied Mark to see if he was getting bored. Gramma Gretta sometimes had a way of doing that to a person.

Instead, she saw a genuine smile on Mark's face and heard him say, "I would love to hear about all the special items you are willing to share."

"See, Ro, other people are interested in these things that I have saved all these years. Now don't interrupt again," Gramma Gretta reprimanded playfully. Still holding the cup of shells, she resumed her story telling.

Rane mouthed, "Thank you" to Mark.

"These shells are from Ro's and my first visit to the ocean. Ro spent hours trying to find the perfect one. She was going to make a picture of flowers using them for a 3-D effect. As you can see, we never got around to making the picture and all I have is all these unused shells."

Rane bent her head and placed her hands over her face.

———

Mark's eyes glistened with laughter as he watched Rane. His heart swelled with an unexpected feeling of love. Every minute he spent with her proved to further his feelings from years ago to the present. She was everything he'd ever wanted in a woman from her sophistication, independence, and proficiency in her work, to her quick-thinking remarks, and show of affection to the people she cherished.

Mark watched as Gramma Gretta selected the framed hand-colored picture. "This is one of Ro's pieces of art a couple of years later. You can see she had some talent when she was younger. She'd drawn this one during her plane ride down here. As you can see, it's torn. Ro, honey, pay attention. You know I muddle up the facts. You might have to help me," Gramma Gretta said, and handed the picture to Mark for a closer look.

"No, you can't tell that story."

Gramma Gretta just smiled, ignored Rane's outburst, and continued. "My sweet, Ro, sat next to a young man during her flight down here and she'd asked this young man to marry her when she got older. She never was afraid to say what she felt."

"This is so embarrassing." Color graced Rane's cheeks when she glanced at Mark. "I told you part of this story last night."

"Now, now, no interruptions, you told me to tell it."

"Okay, I'm sorry, Gramma Gretta."

"Leave it to our outspoken Ro, she went and asked this young boy to marry her. Now mind you, she was only thirteen years old, so she drew him a picture of Disney's Epcot Park and told the young man to meet her there in the future." Gramma stopped talking to take a drink of her lemonade. "This is the sweet part, just like my lemonade. How many years did you tell him?" Gramma Gretta asked Rane, obviously expecting her to finish the story.

———

"Oh, Gramma Gretta, I don't remember. I think it was thirty years," Rane replied and stared at the picture Mark now held in his hands.

She'd forgotten all about the picture and the message she'd written on the missing half but not the image of the handsome young man. Every so often, she'd think of him and his blue eyes, black hair, and his smile. That day came back to her as if it was yesterday.

She remembered she could hardly wait to tell Val all about the good-looking young man who'd sat next to her on the plane. She'd watched him walk down the aisle and it had reminded her of models walking the catwalk in a fashion show. When he sat down next to her, she hadn't been able to utter a single word.

Déjà vu hit her.

She stole a momentary look at Mark as he held her picture. Suddenly she felt like she was sitting next to an older version of the young man from the plane.

It was him! No, it couldn't be.

There was no way in hell Mark could be that same young man.

Nevertheless, what if he were, and after all these years they'd found each other by accident? No way, she kept telling herself. Her Mark couldn't be the same person from the plane. Could fate be on her side?

She regarded Mark more closely and concentrated on his eyes.

She gasped. They were the same shade of blue. She remembered comparing them to the color of the morning sky.

She stared at him to see how he had changed over the years. His black hair now showed some gray strands, but you could tell it still had a hint of the blue-black color she remembered. No wonder she'd been so attracted to him. As a man, he never lost his kindness, air of authority, and sexuality. She understood. It was Mark who'd been missing from her life.

———

Mark watched as a rush of emotions crossed Rane's face.

Was she remembering? Had she made the connections?

Keeping his gaze focused on Rane, he stated, "Gramma Gretta, this is indeed a very special picture. I'm glad you've kept it safe all these years." He paused, still debating if he should let the cat out the bag, then, he continued. "The number of years on the picture is twenty."

Rane's jaw dropped open, and she placed her hand to her mouth.

"How do I know?" Mark smiled at the two women. "I have the other half of this picture in my office back in Minnesota."

"Oh no, this isn't happening," Rane said as tears ran down her face.

Mark handed the picture back to Gramma Gretta then grasped ahold of Rane's shaking hands.

"Rane, I am that boy from the plane. I wasn't sure you were the girl until I saw your half of the picture. I went to the beach to look for you too. I knew you'd turn out to be the woman I'd want in my life. I've waited all these years in hopes you'd show up and here you are, in front of me. I fell in love with you not knowing who you were."

He released her hands and withdrew a diamond ring from his

pocket. Taking her left hand, he slid the ring on her now trembling finger.

"I know you asked me twenty years ago but if you would still like to marry me, I'd be honored."

Rane smiled, appearing too stunned to answer. She nodded as more tears came.

"I was beginning to think you'd never find her," Gramma Gretta announced and then asked in an all-knowing tone, "What took you so long, young man?"

Epilogue

The radiant morning sun shone on the wedding couple giving the illusion of a pair of heavenly angels with the Disney Epcot sphere in the background. Rane and Mark stood hand-in-hand in front of a pastor, dressed in a white robe, who held a Bible.

It was picture perfect and what made dreams come true.

The ceremony took place by Spaceship Earth at the park's entrance. Floating flowers filled the circle water fountain and the front garden featured princesses and princes topiary in their honor.

Mark had arranged with Walt Disney World to have the wedding take place at Epcot Park during off hours. A select few of The World Showcase restaurants would host a lunch reception. She and Mark would be using a trolley bus to make appearances at each of the restaurants for their guests.

The gates would open to the general public at the usual time but by then, they'd be heading back to the villa.

Rane didn't even want to know how much money it was costing Mark, but he was certainly making all her wishes come true.

Several hundred guests sat in rows giving them a full view of the fairy-tale wedding taking place in front of them. In the front row was Gramma Gretta, Anna, Rane's mother, and Mrs. Weber.

Everyone quieted down when the song *"If I Never Knew You"* from Pocahontas began to play. Val stood next to Rane and Philip next to Mark. As soon as the song ended, Rane turned and faced Mark.

She couldn't believe she was standing next to him, about to become his wife. Who would have thought a promise made twenty years ago would come true? They were star-crossed lovers who'd found each other the hard way. How had she known that day so long ago that they belonged together? She'd given up. No, she'd forgotten, but he hadn't.

She feasted her eyes on him, her husband-to-be, dressed in a white tuxedo, which made him even more handsome with his black hair and tanned skin. It all seemed like a dream so unreal she still couldn't believe everything that had happened, and she was about to say *I do* to the man she truly loved.

Rane let her mind drift back to the morning they'd gone to Gramma Gretta's home.

After Mark had placed the ring on her finger, everything happened very fast. Grandma Gretta had cried, and her mom had come home early from work. Philip came in carrying Mark's half of the picture, which he'd secretly removed from his office unbeknownst to him, and they decided to get married in a couple weeks on the promised date.

A whirlwind of activity happened from then on. She and Mark agreed to an unusual invitation featuring a copy of the twenty-year-old picture and sent them out via faxes, e-mails, text messages, Twitter, Facebook, and special delivery to some important guests.

Val nudged her in the back and Rane realized it was time for her to say her vows. They'd playfully changed the order of the traditional vows since she was the one who'd originally asked Mark to marry her years ago.

She smiled and repeated, "Yes, I, Rane Schoen, take Mark Christmenn to be my..."

———

Mark held her hand and listened as Rane spoke her affirmation to become his wife. He couldn't believe he'd actually found the girl from the plane twenty years later.

And that girl had turned into a beautiful woman! In fact, he'd never seen anyone more beautiful in his entire life. Her long hair was up and away from her face, leaving some whips framing her face. He admired the low-cut, off-the-shoulder white beaded lace wedding dress. The gown was very form fitting and didn't leave much to the imagination. But, then again, he didn't have to imagine. He knew what treasures the dress hid.

When Rane finished her pledge, he squeezed her hand and repeated his vows to her.

"Yes, I, Mark Christmenn, take Rane Schoen to be..."

Finally, the pastor pronounced them husband and wife. Mark wasted no time taking Rane in his arms.

"I love you," he whispered and captured Rane's lips in a kiss to seal their exchanged vows. The cheers and hollers of encouragement broke them apart.

He ended the kiss and focused on her now blue-green eyes. He realized that she was showing him her love and knew he'd have a lifetime to take advantage of what her green eye color meant.

She was his true-life dragon. He knew that, like the dragons and their human partners, he, too, had found his life-mate for all eternity.

THE END

Don't miss out on your next favorite book!

Join the Satin Romance mailing list
www.satinromance.com/mail.html

———

THANK YOU FOR READING

———

Did you enjoy this book?

We invite you to leave a review at your favorite book site, such as Goodreads, Amazon, Barnes & Noble, etc.

DID YOU KNOW THAT LEAVING A REVIEW...

- Helps other readers find books they may enjoy.
- Gives you a chance to let your voice be heard.
- Gives authors recognition for their hard work.
- Doesn't have to be long. A sentence or two about why you liked the book will do.

About the Author

Born and raised in the cold and beautiful Minnesota, she escaped to Illinois for seventeen years to raise two boys, and now calls Florida home. She and her husband Andy, who's always her hero, have a new family to worry about; Cookie, an Assui-Po dog, Oreo, a black and white cat who thinks he is a dog, and Chip, a ragdoll cat, that their sons compare to Eeyore.

She loves to travel, read, and bowl. You can catch her writing her next novel at the lanes.

Sonja encourages you to check out her web site for more info and don't be surprised if she lets her Norwegian heritage come through in her stories. You betcha!

www.sonjagunter.com

Also by Sonja Gunter
With Satin Romance

<u>Novels</u>

Waves of Chances

If Yesterday Could Talk

<u>Holiday Novels</u>

Who's Been Naughty or Nice

Avoiding My Merry Birthday

<u>Anthologies</u>

First Class All the Way

in From Florida with Love, Sunsets & Happy Endings

Fast Lane Court Order

in From Florida with Love, Sunrise & Stormy Skies

Love Knows No Depths

(Meet Captain Neil Becker in Waves of Chances)

in From Florida with Love, Sunny Skies & Afternoon
Delights

Apple Pie Delight

in Food & Romance Go Together, Vol. 1